The Whole She-Bang

A collection of Canadian crime stories

by Sisters in Crime: Canada

Edited by Janet Costello

Toronto Sisters in Crime, Publisher

Toronto Sisters in Crime, Publisher

Library and Archives Canada Cataloguing in Publication

The Whole She-Bang: stories by Sisters in Crime: Canada ; edited by Janet Costello

ISBN 978-1-300-26725-6

Detective and Mystery stories, Canadian (English) 2. Costello, Janet

Also issued as ISBN 978-0-9880936-0-7 (EPUB)

Cover Art and Design by Antonia Gorton

Advance Praise for The Whole She-Bang

"Go ahead, admit it. When you think of Canada, you think: polite, earnest, clean. Well the Canadian Sisters in Crime are here to set the record straight, with *THE WHOLE SHE-BANG*, a winning collection of crime stories. Some will make you smile. Others will make you gasp. And some will stay with you long after you turn the last page."

-Sean Chercover, author of *THE TRINITY GAME*

"Good news: murder is alive and well in this entertaining new Canadian mystery anthology. In *The Whole She-Bang*, several bright new voices join established and award-winning crime writers to serve up a variety of stories full of suspense, surprise and satisfaction. Enjoy!"

-Mary Jane Maffini, 2010 Agatha Best Short Story Award for *SO MUCH IN COMMON*

"The women (and one man) of the Canadian Sisters in Crime have assembled a delightfully diverse collection of stories in *The Whole She-Bang*. Every one of these enticingly dark tales, whether by established authors or new names, showcases the talented storytelling and the keen voices of Canadian crime writers. The stories show female characters not so much as victims, but as players in the game of justice."

-Steve Steinbock, reviewer

Acknowledgements:

Thanks to the members of the Toronto Chapter of Sisters in Crime for the inspiration you have provided with twenty years of volunteer work that has kept us moving forward. Thanks also to those who have taken on big projects with no prior experience who provide us with the motivation to do the same.

Thank you to Anthony Bidulka, Karen Blake-Hall, Jeannette Harrison, Nathan Hartley, Joan Janzen, Jude Keast, Helen Nelson, Trish Rees-Jones, Renate Simon, Caro Soles, Robin Spano, and Jo-Ann Stepien, all Sisters to this project. Thanks for the hundreds of hours you have volunteered, accepting the stories, judging, proof-reading, fact checking, editing, providing legal help, formatting and marketing this anthology.

Thank you to Antonia Gorton who created a cover that captured our concept beyond our sultriest visions.

Janet Costello

*For six years, **Janet Costello** has been the editor of* Crime Scene, *the Toronto Chapter Sisters in Crime newsletter. There she has also published interviews, articles and puzzles. She enjoys attending mystery conventions, especially when she can volunteer. Janet works as a commercial insurance underwriter to support her reading habit (and to ensure that habit includes a glass of red wine nearby).*

Table of Contents

Introduction

by Helen Nelson

Chapter President, Sisters in Crime Toronto

Here we are – celebrating our twentieth anniversary as the Toronto Chapter of Sisters in Crime. In this, our Chapter's first anthology, we have one short story for each of those twenty years to present to you as part of the celebration.

We didn't plan it that way. We didn't really set a number. We didn't want to tell our judges that they must pick a certain number of stories. Although we certainly hoped they would be able to choose between 18 and 25. What we wanted was a collection of stories that would represent the depth of talent among members of Sisters in Crime who are resident in Canada.

And we have succeeded! The stories are cozy and noir, humorous and poignant, historical and current. We have amateur sleuths and professionals–cops, private detectives and even–oh, but I don't want to include any spoilers. Our protagonists are women, men and children. Our settings are varied too, within Canada, the U.S., the United Kingdom, Vietnam and an unnamed exotic locale. Our authors are young and young at heart–established authors and those who are being published for the first time. And while we are mostly female, there is also one male author in this collection.

Congratulations to the authors of all the stories selected for this anthology. We're convinced that there are many more great storytellers out there. We hope you are all busy honing your craft.

From the idea's inception, somewhat over a year ago, until publication, this anthology has been produced by a team of volunteers who have put in hundreds of hours, collecting, judging, editing, proof-reading, fact checking, formatting and planning a marketing strategy. Who knew when we started this just how much work it would be? What a wonderful thing we have such a dedicated group in our chapter who have lent a hand in the endeavour. Sisters in Crime is an organization of volunteers and that spirit has shone through in this project.

We have tried our best to follow the rules for anthology publication set out by the international organization of Sisters in Crime. They are rules we agree with. The most crucial ones for us are around the blind nature of the judging process. That is harder to follow than one might think–especially in the age of instant publishing on the internet. But we have done our best and all stories included were selected as part of that blind judging process.

Would we do it again? Absolutely! And we won't wait another twenty years. Who knows, maybe *your* story will be in our next collection. In the meantime let's celebrate twenty years of the Toronto Chapter of Sisters in Crime with these twenty stories. Happy Reading.

Baby, the Rain Must Fall

by Vicki Delany

"It's a crime not to read Delany," says the London Free Press.
Vicki Delany *is one of Canada's most varied and prolific crime
writers. Her popular Constable Molly Smith series (including In
the* Shadow of the Glacier *and* Among the Departed*) has been
optioned for TV by Brightlight Pictures. She writes stand-alone
novels of modern gothic suspense such as* Burden of Memory *and*
More than Sorrow, *as well as a light-hearted historical series,
(*Gold Digger, Gold Mountain*), set in the raucous heyday of the
Klondike Gold Rush. She is also the author of* A Winter Kill, *a
novel for reluctant readers.*

*After early retirement from a systems analyst job in the high-
pressure financial world, Vicki is settling down to the rural life in
bucolic, Prince Edward County, Ontario, where she rarely wears
a watch.*

*Visit Vicki at www.vickidelany.com or her blog about the writing
life One Woman Crime Wave
(http://klondikeandtrafalgar.blogspot.com)*

The moment I got home from work, before even stripping off
my clinging panty hose and unseasonably warm suit, I poured a
glass of Ontario Chardonnay. I was swirling the cool, crisp wine
around the inside of my mouth when the phone rang. I peeked at
the call display. A local number; not one I recognised.
"Hello?"
"Debbie. It's Maureen Kildare."
"Maureen Kildare! Good heavens, after all these years! How
are you?" I could barely get the words out. This was a voice I had

never expected to hear again. And never wanted to.

"Okay."

"Where are you calling from?" I didn't want to know, but I had been raised with a sometimes-inconvenient, full complement of manners.

"My mom's."

"Is she still living in Oakville?" I swallowed most of the wine in one gulp.

"Yes."

"How long are you staying?"

"Until I get a few things sorted out."

The silence between sentences grew. Maureen was never the most vociferous of our tightly-knit high school group. I suppose thirty years spent in and out of prison hadn't turned her into a social butterfly. Not a lot of Canadian women – at least middle-class white women from the affluent Toronto suburb of Oakville – spend that amount of time in jail. But once she went in, Maureen didn't seem to be able to stay out. Or so I had heard - I hadn't spoken to her since the day she was sentenced to her first stretch. I don't think any of the others had either. If there was one social skill our mothers hadn't taught us, it was how to conduct oneself on a prison visit.

I finished the wine and topped the glass up, unable to think of anything more to say. Maureen wasn't trying terribly hard to keep up her end of the conversation. "We must get together one day soon," I suggested, grasping at a conversational convention. "For dinner maybe. Yes, dinner, that would be nice."

"Okay." Maureen's voice was rougher than I remembered. It used to be so soft; she'd always sounded like someone's breathless little sister. But again, I suppose a stretch in the infamous Kingston Prison for Women, known as P4W, would harden anyone's softer edges.

"Well, I've gotta run. Jerry's parents are coming for dinner. Let's keep in touch."

"Next weekend would be nice. Friday?"

"What?"

"Next Friday. That dinner?"

My mind raced. If Maureen wanted to see me, I should take the time to meet her. I owed her that, at least, and what harm could it do, other than to cause us both a few awkward moments? We had been close—once. "Next week's no good. I'm..."

"Yes?" The single word purred into the phone sounding just like the Maureen I remembered.

"I'm…" I could feel my heart beating in my chest. I finished another glass of wine. We'd been great friends once, Maureen and I, best friends in a group of best friends. And we'd abandoned her pretty quickly—me as fast as the others.

I spoke before thinking things through. "I'm going up to Diane's cottage next weekend. We still go every year. Janet, Sue, Cathy, the whole bunch. For a long weekend. Why don't you come with us? It's always great fun. Diane's place is wonderful—you remember. I'm sure everyone would love to see you." I wanted to stuff the words back in my mouth. Everyone would love nothing of the sort. We'd gone on with our lives leaving Maureen to drift in and out of jail and between jail stints to wander the streets of East Vancouver doing God-knows-what.

"I don't have a car. I'll drive up with you. Pick me up at my mom's— she still lives in the same house. You remember where that is, don't you, Debbie?"

"I remember. Have you talked to any of the others—uh—lately?"

"No. But I did see Sue's brother Rob in Vancouver a few months ago. He told me the old gang's still pretty tight."

The phone clicked softly as she hung up.

The old gang, as Maureen so unflatteringly called us, consisted of the five, six including Maureen, who had been best friends throughout high school. We were the brainy ones, the unpopular, unathletic, ungainly bunch who clung together against the contempt or, worse, the indifference of the 'in' crowd at Thomas A. Blakelock High School during the rebellious (for everyone except us) sixties. Our lives had diverged a great deal since, but once a year we gathered at Diane's family cottage on Lake Muskoka for our annual girls' weekend. Every summer since 1972, the second weekend in August saw most of us, and more often than not all of us, heading north. And so our lives were revealed to each other one year at a time as husbands came and left, children were born and grew up, parents died, homes moved, jobs attained and abandoned and careers grew. It had always been a girls' weekend - husbands and children were banned, with a reluctant exception made for breastfeeding infants. Some years we came from all over the country, from around the world even, for our weekend. Every year the ghost of the still-living Maureen, scarcely mentioned, rarely acknowledged, hovered in the midst of our circle of friends like a large dog's particularly smelly indiscretion.

I pulled up in front of the Kildare house. The trees were taller but otherwise it was as I remembered: green lawn as perfect as a golf course, neat rows of red and pink geraniums and petunias strictly confined to the well-tilled flowerbeds. I'd avoided this street for thirty years. I had no desire whatsoever to set foot in that house again, for who knew what bad memories it might still contain. Fortunately I didn't have to. Before I was even out of the car Maureen rushed out of the house, the door slamming behind her. I thought I heard her mother cry, "Maureen, must you always make such a racket?" But that might have only been a wisp of memory. I opened the trunk and she threw her backpack on top of my suitcase.

For a moment I found myself genuinely delighted to see her, and I squealed as I gave my former best friend a hearty hug. She had been quite plump in high school, but today I could feel the sharp bones beneath her sweater. The hug was not returned, and Maureen pulled herself out of my grasp.

"Nice car," she said, settling into the leather seat of the Lexus as we began the three-hour drive to Muskoka.

"When the last of my girls finally left home I realised I didn't have to drive a minivan any longer, so I treated myself to this little beauty."

"Girls?" she raised one eyebrow. "How many?"

"Four," I laughed, pulling into traffic. I rattled off names, ages and present locations and occupations. Then I babbled a bit about my job—vice president of a bank, thank you very much—but Maureen didn't seem impressed. She said nothing more and I finally got tired of the sound of my own voice. The rest of journey passed in silence.

As I did every year, I'd taken the day off to drive up early Friday morning, so the traffic heading into Cottage Country wasn't too bad. Once we passed Canada's Wonderland north of Toronto the congestion of urban sprawl faded into gentle farmland and rolling green hills, and I stopped thinking about traffic and began to worry about what I'd done. I hadn't told anyone, not even Diane, I was bringing Maureen. If they'd told me to uninvite her I simply wouldn't have been able to find the courage to do so.

My mind wandered. Maureen had always been different from the rest of us. We mostly came from affluent families in what was then the most affluent town in Canada. No one in Oakville had been poor, but Maureen's family was about as close as one could come and still be living in that town. Diane's family, on the other hand, was rich. Today she'd go to a private school, but somehow things seemed more egalitarian back then. For reasons not fully understood by any of us, Maureen managed to fit herself into our group. Maybe because she was so terribly smart, even though she sometimes tried to hide it, and maybe because in the first days of grade nine she chased off a group of boys who were laughing at my budding bosom. But Maureen was always one of our group, although sometimes she stood slightly to one side. No sleepovers or birthday parties at Maureen's house. Although I was her best friend, I never saw the inside of her immaculate home more than a handful of times.

High school ended as it must and we went our separate ways. In the fall of 1972, Janet and I were at the University of Toronto; Cathy was at Carleton University in Ottawa taking the journalism program that would get her a job as Middle East correspondent for one of the major U.S. newspapers; Diane was planning her wedding to a junior partner in her father's law firm; and Sue was backpacking through Europe. Maureen, the cleverest of us all, worked a cash register at Kmart.

By the summer of 1973, Maureen was on trial for the murder of her mother's brother. We, except for Diane whose father forbade it, went to court a few times dressed in our most sombre clothes, and sat stoically in the front row trying to offer some feeble degree of moral support.

Maureen's defence was that her uncle had been molesting her for years, and one day she'd had enough and brained him with a fireplace poker. The case was a cause celebre, a nine-day wonder, and everyone predicted she would get off with a suspended sentence. But the defence was lacklustre and the prosecution fiery. They'd successfully argued that there was no evidence of any ongoing abuse or of any attempted rape on the day in question—Maureen had never told anyone her uncle was molesting her, so why should she be believed now? Maureen's mother hadn't helped by telling the court that her daughter sometimes acted 'mature for her age.' The whole town was shocked when Maureen was sentenced to ten years in federal prison.

In the summer of 1974 Diane was the smug, proud mother of a bouncing baby boy; Cathy was first in her class; Sue was at community college studying fashion; I had switched my major to the new field of computer science; Janet had quit university to 'find herself'; and Maureen was incarcerated at P4W.

I glanced out of the corner of my eye at my former best friend. She looked at least ten years older than she was: Her face was deeply lined, sallow skin hanging on chipped cheekbones. The bags under her eyes carried the full memory of thirty years of rough living. Her thick black hair was heavily streaked with grey and as badly cut as if she'd lopped the ends off with a nail file smuggled into jail in a birthday cake. The tips of her fingers were yellow, and she picked constantly at a loose thread in her cheap sweater or at the frayed end of the belt holding up her shorts.

And I knew that by inviting her I had made a terrible mistake.

We were the first to arrive. I didn't have a key to the main building, but it was a warm, sunny day so we piled our bags by the door and walked around to the lake-facing side of the sprawling old cottage. The shed was unlocked and I dragged cushions out to dress the lounge chairs on the deck. From the depths of my cooler I pulled out a bottle of wine, a corkscrew and two acrylic wineglasses. I always travel prepared.

Maureen leaned on the blond wood rail of the deck, gazing out over the sparkling blue expanse of Lake Muskoka. Tiny waves danced in the sunshine. A seaplane cut a path through the clear sky overhead. She held her face to the sun. Either I'd forgotten the shape of her nose or it had been broken in the years since I'd seen it last. She closed her eyes and almost smiled. "This is a nice place," she murmured. "Diane's a lucky lady."

I poured the drinks and held out a glass. Maureen took a long look at my hand before shaking her head. "I don't drink."

I debated pouring her share back into the bottle. But it might spill. I added it to my own glass.

We were stranded in that horrible limbo where we had too much and nothing at all to say to each other; in the end we chose to say nothing. I'd half finished the bottle of wine when we heard a car pulling up the gravel driveway.

I got to my feet, lifted my wineglass jauntily, and stuck a smile on my face like a painter might slap a bit of Polyfilla over a crack in the ceiling. Diane and Janet rushed through the cottage and threw open the wide French doors leading to the deck.

"I knew you'd be here first. You always are." Diane ran towards me with a huge smile on her face and arms outstretched. Janet came behind, talking at nothing. Janet was always talking.

They saw my guest at the same moment. Diane's smile disappeared and Janet stopped mid-sentence.

I stepped towards Maureen. "Look who I found! Maureen Kildare, can you believe it? After all these years, I knew you'd be delighted to see her."

Maureen stepped forward. Not a flicker of emotion touched her worn-out eyes. She did not smile or offer her hand. "Diane. Janet."

Diane sank into an uncushioned lawn chair. Her face had turned white under her rich tan, and she touched her chest with one palm. For a moment I feared she was either about to have a heart attack or throw Maureen and me out of the place.

Perhaps both.

Janet recovered first. "Maureen. It's been an age. Must be five years at least since we graduated high school." Her laugh was as irritating as a jet ski buzzing around a canoe. But at least she laughed. And then she stepped forward and enveloped Maureen in her arms. Maureen stood stiffly under the hug, her arms straight at her sides, her body not bending a single degree. But Janet, dear Janet, who had never quite stopped being the hippie of her youth, appeared not to notice. "Why don't you come and help me carry in the groceries, Maureen. I've brought such a lot. Diane drove, so she gets to rest for a bit." Maureen was dragged along by the sheer force of Janet's personality.

I looked at Diane. "I'd better go and bring my stuff in as well."

"How could you?" Diane hissed. The corner of her left eye fluttered in a nervous twitch.

"Diane, I'm sorry. I didn't know what to do. I thought..."

"You thought..."

She was prevented from finishing the sentence when Janet stuck her head onto the deck. "These burgers are still frozen. Do we want them for tonight or should I put them in the fridge? Oh, good – Sue and Cathy are here. That was quick. Sue picked Cathy up at the airport. Time for some music, Diane. Why don't you put on the album you played for me in the car?" She held the door open. Diane glared at me once more and walked into the cottage as if she were going to her execution. Always the prima donna, Diane was.

Suck it back, Diane, I thought. It's only a weekend. If I can bear it, you can.

Sue and Cathy were also less than thrilled to see Maureen, but they recovered quickly and managed to be civil and even a touch enthusiastic. Maureen didn't seem to care what any of us thought, and she passed the afternoon sitting on the deck gazing out over the water.

Diane had three older sisters, so when we were growing up she had been well ahead of the rest of us in terms of music. She still adored the 'Bobbies' that her sisters had loved – Darin, Vernon, Sherman, Vee—along with Elvis and the girl singers such as Leslie Gore. The rest of us had been more into the likes of the Beatles, the Dave Clark Five, and the Monkees, but we always enjoyed travelling into the past with Diane. She put on her iPod, selecting all her old favourites, and as we sliced and peeled vegetables for salads and prepared burgers and kebabs for the barbecue, we sang and danced to well-remembered music and the mood lifted. Even Maureen came inside and stood at the sink shucking corn and humming under her breath, although she spoke only when asked a (rare) direct question.

We ate dinner on the deck as powerboats rushed by taking weekenders to their cottages or into the nearby town of Bala for a night out. A family of ducks drifted past, and to my surprise Maureen grabbed a hamburger bun and hurried down to the dock to feed them. For a moment I was happy that I had brought her.

"You should have asked me, Debbie," Diane snapped once Maureen was safely out of hearing.

"Oh, give it a rest, Diane," Janet said. "Look at the poor girl. When was the last time you got such pleasure out of the ducks? We can't begin to imagine what the years have been like for her."

Maureen ripped the bun into crumbs, which she scattered over the water. The ducks rushed to the feast and the sound of Maureen's light laugh rose up the hill. It was the first time she'd laughed all day. I wondered when she'd last had a good hearty belly laugh.

Accompanied by a clatter of dishes and cutlery, Cathy volunteered to wash up, and Sue quickly followed her into the kitchen.

"It still wasn't right, Debbie." Diane scooped the last of the Caesar salad out of the bowl with her fingers. "But we can't do anything about it now." She jammed a piece of romaine into her mouth.

I watched the setting sun draw streaks of orange across the darkening water.

Sue had brought a pile of videos. Tonight we would have a choice of The Magnificent Seven, The Great Escape or Baby, the Rain Must Fall. How we had loved Steve McQueen when we were girls.

We decided to watch The Magnificent Seven tonight and save The Great Escape for Saturday. (Did I mention that I also loved

Robert Vaughn—who can forget the Man From Uncle—and Charles Bronson in their prime?) Baby, the Rain Must Fall we agreed to take a pass on. Steve McQueen struggling to make it straight while out on parole—too depressing and much too close to home for this weekend.

The memorable theme music started up, but the mood in the room had turned raw, edgy. Maureen watched Diane through narrow eyes, Diane kept her focus on the screen, drinking a good deal more than was her habit, and Janet watched them both. I opened another bottle of wine and wished I hadn't quit smoking. Only Sue and Cathy seemed to be enjoying the movie.

Finally the grand climax came and our noble heroes were dispatched to their various rewards. We made going-to-bed noises and trundled off to brush teeth, put on pyjamas, and slather on night cream.

Maureen and I were sharing a room. She was sitting on top of her bed, fully dressed, gazing at the dark forest outside the window.

I pulled down the duvet on the single bed and climbed in. "If you're not happy being here, I can take you to Gravenhurst tomorrow to catch the bus for Toronto."

I was trying to be helpful, but my former best friend turned to me and the venom in her eyes took my breath away.

"I'm not going to leave by the back door, Debbie. Sneak away like the unwanted guest I am so the rest of you can finish your lovely weekend."

"I didn't mean..."

"I'm sure you didn't." She closed the bedroom door on her way out.

The day had been a long one, and despite the turmoil I was feeling I fell asleep quickly. I'm not sure what woke me, but I knew someone was up. Maureen's bed was under the window and by the white moonlight flooding in I could see that the covers had not been disturbed.

It was time, long past time, I talked to Maureen. Really talked. I clutched what shreds of courage I could dredge up, climbed out of bed and crept into the hall. All was quiet, except for the chirp of crickets in the woods and the soft murmur of women's voices on the deck.

The blinds had been left open and I could see two figures standing outlined against the dark of the forest and the lake beyond. Diane was dressed in a semi-sheer nightgown, an expensive, fluffy concoction of white lace and peach satin.

Maureen still wore her khaki shorts and tattered polyester sweater.

The warm night air had a close, almost liquid feel, so the windows had been left open to catch a breeze. I edged closer, staying out of sight behind the gathered blinds.

"I want to see him," Maureen said.

"No. It's too late. Too much time's passed. I won't allow it."

"I don't need your permission, Diane."

I couldn't imagine whom they were talking about. Had Maureen had an affair with Diane's ex-husband? They were divorced so long ago, hard to believe Diane would care.

"He doesn't live at home. I won't tell you where he is. You can't find him."

They must be taking about Eddie, Diane's son. Why would Maureen have the least bit of interest in meeting Diane's son?

"Don't be ridiculous. Of course I can. Are you going to spirit him out of the country? I'd rather you spoke to him first. It would be easier on him that way, don't you think? But with your help or not, I will see my son."

I sucked in my breath and slapped my hand over my mouth.

"My son. He's my son. Not yours." Diane's voice was low, angry and full of pain. "You gave up that right the day he was born. You agreed to."

"I agreed to nothing. They'd take my child away whether I agreed or not, I was going down for ten years. What say did I have? When your mother and father came to talk to me, I was happy to let you have him. I didn't agree to lose him forever; your father told me I could visit when I was released. Any time I wanted, your father said. Even though he was the offspring of that bastard uncle of mine I wanted my son to grow up knowing who his real mother was, and your father agreed. But when I arrived at your parents' house your father shut the door in my face while your mother called the police. Did you know that, Diane? Did you know what they promised me? Did you know they lied and had the police drag me off their property and put out a restraining order on me?"

"My father only wanted..."

A cigar boat came by, in the dead of night much too close to the shoreline for safety. The roar of its engines drowned out the rest of Diane's sentence.

"...out of here tomorrow. I'll call my father; he'll make sure you never see Edward. Never."

"Oh, Diane," Maureen said, her words almost whisked away by

the light night wind. "I don't mean you or the boy any harm."

"Be gone tomorrow before breakfast." Diane stalked down the steps towards the lake, leaving Maureen standing alone in the beam of the single light shining above the French doors. I ducked into the bathroom, not wanting to be seen.

Maureen didn't come to bed, and I lay awake most of the night. Poor Maureen. How she must have suffered all these years. She would have been pregnant when she was on trial; she had certainly packed the pounds onto her already chunky frame—jail food and stress, we all assumed. Diane and her husband went to Vancouver for a few months shortly after Maureen's trial ended. When they returned to Oakville, they were the proud parents of a baby boy—the only child Diane would ever have. I never thought anything of it—we all knew girls who'd 'gone to stay with an aunt', but none of them were married or came home with a baby!

I must have dozed a bit, for just as the rising sun touched the edges of the blinds, I was jolted into wakefulness by a full-throated scream. I grunted, grabbed at my blankets and rolled over, but the scream was repeated and then a second voice joined in.

I stumbled to my feet and ran onto the deck. Sue and Janet were scrambling down the stairs towards the lake. Janet moved so fast she tripped and took the last couple of steps headfirst. Sue didn't even look over her shoulder to see if her friend was all right.

Something was in the water. Something diaphanous and white with a touch of peach. Diane's night-gown. Floating serenely on the glass-like surface.

Sue hit the water in a perfect dive. Janet struggled to her feet and, ignoring the blood flowing freely from a wide gash across her knee, ran to the water's edge.

"Christ, it's Diane." Cathy stood beside me.

"Call 911," Janet shouted up at us. "Quickly."

Cathy did as she was asked, and I hurried down to the water to see if I could help. Sue had hooked one arm around the limp form and was swimming towards shore pulling the burden behind her. Janet and I dragged it onto the rocks. Sue clambered out of the lake and crouched, hands on knees, gasping for breath, while water streamed off her Mickey Mouse shortie pyjamas. Janet immediately started performing CPR, but anyone could see we were too late.

"Oh, my God. What happened?" Maureen touched my shoulder. She was dressed in the clothes she had been wearing the day before. They were rumpled and dirty; her short, badly cut hair stood on end, and her hands and knees were caked with mud.

"You!" Sue faced Maureen, her hands placed firmly on sodden hips. Janet continued the steady rhythm of trying to bring the dead back to life. "What do you know about this?"

"Hey," I said, stepping between them. "Maureen had nothing to do with this. Diane must have slipped on the dock in the dark and fallen in. Easy to do. Maybe she hit her head."

"Ambulance is on the way," Cathy shouted down. "I'll meet them at the road."

Maureen said nothing.

Janet sat back on her heels. "We're too late," she said with a sob. Forgetting Maureen, Sue crouched beside her and took her in her arms.

"I'm going up to get dressed," I said. I could think of nothing else to do.

Maureen shut the door of our bedroom behind her. "They'll be able to tell, Debbie. The police. You wouldn't believe what investigators can read in a footprint or a small bruise. They can tell if someone was alone and hit their head when they fell. Or if they had company and were hit by something before going down."

"I didn't mean to," I said, pulling on a clean yellow T-shirt dotted with blue flowers, "but I was so angry at the way Diane spoke to you. I tried to tell her you deserved better. She said her father wanted a grandson so much and they'd always known she wouldn't be able to have children. She said it was your fault you lost your son. I hadn't known you had a baby. Why didn't you tell me?" I collapsed onto the bed and started to cry. "I'm so sorry. I tried to make it right. Now she's gone you'll be able to see your boy."

"Oh, Deb. Don't you understand? The police will blame me straight away—me, an ex-con, a convicted killer; they won't even bother looking at anyone else. They're smart. But blinkered."

"I'll tell them what happened. If I have to. You didn't do it."

"No. I didn't. I hated Diane for the way her family treated me, but I didn't wish her dead. You can't to go to jail, Debbie. You have a great job, a caring family. I can. I've been there often enough. Tell you the truth, I don't like it much on the outside. There's nothing for me here. Diane showed me that. My mother told me I have to be out of her house when I get back."

"But..." I blubbered.

"No 'buts', Debbie." Maureen sat on the bed beside me. "I'll take the fall for you." She stroked my hair. "Like I did that night when Uncle Fred dragged you into the rec room and you killed him."

"I didn't mean..."

"I know you didn't. Who would have thought the jury wouldn't believe what he'd been doing to me all those years?"

In the living room someone switched on music. Diane's mixes of old favourites: The title song from Baby, the Rain Must Fall was first up.

Steve McQueen couldn't make it out of prison either.

The Troublemaker

by Lynne Murphy

Lynne Murphy describes herself: I am a retired journalist. Founding member of the Toronto Chapter of SinC. Prepublished novelist. Have been reading mysteries for almost 70 years.

Roger Trombley loved his job as concierge of the Cottonwoods Condo, "one of Toronto's finest residences." He liked wearing the navy blazer with its brass buttons, which he felt made him look rather nautical. He liked opening the door for the elderly residents and helping them with their parcels. He loved dealing with the tradesmen, making them wipe their feet and clean up after themselves. He was a very happy man.

Bessie Bottomly loved her position as head of the volunteer garden committee at the Cottonwoods Condo. She was never happier than when she was presiding at a meeting of the committee, which she ran according to Robert's Rules of Order, in spite of the fact that it was a volunteer committee. She liked telling the landscapers what flowers to plant and where to plant them, but the meetings were the best part of the position.

Peter Kruger loved his role as troublemaker at the Cottonwoods Condo. In the six months since he had moved in, he had received numerous warnings and three letters from Management, asking him to cease and desist in his various activities.

One of these activities was turning off lights in the public areas to save electricity.

He did this with great regularity. Another was crawling into the dumpsters to see if people were recycling properly. Much to his delight, some days he found newspapers or plastic containers in with the garbage. Sometimes he even found corrugated cardboard. Those were the times he drew a red circle around the date on his calendar.

He had become an irritant in Roger Trombley's pleasant life. At first, Bessie Bottomly listened to Roger's complaints with sympathy but they didn't really rouse her to action. That was before Peter Kruger decided to interfere with the gardens.

He hadn't bothered to come to any meetings of the garden committee, just appeared one day with his own shears and started trimming the shrubs. Maisie McClain saw him from her balcony and phoned Bessie right away.

"I don't think it's the landscape company," she said, though her sight was not all that good. "It looks like that odd little man who lives on Olive's floor. And I think he's trimming the saskatoon bushes. Surely that can't be right in June?"

Bessie's balcony faced the back of the building so she couldn't check on this from her own apartment. She threw on her sweat suit, took the elevator to the ground floor and rushed out the front door. Sure enough, there was Mr. Kruger, hacking away at a saskatoon bush. Evidence of his violence lay on the ground around him.

"What do you think you're doing?" Bessie shouted.

Mr. Kruger stopped in his depredations.

"These have bloomed," he said. "I'm cutting off the dead flowers. They look untidy."

"Those are saskatoon bushes not lilacs," Bessie said. She could barely speak, she was so angry. "The flowers turn into fruit. Surely any idiot knows that."

No woman was going to call Mr. Kruger an idiot. He turned around and took another piece off the branch he had been working on. Bessie was a large woman with a commanding bosom and Mr. Kruger was a small man. But she thought better of trying to stop him herself. Those shears were lethal weapons.

"I'm calling Roger," she said and rushed inside to use the answer phone to the Concierge's desk.

Roger arrived in short order, buttoning up the brass buttons on his navy blazer. By the time he got there, the saskatoon bush was just a stem and a few pitiful leaves. Bessie was almost in tears.

"Mr. Kruger," Roger shouted, "you have been asked not to prune the bushes. The landscapers are responsible for that. Under advice from the garden committee. Mrs. Bottomly is head of the garden committee. Please leave that bush alone."

Mr. Kruger took one more mighty chop at the bush and

stepped back to view his handiwork.

"Very well," he said. "But since the garden committee is just volunteers, I think I have as much right as anyone to work in the gardens."

He headed off toward the back of the building in the direction of the dumpsters.

"This is awful," Bessie said. "What can we do, Roger?"

"I'll make sure he gets a letter from Management," Roger said. "This will make four since he came here."

At exercise group the next morning, Bessie told the ladies about Mr. Kruger's vandalism.

"He was like a plague of locusts attacking that poor little tree," she said. "He doesn't seem to pay any attention to the letters from Management. What are we going to do?"

"I think he's been planting orange marigolds around the trees out front," Olive said. "At least they keep showing up. And I know how you hate orange marigolds, Bessie."

"I'm almost sure he's the person who keeps turning off the lights in the recreation centre," said Isobel. "You know I always go down to swim at seven and he gets there at six. You can tell by the sign-in book. And the light in the ladies' change room has been off every morning these past few weeks."

Bessie pondered that. Then she stood up and marched down the hall to the ladies' change room.

"It's just as I thought," she said when she came back. "He has to step inside the ladies' change room to turn off the light. Suppose one of us was in there naked?"

"Oh, Bessie!" they all said. They went on to talk about other things: Shirley, who had gone into hospital and likely wouldn't be coming back to the condo to live, even if by some miracle she was able to walk again; Evelyn, who had moved into a retirement residence and met some old goat there who was probably after her money. They forgot about Mr. Kruger for the moment.

But Mr. Kruger had not been swayed from his path of recycling, energy saving and garden improvement. Lights were turned off. Cardboard was pulled from the garbage dumpsters. And orange marigolds continued to show up wherever there was a tiny space in a flowerbed. No matter that the garden colour scheme was a carefully planned pink and blue and mauve. Bessie began her own guerilla campaign. She couldn't bring herself to kill a flower but she moved all the orange marigolds to a neglected bed at the back of the condo where no one ever went. The next day the marigolds were back in their original places, looking somewhat the worse for wear. Bessie moved them again.

"Mr. Kruger will wear out before I do," she told Roger. But Isobel was the one who brought things to a crisis point. The lights continued to be off in the ladies' change room when she went for her seven o'clock swim. One day she tripped over a pool noodle someone had left on the floor, fell, and hurt her wrist. She complained to Roger.

He took care to watch the security camera trained on the ladies' change room door the next morning. Sure enough, at six a.m. Mr. Kruger could be seen, stepping inside and apparently, flicking a light switch. Then he reappeared.

"We've got him on film," Roger said to Isobel and Bessie. "Management will have to write him another letter."

"Leave it for a few days," Bessie said. "I want to talk to the girls."

She was developing a plan to deal with this irritant in the smooth flowing life of Cottonwoods. That morning at coffee after exercise class she, Isobel, Olive, Maisie and Charlotte talked over the plan.

"He doesn't pay any attention to the letters from Management," Bessie said, "so we need to give him a good shock. Here's what I think we should do. We get down there before he does and take off all our clothes...."

The ladies listened to her plan, wide-eyed. Then they looked at each other with a mixture of horror and delight.

"I'm game if the rest of you girls are," Maisie said. "Luckily, I can't see a thing without my glasses, so he won't recognize me."

No one pointed out the lack of logic in this statement. But Charlotte was worried.

"He will recognize some of us," she said. "Think how embarrassing that will be if he tells everyone."

The ladies thought. Then Olive said, "I have an idea. You know those masks we have left over from the Halloween party? We can wear those. Then he won't know who we are. I'll get them from the cupboard."

Everyone wanted the Snow White mask except for Bessie, who felt that with her height, she was better suited to Chewbacca from Star Wars. The ladies finally agreed that Charlotte should be Snow White, since she had been beautiful, and indeed, she still was. The others settled on Mickey Mouse, Ronald Reagan and a generic cat.

Bessie looked at her little group of masked ladies and smiled to herself. Peter Kruger wouldn't know one of them.

"Well, that solves that," she said. "Is everybody in?"

"All for one and one for all," Charlotte said gamely. She was fond of reading historical romances.

The ladies met the next morning at ten to six in the ladies' change room. They all stripped to the skin, wrapped themselves in towels for warmth and donned their masks. They lurked around the corner, out of sight of the change room door, trying hard not to giggle.

"It's just like a surprise party," Isobel whispered. "That one we had for Dolly's ninetieth birthday where we all hid and then jumped out at her."

There was a moment of silence and then Bessie said, "Dolly should have told someone she had a weak heart."

Promptly at six, the door to the change room opened and Mr. Kruger stepped in with his hand outstretched toward the light switch. The ladies threw off their towels and leapt forward, screaming, "Pervert." Mr. Kruger shrieked, took a step backward, tripped over his plastic flip-flops and fell heavily to the floor. His head made a clunk like a baseball bat connecting with the ball when it hit the ceramic tiles. He twitched a few times and then lay still.

"My God," Olive whispered, "I think we've killed him."

"You were a nurse, Charlotte," Bessie said. "See if you can find a pulse."

All the bare naked ladies took off their masks and knelt on the floor around Mr. Kruger except for Maisie who had arthritic knees. It looked like some ancient witches' coven. Charlotte felt his neck.

"There isn't any pulse," she said, after a long moment. "And I can't stand to give him the kiss of life. What on earth are we going to do?"

Bessie rose to the occasion.

"Isobel, you can move the fastest. Go get Roger. He has CPR training." And as Isobel opened the door to rush out, she snapped, "For pity's sake, put your robe on."

The ladies busied themselves getting decently covered while they waited for Isobel to return with Roger. They also put the "Pool Closed for Cleaning" sign outside the door. When Roger arrived, he tried for a pulse and put his ear to Mr. Kruger's chest. Then he shrugged.

"I'm afraid he's beyond helping," he said. "I suppose I should call 911."

"We'll look like such fools," Bessie said. "Olive, your husband was in politics. You know what the Press will make of this. Couldn't we drag him into the men's change room and pretend he hit his head there?"

"What if his family sues the building?" asked Olive. "They could say there was water on the floor or something and he slipped."

Roger sat back on his heels and thought about it.

"I think I have an idea," he said. "First of all, I'll go down and turn off the security camera for this area. There's a full dumpster right beside the emergency exit from the pool. Cover him with towels. I'll get the dolly and move him out there. It will look like an accident. He's been warned about going into the dumpsters so the building shouldn't be held responsible."

Olive said, "You realize that we're breaking the law if we do this?"

"But no one's going to squeal," Bessie said, "Olive, you know what happens to squealers?"

"What? What happens to squealers?"

"They don't—they don't get invited to the pot luck suppers."

"Nobody's going to squeal," Charlotte said.

"Then that's all right," Roger said. And as he left, Bessie heard him murmur, "I'll say he must have been poking around in the dumpster again. He fell backwards and banged his head on the concrete."

And that is how Mr. Peter Kruger was found dead beside a dumpster at Cottonwoods Condo by the driver of the recycling pickup truck. Everyone accepted Roger's explanation. The garden committee from the condo sent an enormous wreath of orange marigolds to the funeral home.

On The Way To Hue

by Sue Pike

Sue Pike has stories in all seven of the Ladies' Killing Circle anthologies and was co-editor of Fit to Die, Bone Dance *and* When Boomers Go Bad *(RendezVous Press). Her stories have appeared in* Ellery Queen's Mystery Magazine, Storyteller, Cold Blood V *as well as* Murder in Vegas *(Forge),* The Deadly Bride *(Carroll & Graf) and* The Best American Mystery Stories, 2006 *(Houghton Mifflin). She won the Crime Writers of Canada Arthur Ellis award for Best Short Crime Story of 1997. In 2007 Sue started her own publishing house, Deadlock Press, and put her anthology skills to the test by collecting and editing stories for* Locked Up, *tales of mystery and mischance along Canada's Rideau Canal Waterway.*

Le Duan Street was teeming with motor scooters, cars, old trucks and battered cyclos. But the main obstacle between me and the Hanoi train station just across the road was a flood of bicycles tearing down the incline. I paused and my companion bumped into me again.

"Damn it all, Maureen," I shouted over my shoulder. "Back off!"

My heels were sore from the pummeling of her black boots. The woman had no sense of personal space and no idea of proper attire. It must have been ninety degrees and here she was, decked out in heavy canvas pants, some kind of secondhand flak jacket and a pair of so-called Viet Cong boots she'd found for sale on the sidewalk outside our hotel yesterday.

I looked down at my own feet. A purple lump was forming on my left ankle and this time she'd managed to rip the strap on my sandal.

"Sorry, Liz." Maureen crept up beside me. Her pale, powdery skin was pleated with wrinkles.

I caught her wrist. "How old are you, Maureen?"

"Seventy."

"Right." I interrupted her. "Me too, and I sure didn't sign onto this trip to take care of someone else. We're just fellow-travelers. Okay?"

She cringed. "Sorry. Sorry, Liz. It's just...everything's so frightening."

"Well, why in heaven's name did you come on this tour?"

She mumbled something but I couldn't hear.

"Look," I sighed. "We're nearly at the station. Get ready to dash across as soon as there's a break." I wished I had a rope for her to hang onto. That was how I'd corralled my kindergarten kids in Sacramento years ago.

A group of pedestrians gathered beside us and as soon as they moved forward I lunged too, darting and weaving with them.

"Oh...oh...oh." I heard the cry coming from behind me and felt a tug on my backpack. I grabbed the straps with both hands and managed to drag Maureen to the other sidewalk and up the steps to the station.

I paused to let my eyes adjust to the gloom and then made my way to the information desk, trying to keep my broken sandal on my foot and at the same time stay out of range of her boots. The din inside the station was deafening and I had to shout the word "Hue" to the stone-faced official behind the desk, pronouncing it "way" as the guide book instructed. The uniformed man stared at me and I pulled my ticket from my pocket and pushed it across the desk. He examined it and then looked over at Maureen, who was gazing up at the ceiling.

"For God's sake," I hissed. "Give him your ticket."

"What?" She tilted her head to one side like an anxious spaniel.

"Your ticket. He won't let you go without your ticket." I took a deep breath. The air tasted of singed metal.

Maureen dropped her pack to the floor and began to rummage inside. I could feel the impatience of the crowd behind us but I didn't have either the nerve or the language skills to try to explain. I glanced at my watch. Seven o'clock. We'd be lucky if we made our train. Finally Maureen produced a much-folded piece of paper and the clerk, holding three fingers aloft pointed towards the tracks. I turned away and felt the familiar blow, this time on my right instep.

"Sorry!" squeaked the voice behind me. I gritted my teeth and

34

tried to run but after a few yards I kicked my shoes off and sprinted barefoot toward Track 3. A woman in uniform glowered at us from her position in front of the first door we came to, made a big show of tapping her watch and then began to shout at us in Vietnamese, pointing down the train. We scrambled over to the first open door and hauled our packs aboard just as a whistle sounded and the train lurched into motion.

I limped down the corridor until I found our cabin. It was a tiny room designed to sleep four with double berths against each side wall and a single window between. I threw my pack onto one of the lower bunks, extracted a wet wipe from my pocket and sank down on the thin mattress to scrub the grit off my feet. Maureen dithered in the doorway.

"Um. Which one is mine?"

"Take your pick," I said, examining my bruises. "We have the room to ourselves." Another couple from the tour was supposed to share with us but a malfunctioning pacemaker had sent them back to Chicago early.

"Well," she paused and looked around as though faced with innumerable choices. "I think I'll take this other lower bunk."

I swung my sore feet onto my cot, shoved the pillow behind my back and pulled a book and my reading glasses out of my bag.

I'd only managed to read a paragraph when I sensed her presence hovering over me. "Liz? Where are the washrooms?"

I put my finger between the pages. "You know what, Maureen? I've never been to Vietnam before and I've certainly never been on this train before. I don't know any more about the layout than you do." I adjusted my reading glasses and opened my book again.

"Well, then. I guess I'll just..." I sensed her hesitating in the doorway, but kept my eyes locked on the page.

When she was out of sight I massaged my neck with one hand and searched through my bag for my slippers and a couple of aspirin with the other. How in the name of heaven had I gotten myself into this situation? But I remembered exactly how it had happened.

Debbie from the tour company had called one evening a month or so ago to say a Canadian woman had just signed up for our seniors' club tour and was hoping to save herself the single supplement. Since I was the only unaccompanied woman on the trip would I consider being her roommate?

I told Debbie I'd get back to her and then spent the next hour cooking up worst-case scenarios. When the most annoying thing I could imagine was an elderly woman who hogged the bathroom and talked too much, my frugal side took over and I called her back in the morning to say sure. I could certainly use the savings, I reasoned.

None of my imaginings had prepared me for this child in a woman's body. It was just bearable while others on the tour were there to share the burden, to take turns sitting beside her on the bus tour through Thailand, to talk her through the currency. I only had to put up with her at night and usually found a way to bury myself in a book and feign deafness.

It was when we were the only two on the tour supplement to Vietnam that I knew I had a problem. She had trailed along behind me in Hanoi, tiptoeing across intersections, peppering me with questions I didn't know the answers to. Where could we buy food? What was the name of that bird? That building? That street? The boots were meant to protect her from the rats that she, and only she, saw in every alleyway.

This overnight train trip and another day and a half in Hue would drive me mad if I didn't take control of the situation. I threw the book aside and swung my legs down. We'd picked up some spring rolls and biscuits at a street stand. I wiped the table with my sleeve and fished the parcel out of my pack. I would establish some ground rules about the next few days while we ate.

I stared out the streaked window while I waited for her to return from the toilet. We'd left Hanoi and its suburbs behind and were moving through a lightly populated area of plain concrete houses, many with an open room the size of a garage showing shelves of vegetables and dry goods for sale. Families hunkered in doorways. Some were watching television while others seemed to simply perch, waiting for customers. Children in shorts and plastic sandals played on the dusty driveways and waved to the train as it passed, like children the world over. In the distance I could see the purple shadows of a mountain range. Before long we were in open country with women working in rice paddies, still wearing the traditional cone-shaped hats although the sun had set and dusk was settling in.

I was starting to wonder what had happened to Maureen when she appeared in the doorway, her pinched little face flushed. "The brochure said there would be a modern washroom. All I could find was a filthy room with a hole in the flo—"

"Right," I interrupted her as I arranged the food on the table. "Let's eat."

"I can't. I feel sick." She stretched out on her bunk and turned her face to the wall. Her wispy grey hair trembled slightly and I wondered if she was crying.

"Well, I'm going ahead. I'm hungry." I ate my rolls and was just finishing up a second biscuit when Maureen pushed herself up to a sitting position.

"Well, maybe just a little." She picked up a spring roll and gave it a mouse-like nibble.

I put my biscuit down. "Maureen, we need to talk about something." I used my firmest schoolteacher voice. "You are seriously getting on my nerves – following me around, clutching at my sleeve all the time, waiting while I open doors for you. I didn't come on this trip to be your nursemaid."

"Sorry." She ducked her head. "I'll try harder."

I wiped my mouth and reached for my book.

"Um. Liz? There's something I want you to have."

"No, Maureen." I slapped the table hard. "You're not getting it. I don't want presents. I don't want anything at all except the freedom to enjoy myself without having to be responsible for you. Do you understand?"

"Sorry."

"And stop saying you're sorry. What is it about you—?" I almost said 'Canadians' but stopped myself and retreated to the far corner of my bunk with my book.

The train had been slowing for a while and now it stopped at Thanh Hoa Station. Within minutes, swarms of people drifted down the corridor past our open doorway slowing to stare at the two elderly white women. I looked away until a small boy marched into our cabin, pushed ahead by his parents. He held his hand out in the typical begging motion and Maureen dropped some Vietnamese coins into it. The Dong weren't worth much and the little boy continued to stand, his feet planted stubbornly in the middle of our room and his hand still out. "U.S. Dollar," he said in a whiney, singsong.

I lurched to my feet, turned him around by the shoulders and marched him back to his parents, slamming the door shut behind them. "U.S. Dollar, indeed."

Maureen pressed a finger onto some biscuit crumbs on the table. "Oh, I don't know. They have no reason to like Americans. Why shouldn't they try to get as much as they can?"

Maybe if I hadn't been so tired I would have let it go. I would have climbed beneath the covers and gone to sleep. But she was getting under my skin. "Right. Here we go. The anti-American speech."

She stared at me, frightened by my outburst. "I just meant

37

people who look like us."

But I wasn't about to be mollified. "And what do you know about it anyway? Canada wasn't even part of the Vietnam war."

"But we were in a way."

"Oh sure. A few hundred volunteers. That hardly counts. I lost my beautiful kid brother. One day he got his draft notice and the next day he was gone."

A rap on the door made us both jump. A porter brought in a teapot and two tiny cups on a tray. He set them down on the table and stood smiling into space while Maureen fished in her pocket for more coins to hand him. The Dong weren't having much effect tonight so I found a dollar in my bag and shoved it into his open hand.

After he'd left Maureen leaned close to the teapot and sniffed. "Can we drink this?"

"Oh for heaven's sake. It's been boiled." I grabbed my toothbrush and bolted down the corridor and across the gap to the next car where I found a European-style WC with a clean toilet, sink and paper. For one delicious moment I thought about keeping this treasure to myself and then I shook my head. What was the matter with me? Why was I letting this mousy little woman get to me?

Returning, I saw thin slivers of light under the closed doors of a couple of cabins but otherwise it was dark and the only noise I could hear above the clatter of wheels was the reedy sound of Asian music coming from someone's radio. I checked my watch. It was after eleven. The next stop would be Vinh early in the morning. I might still get a little sleep.

Maureen had switched off the single light in our cabin and when I closed the door behind me it was like being swallowed up in black velvet. I groped my way to my bunk and chucked the backpack into a corner before kicking my slippers off and crawling under the sheets.

"Liz? Why did you come to Vietnam?" Her voice coming out of the darkness made me jump.

"Christ, woman! I thought you were asleep."

"Me? I hardly ever sleep. They say we don't need much sleep at our age but I have to say I miss it." She paused. "Why Vietnam?"

Oh what the hell. I wasn't such a great sleeper myself. I pulled myself up to a sitting position and shoved the pillow behind my head. "I wanted to see if I could make sense of what happened here forty-some years ago. What happened to my whole generation." I hadn't talked about this to anyone for a long time. It felt right, somehow. "I was a bit crazy in the 'sixties, you know? Civil rights. Women's lib. Anti-war. Free love. Name any bandwagon and I was on it. There was so much to protest then. So many wrongs to make right."

"I watched some of the marches on television. Kent State. Washington." She sounded breathless and now that my eyes had adjusted to the darkness, I saw she was sitting up too, her face a pale and cratered moon floating over the bunk.

"There was a lot of dope," I continued, "but television was our drug of choice. We'd make placards in the morning and march all afternoon and then rush back to somebody's place to watch ourselves on the news. Those black and white flickering images were our real addiction." I poured some tea into a tiny cup. "And I've never felt more alive. We thought we were doing something new and meaningful. We were making history."

"But?"

"Oh well, you know how these things go. Everything got out of hand. We got more and more daring and the cops got more and more angry. The violence wasn't restricted to Kent State. God, no! We only had to go to any major city and we could stir up a revolution." I grimaced at the memory. "I've consumed more tear gas in my lifetime than today's kids have soda pop. I've been dragged by my feet over rough pavement until I bled, but I kept going back for more." I took a sip of the lukewarm tea. "And then one day, one of the cops caught me. He shoved his baton in my chest. Hard. It hurt like hell, knocked the breath out of me and I went down like a sack of potatoes. I looked up into his face and saw pure hatred there. He held me down with the baton while he kicked me. Same breast. Broke a couple of ribs that time."

"That's awful."

"I was out of commission for quite a while. They were able to tape my ribs all right but his steel-toed boots had ripped the tissue in my right breast. I had reconstructive surgery but the damned thing never looked right again." I rubbed the scar tissue on my chest.

The pale disk was bobbing up and down in agreement or sympathy. I couldn't tell which.

"So anyway, I went home and finished my degree and just before graduation I got a phone call from one of my friends. They were organizing a march. Could I come? This would be the last one, they promised." I finished the tea in my cup and set it down on the table. "I'd already got the job with the Sacramento School Board by then and I knew I had to stop this, to grow up, as my father was so fond of saying. But it was like any addiction. I couldn't seem to stop. I took the bus east for one more march. One more trip." I sighed. "And what a trip it was. We were stoned, singing, dancing down the street and then I looked up and saw him. Same boots. Same baton. Same hatred on his face."

"Same policeman?"

"You bet." I closed my eyes and allowed my mind to drift into the scene. "I shouted to my friends and we swarmed him, separating him from his pack. We were so smooth. So agile in those days. I'd stapled my placard to a stick that I'd pulled out of someone's garden. I hadn't noticed at the time that it was sharpened at one end. I just meant to shove it at him, exactly where he'd pushed his baton into me. It was a hot day and he was only wearing the light cotton uniform with a couple of shirt buttons undone. He must have recognized me because he lunged at me just as I was going for him. I was as surprised as he was when I felt the point going through his skin and then into his flesh. He fell and we ran. We went back to my friend's apartment to watch the footage on TV and it was only then that we heard he was critically injured. The next day he died."

I could hear Maureen's quick breath from the other bunk. "Did they catch you?"

Someone walked past our door humming an Asian tune, high-pitched, atonal. I listened to the footsteps receding down the corridor and when it was quiet again I said, "No. It was too confusing. No one was able to describe us."

"What happened?"

"I took the teaching job in Sacramento and my friends and I drifted apart. I got a call a few years later from one of the guys but we couldn't think of anything much to talk about." I took a deep breath. "So that was that. I lived alone. Taught school. Retired. But the worst thing was I lost my only brother to that war. My sweet baby brother." I rubbed my sore heels. "I blamed my father for making him go. He always thought Tommy was too sensitive, that war would make a man out of him. Told him so many times."

We sat in silence for a long time until Maureen said, "I killed a man too."

"Oh, come on." I laughed.

"I did."

"Okay. I'm listening."

"Liz? Can I come over to your bunk? I'll sit at the far end. It's just...I've never talked about this before."

I saw her shadow move across and felt her settle onto the other end of my bunk.

"I was twenty-nine in 1970 but I'd already been married for twelve years and I was kind of lost, unhappy, you know? All the other women my age either had babies or a job." She was quiet for a moment and then made a clicking sound with her tongue. "Well, it turned out the baby wasn't likely to happen. Not with Robert anyway."

"Robert is your husband?"

"He was. We divorced later and he died a few years ago" She pushed her back further into the corner. "But at the time we were living together in Ottawa and going to a church there. They had this outreach committee that was helping draft dodgers." The train was slowing and lights flashed by the windows as we pulled into Vinh. It felt like one or two o'clock in the morning but I couldn't be bothered checking my watch.

"American kids were pouring over the border in those days to escape the draft," she said. "And they needed places to stay, jobs, food. The organizers assigned half a dozen young men to our congregation for billeting. I remember going to the bus station with Robert to pick up our boy. It felt dangerous somehow, like a spy movie."

She paused and I waited for her to go on.

"He turned out to be just a scared kid, really. He was against the war but at the same time he hated letting his country down and disappointing his father." The train started up again and I could see Maureen in the fluorescent glow from the light standards strung along the track. Her eyes were tight shut now, her arms pressed against her stomach. "I thought he was settling in fine. We'd found him a job with a construction crew and he was starting to make a few friends, but then just a few weeks after he arrived his father called. I was in the kitchen and he was outside fixing the fence at the back of the garden. We didn't have portable phones then so I called him in and I went upstairs to give him some privacy. But then I heard him crying—really sobbing, so I ran downstairs. He was sitting on the kitchen floor with his head in his hands. I remember the sunlight from the window shining on that red hair of his, making it glow like an ember. He told me his dad had called him a coward, a pussy. Horrible, hurtful things."

"What?" I'd been drifting off but something she'd said jerked me awake.

"I hugged him and stroked his hair and before either of us knew what was happening he was hugging me back." She paused and shifted on the bunk. "I still remember that feeling. It was like

41

a dull pain in my stomach. Robert had never been much good in that department so it was all new for me and I was—well I was overtaken, I guess you could say."

"Hold on a minute." There was something nagging at me.

"Oh, I don't blame Robert," she went on as though I hadn't spoken. "It turned out he was gay. I'd never even heard of anyone being that way and I don't think he had either, but it certainly helped us to understand what went wrong between us."

"But the boy?" my tongue was thick and I was having trouble with the words. "What about the boy?"

"Well, we made love and I got pregnant." She clicked her tongue. "Simple as that." I heard her rummaging around in the pockets of her ridiculous flak jacket for a tissue.

I was wide awake now. "Maureen? What are you trying to tell me?"

"At first he seemed pleased, excited even. We started to make plans. I'd leave my husband and Tommy would get his landed immigrant status so he could work properly." She blew her nose. "But he was only nineteen—just a kid as you said. I could see that it scared him. I began to wonder what he was more frightened of, me and the baby or the thought of going to Vietnam. "

I think I must have made some kind of sound but she was lost in her memories, rocking back and forth.

"I wanted us to go away someplace. You know? Someplace where we could talk things over. My family had an old cottage in Eastern Ontario where I'd spent my summers as a kid and I wanted Tommy to see it." She was almost incoherent now, her words running together in an unbroken stream.

"It was still cold up there in May and the tourists didn't come until summer. There was nobody else for miles."

"No. Please." I needed her to stop before it was too late.

"We went to see an abandoned mica mine that my uncle had taken me to when I was little. Now they are just deep holes in the ground a few meters wide that the mining companies never bothered to fill in. The area was overgrown with juniper and sumac and no warning signs at all. You could stumble into one of them if you didn't watch your step."

"You killed him." I said, trying to staunch the terrible flow of words.

"He said he was going back to the States to sign up. I couldn't let him do that. He had responsibilities now." She was sobbing, her words coming out thick and moist. "I was slapping him, pushing at him, trying to make him understand and all the time he was backing away from me, trying to avoid my hands and when I realized how close he was getting to the edge of the mine I shouted to him but he slipped over."

I jammed my fingers in my ears, willing her to stop.

"I tried to get help. I screamed but there was no one around. You have to understand how dense the forests are and how isolated it is up there. The mine was so deep and the water was so cold." She was rocking faster now. Back and forth. Back and forth. Her head thudding against the wall of the cabin. "He never made a sound after that first yelp when he slipped. I tried calling him but he must have hit his head going in and then the cold..." She had finally run out of words.

I forced air into my lungs and shut my eyes trying to form a picture of him in my head but I couldn't make the parts fit together. The red hair, the freckles, the sunburned nose. It was so many years ago. "I never knew what became of him."

"Your father knew where he was." Her voice was hoarse from crying. "I heard Tommy give him our address."

I took a long breath and let it out slowly. The old bastard had taken that knowledge to his grave. I found a tissue in my pocket and blew my nose. I was numb, somewhere beyond tired, beyond feeling. "How did you find me?" I asked finally.

"I used the internet. That Classmates site. I remembered the name of Tommy's high school. I found your Facebook listing there and that's how I knew about this trip."

"And the baby?"

"Robert made a deal with me. The baby and I could stay if I'd let him see this man he'd met." She sighed. "Once she was born he loved her, of course. Who wouldn't? She was so sweet and he turned out to be a good dad. She adored him."

"She?"

"Sarah Elizabeth." She whispered the name. "Oh Liz. She's so much like you. Strong, opinionated. All the things I'm not."

I tasted the name. Felt it fly into the closed and bitter places in my heart, forcing light and air inside. Sarah Elizabeth.

"She's almost forty now. Married with a couple of kids of her own. They live in San Francisco." She clicked her tongue and I could hear the smile in her voice. "Imagine me with American grandchildren."

"Sarah Elizabeth." I hadn't realized I was saying it out loud until I heard my own voice.

"She's a teacher, like you. High school English. And pretty political too. Robert used to call her a firebrand. You should hear her on the subject of climate change. Oh my goodness."

It was getting light in the cabin. Dawn. Maureen stood up and stretched.

"Liz? Remember I said I had something for you?"

I nodded. Too tired to speak.

She pulled her bag from her bunk and after a few minutes of searching withdrew a snapshot and handed it across to me. "Here she is."

I held the photo up to the dim light from the window. It was like looking at a picture of me all those years ago, only there was a softness about the eyes that I had never had and her smile was full of love and affection.

Maureen was still standing, clutching the table for support and peering down at me. "I wanted her to have some family, besides me."

"She knows about Tommy?"

"She does."

I stared out the window. The train was passing through the Demilitarized Zone now. Water-filled craters dotted the landscape where B-52 bombs had blown the earth away. I wondered if this was what the abandoned mines in Ontario looked like. Tommy might have died right here, I thought. So many did.

"Would you like to meet her, Liz?"

I couldn't take my eyes off the bomb craters. Tommy would have hated the bombs. He wasn't a coward. My father was wrong about that, but he'd been a sensitive boy. He would have hated war and hated having to kill others. At least he hadn't had to put up with the prolonged terror, the noise and filth of this horrible war.

I turned away from the window and took a deep breath. "You think she might want to meet an old battleaxe like me?"

"Oh Liz. She would. Of course she would."

The Hard Way

by P.M. Jones

P.M. Jones, *always an avid reader, devours eloquent words and quirky tales with gluttonous velocity. In 2012, she shared her other secret passion - her love of writing. Her other, more well-known passions include creating spicy gastronomical feasts from around the globe to the rhythm of excellent music at a seaside retreat, while enjoying a glass of fine red wine in the company of good friends. From her experiences as a traveler, a woman of many different careers and the priceless gift of motherhood, P.M. Jones has much to offer as a writer. After honing her craft and experimenting with many different genres, writing mysteries seemed to be the right fit. Whether light and comical, historical, or ominous chillers, she loves to weave a multifaceted tale of intrigue. P.M. Jones lives outside Toronto and is busy writing and following one of her favourite sayings, "Live Life Like You Mean It!"*

Sitting in a coffee shop, I watched the line. Everyone had a cell phone or electronic device in hand. Talking. Texting. Surfing. Gaming. No one was comfortable speaking to the person in front or the person behind. Eyes were down, never making contact, no matter the proximity to other bodies in the room. Nobody noticed anyone anymore. It rankled.

As a police detective, it was second nature to me to note the details in a room. I immediately felt a wave of guilt for discounting humanity as a whole. I supposed, if there had been a young child or a senior in the queue, they would have looked around to see who seemed interesting or 'connected'... would have interacted with another beating heart, an interesting mind, friendly eyes. I tucked my phone into my purse, determined not to be 'one of them' as I enjoyed ten free minutes before I had to head into work. I smiled at the people occupying the table beside me. A young kid smiled back.

My purse vibrated and chimed. I ignored it.

It did it again. And again.

I swore under my breath and reached for my bag. The woman with the young kid, a toddler and a baby in tow, shot daggers at me with her clear blue eyes before swiping the crumbs off her table into her napkin, and dragging her impressionable young out the door. Guess my cursing was louder than I thought.

Seeing the caller I.D. I knew I had to answer, but I didn't have to like it. "I'm trying to enjoy a goddamn cup of coffee, here."

"Take it to go, Shannahan." Gruff, apathetic voice. My new partner, Bruxton. "We've got another one. Young woman. High profile. Same M.O... All hands on deck."

I grabbed my coffee, already in a takeout cardboard cup, and headed out the door, mentally cursing the existence of mobile phones.

As I bitched my way across the parking lot, I threw in another bunch of individuals who deserved a good mental thrashing. My boss, the dry cleaner who lost my little black dress, the cranky old lady who always let her dog crap on my lawn, the perpetrators of hideous crimes, and just for good measure, the idiots who invented pantyhose and the underwire bra.

One week, two unsolved homicides, one ulcer, and two hundred-something cups of crappy coffee later, we were no closer to identifying the perp, never mind catching him.

The murders were down to an Unsub who deserved some in-depth profiling, a lifetime behind bars and some serious psychoanalysis.

The ulcer belonged to my Captain who worked his department like a 'Risk' game board. Unquestioning soldiers, a target in sight and everyone else in the world breathing down his back.

I empathized with my Captain. But I couldn't sympathize with him. All my stores of sympathy were reserved for myself on a bad day, and for the victims and families of the crimes I investigated, on a worse day.

Shutting the door behind me as I entered his office, I remained standing as Captain Humphries paced around the room, popping antacids like tic-tacs. "Where are you on this latest, Shannahan?"

he barked.

"Same place. No good leads. No forensic evidence." I rocked back on my heels, trying not to rock back too far lest he notice the red soles and deduce that I spent a quarter of my salary on shoes.

"Two dead women in the same number of weeks. Red silk scarves tied around their necks. Screams 'serial killer' to me."

"Maybe. It either is what it appears to be or it isn't," I observed. Not receiving a reprimand for being a smart-mouth or a dressing down for stating the obvious, I continued. "Either there's serial killer out there, or we're dealing with someone who wants us to believe there's a serial killer out there. The latter of the two would lead me to believe there is a definitive motive for one of those murders. Maybe the first two victims were killed as a 'blind' and there's an unknown target who's walking around on borrowed time as we speak."

"See, that's why I like you Shannahan. You spell it all out so plainly. No grey areas. Go find me a killer. And make it quick. In black and white."

I walked through the parking garage, brow furrowed, lips set, eyes unfocused, oblivious to my surroundings, puzzling over the problem before me. I was overworking the situation. That's what professionals do, I rationalized. Intellectualize and analyse every known possible outcome, like a game of chess. I let my mind go blank, pretending to know nothing about anything. Which was actually true.

I went home to bed.

"A good mystery show has to take up at least two and a half hours of your time," I said.

"It does not," Bruxton opposed. We'd been arguing the point of a good half-hour show versus a full length movie all the way over. My partner and I had nothing in common. He was twenty years older than me and liked to operate 'old school'.

"Look at any good movie you've ever seen," I said. "It takes time to get to know the characters. Build up a plot. Have some emotional connection. Sympathy. Love. Hate. Understanding. Opposition."

Bruxton pulled himself out from behind the wheel and we ambled up the wide stone steps together.

Nodding to the officer on duty we proceeded through the massive double front doors of the house. I wondered about the purpose of the huge doors. Giants coming to dinner?

"What about Gilligan?" he asked.

"What? About... Huh?" I never knew what the hell he was going to come out with. We'd been working together for two months and just about everything out of his mouth confused or irritated me.

"Gilligan's Island. Everyone loved that show. It had an unending plot, a mystery until the end at each half hour. Characters you could identify with. It had glamour, suspense and a hint of naughty romance... Ever wonder why everybody asks who you'd rather 'do'? Ginger or Mary Ann?" Bruxton was smiling like a forty-eight year old frat boy.

I'd seen re-runs and even though I'd never been asked the question about 'doing' the movie-star or the farm-girl, I got what he was saying. "Point conceded. It was a brilliant masterpiece of serial television."

I bent down and plucked a piece of dried grass off the corpse and tucked it into an evidence bag.

This was the third dead female in as many weeks. She was a young woman. Not over twenty-five, at any rate. Her fingernails were painted a virulent blue. Almost the same colour as her lips.

The blade of grass was troublesome.

"Hmph," was Braxton's eloquent reply to me. Over half an hour of listening to him make a point, I finally cave, and all he can do is grunt. Frustrating. I watched him as he stood surveying the room through narrowed, calculating eyes. To most rookie detectives, he probably would've looked intimidating. Hugh Bruxton was a veteran on the force, with twenty-four years experience under his belt. That, plus too much fatty food and beer.

I noted the body was positioned in a very sensual pose. A position the crime scene photographer would probably drool over. I had to assume they did, sometimes. Why else would a person do that kind of job? I wondered if everyone else on the crime scene wondered the same about everybody else here.

"So, is she Ginger or Mary Ann?" Bruxton asked.

I looked at the victim's face. Chestnut hair braided down her back into one long plait. Full lips and a bit of make-up. Not full war-paint. But enough to accentuate her long dark lashes and high cheek-bones.

"I'd say an even mixture of the two. Innocent looking, but she wanted to be seen as 'sexy'," I observed.

Standing up, I snapped off my latex gloves. Such a detestable waste. This beautiful young girl, cut down before she could figure out who the hell she was.

"Bag and tag team's here," my partner said. I mentally cringed at the thought... and the statement. I shook it off, like water off a spring-born pup in October, discovering the hard way just how cold water could be.

A week had gone by without any leads. Now in week four, if the pattern continued, another young woman's life would be taken. I wasn't looking forward to tomorrow, if I couldn't do my job today and get this maniac off the streets.

I'd seen photos and files of Vics 'One and Two'. Red silk scarves. I'd been to the crime scene at the big double-door house. That woman had been identified as Nancy Young. She was the daughter of some big-wig in the medical supplies business. The father and mother had been out of town.

This was the pattern. The first two victims were also attractive young women, found at home, alone. Captain Humphries was frantic, putting everyone on this case he could afford. The mayor was breathing down his neck. It was an election year and press conferences whipping the general public into a frenzy did not make for happy voters. If there was a serial killer in our city, he wanted him found yesterday.

I pulled up at the first address on the file which listed Nancy Young's acquaintances and parked curbside. A manicured lawn and professionally landscaped gardens paraded the way to the front door of a sprawling Georgian Colonial. Nancy Young's friend, Leila Leibowitz, lived at home with her parents and two younger brothers. Leila answered the door with a puffy face and red-rimmed eyes. I gave her a slight smile, telling her I was sorry with my eyes and my demeanor.

"We can talk in here," Leila said, leading me into the living room. The house was deadly quiet with the exception of a clock ticking from somewhere unseen. It was a large house, a few blocks from where Nancy lived. I wondered where her parents and brothers were during what was surely the worst time of this girl's life.

"I know you're upset about Nancy," I said. "But we need some help to find the person who did this to her. I want to know if she had a boyfriend, or enemies of any kind, or met anyone new that sticks out in your mind?"

"Nancy hasn't dated anyone since Bradley. That was three months ago. She was pretty broken up about it. He was a jerk, but she really thought he was The One. I told her, I said, 'Nancy, you

49

can do sooooo much better than that idiot'. But did she listen? No. She stuck by him after he got fired for not showing up to work for the umpteenth time 'cause he was hung-over, and even after she found those text messages on his phone." Leila looked disgusted.

"Text messages?"

"Yeah. He signed up for one of those 'Sexting' messages things. You know, the ones you see advertised on late-night TV?"

I felt my lip curl back involuntarily. "I know the ones you mean. So what finally did it? Why'd they break up?"

"Brad hooked up with some slut working as a 'waitress' at the Golden Rail."

"The strip club?"

Leila nodded her head, yes. I took down Bradley's info and moved on.

"So did you and Nancy hit the party scene since she and Brad split? Clubbing or anything like that?" It's what I would've done, if my best friend had just broken up with her boyfriend.

Leila nodded again, her brown hair hanging in a lank curtain around her thin, splotchy face.

"I figured she should get out there and have some fun. She never realized how pretty she was. The jerk, Bradley," Leila spat, "was always putting her down, telling her that her nose was too long and her feet were too big. He had her convinced that she was a big ugly cow. And she wa... was, was so pretty. She was a wonderful, kind person. I'm going to miss her so much."

Leila broke down and sobbed. There was nothing more to be achieved in talking to her. She told me she'd call if anything sprung to mind about Nancy's last few days.

I headed back to the station to pick-up my partner. Bruxton had a standing appointment every Wednesday afternoon, and I figured he'd be back at his desk by now. I didn't want to interview this 'Bradley' person on my own. He sounded like an asshole. I wasn't hesitant to go on my own because I was scared. I was afraid of what I was going to say to the guy and get written up again.

Not giving a rat's ass who saw the red soles, I kicked my shoes off under my desk.

I was poking through the notes, re-reading the waste of time interview with Bradley the Jerk. All we'd gleaned from him was how really shitty he was as far as human beings go, but nothing to pin a charge of murder on. He was dumber than a brick and I couldn't see him walking away from a crime scene without leaving a whack of evidence behind.

It was two days until another murder if the time-line continued. I spread the crime scene photos out on my desk and pinched the bridge of my nose as I closed my eyes, willing the little devils with sticks poking at the back of my eyeballs to go away. I felt a migraine coming on.

The photos were graphic and disgusting. Three lovely young women with bright futures ahead, strangled and raped post mortem. Repulsive. The crime lab was working hard, trying to find something. Anything. We had no physical evidence aside from the blade of dried grass. Whoever murdered these girls knew what they were doing. No semen, no hair, no fibres. Nada. The women had been stripped of their clothes, which hadn't been found.

Coffee. I needed a jolt. I left the photos where they were and headed over to the crappy machine in the little nook at the back of the room.

Cup in hand, I headed back to my desk, determined to find the key to what linked these women together, thus leading me to the heinous killer.

Bruxton was out digging for more dirt on the first two victims, feeling unsatisfied with the depth of interviews which took place before we knew we had a serial killer on our hands.

I nearly jumped out of my seat as a hand reached around from behind me and pointed at the photo of Nancy.

"I thought I got a good angle on that one."

I spun my head around and found Kenny Ulrich standing behind me. How had he managed to sneak up on me? Probably I was too immersed in the files.

"I wouldn't give you too much credit," I said, turning back around to look at the photos.

"Why not?" Kenny asked, bristling. Whatever.

"The pose. I take really crappy photos with my little digital, and even I could have got a good shot here." I couldn't believe I was discussing the merits of a 'good' crime scene photo.

"You don't know what you're talking about." Kenny strode off, shoulders high and square, bony beneath his plaid shirt. Nobody ever said I was the sensitive type.

My cell phone rang and I answered, not recognizing the number on the read-out.

"Shannahan," I answered, as I walked my way through the covered parking garage to my car. The connection wasn't good.

Static crackled at the other end.

"Hello?" I hollered into the phone, hoping a louder voice would clear up the bad line.

"Hello? Detective Shannahan?" I tried to place the voice.

"This is Leila. Leila Leibowitz. Can you hear me?"

"Loud and clear," I said, hanging out the side of the garage to avoid a dropped call.

"I remembered something. Something about Nancy."

"Go ahead," I said, balancing my phone between my ear and my shoulder as I searched through my oversize purse for a pen and my notebook.

"Well, we went to a club the weekend before she... you know. We went to The Station, downtown. You know the one I mean?" I hadn't a clue, but urged her to continue. I'd look it up later.

"Well, they had this photographer there. He was taking pictures of people on the dance floor and selling them for twenty bucks at the front door."

"And Nancy bought one?"

"No. But she did go look at them. There were a few people looking at photos too, and everybody thought Nancy looked real good. She was always very photogenic."

I was baffled, wondering what the hell she was getting at.

"Okay, so what prompted your call?" I hated beating around the bush.

Leila cleared her throat and said 'Um' way too many times.

"It's okay, Leila. Even little details sometimes make a huge difference. I appreciate the fact you've been thinking about this. You've obviously got something on your mind." I was forcing myself into her shoes and even though they didn't fit right, I had to walk a mile in them before I passed judgement.

"The photographer said he was looking for models. Nancy looked pretty flattered by that. After how Brad made her feel I thought it was nice she was feeling good about herself again."

"Did he give her a card? Ask her to get in touch? Get her number or her name?"

"No."

"Okaaay..."

"But a couple of days later Nancy said she might look into this modelling thing. I was really happy for her and told her to go for it."

"Did she?"

"I don't know. But knowing Nancy, once she got an idea in her head she saw it through. I thought it might be important. You said

52

to call if anything stood out in my mind, and well, that kind of did," Leila said apologetically.

I trudged back upstairs to see if there was anything in the files about the web-search history of the three Vics. Nothing jumped out at me. Nor were there any common denominator emails. Nothing to connect the dots. I put a call into the other two teams working the cases and waited for a call back, which came in shortly after. I wasn't expecting much and that's exactly what I got. General search histories were wiped out these days, 'in-private' browsing used with regularity by most people, afraid of being attacked with computer viruses.

I sat back in my chair with my hands behind my head, thinking. Something. Something was there... just beyond reach, driving me crazy – like an itch I couldn't reach.

I reached for the phone and called Bruxton. He answered on the second ring, sounding grouchy. Surprise, surprise.

"You find anything out about modelling searches done on the other two Vics? From friends or family?" I asked without preamble.

"Hold on." Sounds from the other end sounded like Bruxton was shifting the phone to his other ear. I heard paper being shuffled.

"Just double checking my notes here," he said. "I don't recall anybody saying anything like that. Nothing in my notes either. Thought I'd better check to make sure. What's your angle?"

"I don't know. I just heard from a friend of Nancy's who thought she might have looked into modelling recently. All three of those girls were attractive and young. I thought maybe that was the tie-in. Just a shot in the dark," I said, feeling disappointed. I was grasping at straws. But something was niggling at the back of my brain. Frustrating.

"I'll let you know if anything turns up like that," Bruxton said, sounding a little kinder than usual. "We'll get him. Keep on looking for the thread."

Later, I sat at my desk, feeling downtrodden. I had revisited the files fifty times. I'd read and re-read the interviews and reports. I'd gone over the forensic evidence and looked at each photo under a magnifying glass. Literally.

The only commonality I came up with was the way the bodies were posed. Sensual. Erotic. Like they were posing for the camera in death. I was annoyed that I had been left with no tangible clues... and then it hit me. That was the common feature. No forensic evidence. Smart killer. Someone who knew what we'd be looking for.

I sat up in my seat, and slapped my hand down on my desk. Holy Shit! A crime scene photographer would know exactly how we did things. These women had been posed!

I speed dialed Bruxton.

"What do you think of Kenny?"

"Kenny who?" Bruxton sounded pissed off again. Probably he'd had a few beers and was sitting in his undershirt catching a ball-game.

"Kenny Ulrich. The crime scene photographer."

"You still on that angle, Rae?" Bruxton had never once called me by my first name, Rachel. Never mind the short form.

I ran a hand through my auburn hair. I'd ripped the elastic band out two hours ago, staving off the pony-tail headache.

"You ever get a gut feeling on something, Bruxton?"

I waited a moment, listening to silence on the other end of the line, wondering if I'd offended my partner by not using his first name too. Screw it, I thought. No reason to start getting all mushy here. We're just having a conversation for chrissake.

"Plenty of times. Why the hard-on for Kenny? You look into his eyes and see the devil inside?"

I disregarded the obvious reference to body parts which I did not actually possess. "It's the poses. The perfect way these girls are set up to be photographed. No forensic evidence. We're dealing with a Perp who knows what not to leave behind."

"Everybody knows that now. All those shows on TV. Plus half the world thinks they're photographers, what with digital cameras and such. Not much to go on."

I sighed. I knew my theory was weak. Worse than weak. I felt like a three year-old trying to arm-wrestle a strong-man.

I'd finally given up and headed home. I was exhausted. I stripped off my damned heels, navy skirt and blouse and draped my jacket over the back of the armchair in my dining room.

I headed into the kitchen and hauled a container of chow mein out of the fridge. I ate it cold, out of the carton, standing at the sink. I padded into the bedroom to throw on some sweats and made it as far as the bed.

Half an hour later, the phone startled me awake.

"Shannahan," I mumbled into the phone.

"You might be right." It was Bruxton. "I did a little background check on Kenny. Got some unsavory stuff in his past. Sealed records from when he was a juvenile. There was a matter between him and a local girl from his hometown. Thrown out of court due to lack of evidence. He was cleared, but the girl said he got aggressive – tried to get busy with her while taking some pictures for their high school yearbook."

"How'd you get the records?" I asked.

"Been doing this forever. I have managed to make some friends in the right places. There's more. He was charged with taking nude photos of minors – he had them sign disclaimers stating they were of age. He got off," Bruxton said. It sounded like there was hint of laughter in his voice as he said 'he got off'. Gross. I murmured something unintelligible into the phone to disguise the gagging.

"You sound out of it. You sleeping or something? It's only eleven o'clock on a Friday night. Figured you'd have a better way to spend your time on the weekend, Rachel. Either working or maybe out on a date. Jeez."

Well that got my goat. Didn't have a clue what that saying meant, but it felt appropriate.

"I'm working. Bring the information over here if you're up for it," I said, before fumbling for the 'end' button on the cordless.

Bruxton disconnected before I could.

I pulled on sweat pants and a ratty old t-shirt, waiting for Bruxton to arrive. I was practically bouncing, anxious to see what he had dug up on Kenny.

My heart was hammering, adrenaline coursing through my veins, making my body feel like I'd just downed some illegal substance. Or six Red Bulls and vodka.

I couldn't sit still. I put on a pot of coffee, knowing it was the worst thing for me, but I couldn't resist the craving. I walked over to the dining room table and extracted my cell phone from my purse. Dead. I plugged it in to the charger in the kitchen. I was waiting on an email report from the crime lab. Everyone was working around the clock on this one. No one wanted to get the call about another dead girl. I knew I was on the right track, more or less. All I needed was one tiny tangible clue. I was determined to nail this prick.

My feet were at my front door before I knew it when I heard the knock. Bruxton looked like shit. No surprise. He was six hours past a five-o'clock shadow and his shirt was un-tucked on one side.

"You bring the info?" I said, standing aside as he stepped in.

"You look like hell," Bruxton said, giving me an appraising once over. I looked down at myself, then caught my reflection in the mirror. My hair was frizzed out to massive proportions, and there were dark circles under my eyes.

"Whatever," I said. "Coffee?"

"Sure," Bruxton said, moving into the living room. His eyes scanned the room. Such a cop.

I pulled two mugs out of the cupboard and opened the fridge. "Cream? Sugar?" I called out.

Silence.

"Yo. Bruxton..."

"Black."

Reaching for the coffee pot, I noticed the red diode flashing on my phone. A message from the lab. Still no DNA, no fibres, no physical evidence. I scrolled down. The blade of grass had been analyzed. It was Timothy Grass, with traces of other farm forbs, also known as hay.

I stood there, like an idiot, trying to figure it out. Hay? Why would a girl be found murdered in a mansion with a blade of hay on her when the killer had been so careful before? I filled the two coffee mugs and toted them out to the living room.

Bruxton took his and sat down on my sofa, with one leg crossed over the other. I knew I looked puzzled and I wasn't surprised when he questioned it. Bruxton's eyes were flat black and hard.

"I just got a message from the lab. The grass was hay."

"So?"

"So I can't figure out why a killer, a very, very careful killer would leave a piece of hay behind. It doesn't make sense." And then it all came together. The conversation I'd had with Bruxton at the last crime scene came racing back to me. A chill ran down my body, causing goose bumps to spring up on my arms. "I'm going to grab a sweatshirt. One sec," I said, moving toward the bedroom.

I'd seen the look in Bruxton's eyes. Soulless. I'd seen it before. He had the devil inside. I moved to my closet door, and yanked it open, pulling a shoe box down from the top shelf. I felt like a damned fool, getting myself into this spot.

"I'm proud of you Rachel," Bruxton said, moving into the room. He had a red silk scarf in one hand and a long piece of wire in the other.

I swallowed down the bile that had risen in my throat. I

squared my shoulders and looked him straight in the eye. "You're sick Bruxton. You don't know what you're doing. You'll never get away with it. I've got security cameras and you've left DNA all over the place. This isn't like the last three."

"Three?" Bruxton shrilled, an octave higher than usual. "It wasn't three. Three with the same M.O... I've changed it up every time before. A strangling, a beating, a drowning here and there," he said with a note of pride through a twisted grin.

I felt like every nerve ending in my body was jumping. I'd met crazy – but this was sick-crazy. Wacko crazy.

"This time I was going with a theme. Mary Ann and Ginger. You're a ginger. It took you a long time to figure it out. I gave you a clue. I left some evidence."

"Why?" I asked, feeling around on the floor of my closet with my left foot. I cursed myself for owning so many damned pairs of shoes. I almost laughed, hysterically, at the thought.

"You know where I go every Wednesday?" Bruxton asked. He was taking small steps toward me. I shook my head, no. "Therapy. I see a shrink. She tries to get me to talk about my job and my feelings. My whore of a mother and my father, the abusive drunk. Boo-hoo." Bruxton mock cried, pretending to rub his eyes dramatically.

My toe hit the metal heel of my gun. I drew in deep breath. I had to try and keep my head, or the crazy guy would win.

"Why though? I mean, what's the point? We see enough senseless killing every day," I said, buying time.

Bruxton laughed, high and shrill. That was the worst sound I'd ever heard in my life. My hair stood on end, I was sure of it.

"Right, Rae-Rae. Detective Shannahan. It's not senseless killing. It makes sense to me. That's the point. Those girls... the dirty little Sluts – they wanted it, and I was just the man to do it. Kind of old-school, but I knew they'd appreciate it.

"I took out ads in the personals. Nothing on Craigslist or Kijiji, no internet porn crap. Old fashioned print ads. 'Models wanted for print and film'. People still trust the black and white. Especially innocent, old-fashioned girls who really want to be dirty little Sluts."

I ducked down and grabbed my thirty-eight as Bruxton lunged. We both knew it was a moment of do-or-die.

I wasn't ready to die. Bruxton found that out, the hard way.

The Cookie Caper: An End of the Road Adventure

by Helen Nelson

*In her day job **Helen Nelson** is a project manager and IT consultant. At night and on weekends she morphs into a reader who has a strong commitment to the mystery community. She has spent the past four years as president of the Toronto Chapter of Sisters in Crime. Helen began her storytelling career with ghost stories she made up for younger cousins. Family lore has it that the stories gave the cousins nightmares, and got Helen in a bit of hot water. The storytelling continued – but mostly as a background activity to her reading. Some of her many nieces and nephews have been the recipients of stories just for them, but the stories in this anthology are her first published works.*

Do you think my name sounds like a boy's name? I looked Taylor up on the internet and it wasn't in the most popular names for boys at all. It was number 583 for girl's names in 2001. That's when I was born. I am glad I was not named Emily or Madison. Those names were number one and two. In Toronto there were three girls named Emily in my class and two named Madison. Here there is no one named Madison and only one named Emily. But those names are pretty popular so you never know when more might show up.

I am 8 years old. I like adventures and big words. I live in the North. It is a long way north, north of Toronto where I used to live, north even of North Bay. I think we are at the end of the road. But my parents say the road goes on for a long way yet. When we came here my parents said they hoped I would have fewer adventures. I think maybe I'll have more.

I think my mother does not like adventures. Sometimes she says she is too old for adventures. Do you think it is because she is 53? Other times she says she must like adventures because she had me when she was 45 and my father was 50. Maybe they like to have adventures a little bit because they bought this bakery in the north and moved here from Toronto. I had to come with them and leave behind my best friend Madison S. – not Madison C., she's useless.

It is cool to live in a bakery. My mother and father make bread every day. They make lots of other things too. My favourite is the chocolate chip cookies. They have lots of chocolate chips in them and NO oatmeal or raisins, which I hate passionately. I especially like it when, if they cannot sell them all, I get to eat a few.

We came here in February. Only people who live around here were buying our bread and cookies and things then. Now it's July, school is out and the tourist season has begun. There are not very many tourists. My mother and father are disappointed that there aren't more. Maybe they thought there would be a lot and they would be rich. But my Mother says that really they just hoped to make a decent living and have a good place for me to grow up.

I like having a big yard too. Our yard in Toronto was miniscule. Mostly there were just flowers there. Here there are a lot of trees and some vegetables and even more flowers. And it is nice to be by the lake. But I can't have adventures in the lake. I had to promise not to go in the lake by myself. My grandfather says a promise made is a debt unpaid. I don't know what he means. My mother and father say the consequences would be dire indeed if I were to break my promise. I know what that means! I would be in big trouble. Anyway, I always keep my promises.

When the first bunch of chocolate chip cookies disappeared overnight, my mother and father were not happy. They thought it was me who ate the cookies. They thought I was a thief. But it was not me who stole the cookies. I told them I sleep at night. I do not get up to eat cookies. I don't think they really believed me even though I cried and promised them that I did not eat the cookies.

Then, when more cookies were missing another morning, and again the fingers were pointed at me, I said enough is enough. I am going to be a spy. Like Harriet. I will find out who is eating the cookies. Mother and Father will be able to make them stop and they will be pleased and grateful that I was able to find the real thief. And it will be an adventure. This adventure is OK because it's not in the lake and I won't be eating cookies. I did not say I would never get up in the night to be a spy.

Being a spy takes patience. On Monday and Tuesday there were no cookies left, no bread left. There was nothing for the thief to take. On Wednesday night I got up and crept part way down the stairs. I think I waited for hours. I had planned to peek over the stairwell edge if I heard anything. I almost fell asleep on the stairs, so after a while I went back to bed. In the morning all the cookies were still there.

On Thursday night, I tried again. I startled from sleep on the stairs when I heard the back door open. I peeked over the stairwell and was completely surprised to see a big black bear come into the bakery. I did not scream. Oh no – I knew the bear wanted to eat cookies, not me. But really I was too petrified to scream. And I was too scared to move at first. When the bear had a bunch of cookies, he sat down to eat them on the small ice cream freezer.

So I swallowed hard. I crept up the stairs to my parents' bedroom. Like a mouse.

"There's a bear eating chocolate chip cookies in the bakery," I said as I woke my mother up. "His fur is messy and he smells atrocious."

"Taylor, you've just been dreaming, go back to bed." I think my mother doesn't have a good imagination.

"No really, Mom, there is. He's eating the cookies. He's sitting on the ice cream freezer. Just listen to the cacophony from downstairs." Well it was not really that loud, in fact the bear was too busy eating cookies to be all that noisy but I really love that word, don't you?

But by then my Mom was awake and she could hear the bear moving around downstairs. I still don't think she thought it was a real live bear, but she knew that something or someone was in the bakery. Here's the thing, though. It's like I said, my mother does not like adventures. She would not come down with me to see who was stealing the cookies. I told her the bear wanted to eat cookies not us. She said she didn't care; she was not planning to meet up with whoever was down there. She did not care if it was a bear, a spider or Santa Claus. She woke up my father. He didn't want to go downstairs either.

After a while the hullabaloo downstairs stopped and after a few more minutes we did go a little ways down the stairs to check on things. Okay, they did and I kind of followed them even though they told me to stay put. And when there was nothing in sight but the empty cookie tray and the ice cream freezer we went down the rest of the stairs and carefully looked around. The bear was gone and the back door was open.

My parents called the police who called the wildlife people. Yes, the wildlife people thought it could well be a bear. My parents were not happy. My mother wanted to know why the bear just did not knock over garbage cans, why it had to come into the bakery and eat chocolate chip cookies. But, really, if I had a choice between garbage and chocolate chip cookies I know what I would pick. I bet you know what you would pick too! I guess that bear was pretty smart, even if he was a thief.

The wildlife people said they would outsmart that bear with a trap. We had to purposely put out some chocolate chip cookies and leave the house. I didn't want to go anywhere. I had detected that it was a bear stealing our cookies and I really wanted to see them catch him. It would have been a better adventure.

Two nights after setting the trap the wildlife people caught the bear. But he didn't get any of the chocolate chip cookies before they apprehended him.

Still it was fun to stay in the hotel for two nights – almost an adventure. My mother and father just thought it was expensive. Sometimes they are not much fun.

The morning we went back home, the wildlife people and I ate the cookies. The bear is in custody. And I'm looking for another adventure. I am a good detective, don't you think?

The Hunter

by Karen Blake-Hall

Karen Blake-Hall has loved mystery suspense stories since she was a child. She is a member of Sisters in Crime International, Sisters in Crime – Toronto, Sisters in Crime Toronto Executive, Romance Writers of America, Toronto Romance Writers - Kiss of Death Chapter and Fantasy, Futuristic and Paranormal Chapter. When she's not at her day job she's writing or spending time with her husband, children or grandchild. She lives outside of Toronto with her husband and a Jack Russell Terrier who rules not only the street but the universe.

I hunt.

Mankind has hunted since the beginning of time because, without the hunt, we would have become extinct. But that hunt was for food, the continued existence of the species. That ancient hunt was a noble hunt, for survival, for the continuation of the bloodline.

Tonight, I hunt.

But whether it is as noble a hunt is for you to decide.

I hunt, not for the usual things people in this city hunt for. I do not need a taxi to whisk me home to a loving family. I have none. I do not need to hunt for the camaraderie of a noisy bar with booze to loosen my inhibitions for unlike most, I have to struggle to keep my cravings in check. No, my hunt is a solitary one, one that most people never know. Nevertheless, my hunt is my existence because without my hunt, I am nothing.

Through the crowded aisles I forage, bumped and pushed by people I don't know, people I probably wouldn't like if we met under different circumstances, but my quest, the reason for my existence, keeps me true to my course.

I see the usual people, doing the usual things, for people are creatures of habit, nothing more. Yet there is that one that attracts my attention, that one that I must follow. I cannot explain why I cut that one from the herd, why that one is my prey for it is an instinct, a natural reaction that triggers me into action.

They walk with their heads down for no other reason than there is no need for them to look, to see the beauty of their surroundings, for that is of no interest to them. They will not change their routine. Like lemmings heading to the sea, they do not understand their fate, or destiny, if you prefer. But I understand their destiny for it is entwined with mine.

I have heard people say that waiting is a cat and mouse game. The cat with the patience of a saint waits for a little dumb mouse to wander into its path. Now I'm not sure that the cat possesses the intelligence that it is ascribed. Is it patience or laziness to wait for your dinner to come to you? Most other predators search for their food. Anticipating the fight to the death only heightens the quest for nourishment because nourishment without accomplishment is empty.

So I wait for my experience to start. I see the usual people, nothing outstanding and yet I know there will be that one that triggers me to follow. The wait is hard for I long for the chase to begin.

Movement catches my eye. Is it time? My senses go on high alert. My muscles tense, filling with energy for the pursuit.

No, that is not the prey I want. I let them go about their life, unharmed for another day.

Scanning the area, I become impatient, for unlike the cat I don't want to wait for my dumb mouse to walk past. The hunger in me for the hunt increases, I want to pace like the caged beast but the pacing will alert my prey; if alarmed the prey will melt back into the crowd and my quest will go unfulfilled.

Movement again. Yes. Yes.

He looks, so I avert my eyes. He is in my crosshairs but I will not let him know. He looks away. Good. The unsuspecting prey is the most fun.

I stand. Wait. Not wanting to spook him before it is time. I follow a few steps behind so as not to alarm him, for the hunt is about cunning, to allow the prey to be unaware, almost happy in their last moments. I believe in happiness for I am at my happiest during the hunt so I allow them to enjoy their happiness as well. After all, what is the harm?

He starts to walk, so do I. He pauses, so do I, for I will not spook the prey. The chase is most satisfying while in my control. I will run if necessary for I will not lose my prey but for now I will allow him to enjoy his moment, his thrill if you will.

For what is life without thrills? I do not want to think of life without my thrills because thrills make the hunt more satisfying.

He stops and looks around as if he senses me but I know he doesn't see me for I move like a ghost, a shadow, nothing more.

I see a small smile form on his lips. One forms on my lips as well but mine is based on truth and his is fiction only. He is unaware of this truth but it is a truth nevertheless. The cold hard facts of life never lie. I know he will not get away, no matter what he thinks, whether he is thinking at all is not my concern.

At the end of the day or the end of the hunt as you will, he will be prey and I will be his captor.

He pretends to look at things as he walks past, fondling, caressing but in truth he is working his way to freedom. I will stop his quest. It will never happen for him. I am stronger and smarter, my little prey will not see me coming until it is too late.

He stops, as if sniffing the air for danger. We are animals after all, so our instincts for sensing danger have not changed. We pretend we are superior, not like the other animals but we aren't any different. We have our leaders, our guards, our followers and our weak. I do not prey on the weak for they are not worth the chase. The strong, the would-be leaders are the ones that quicken my pulse and my prey has quickened mine.

Acting coy he stands, waiting for the elevator. We both know I cannot follow him into the small box without being seen. I laugh to myself for he hasn't outsmarted me. I race down the secret staircase taking three steps at a time. I know just how long I have to reach the bottom and get into my next hiding place before the elevator doors open.

Near the bottom of the stairs I catapult myself over the railing gaining speed, for speed is of the essence. Now locked in a race of time that I must win in order to continue the hunt, I dash through the doorway into the main area of the building.

Quieting my breathing, I walk to the pillar and wait. The elevator doors open as if the Gods are working with me but I do not believe in them nor do I need their help. A woman pushes a baby carriage out of the elevator first, smiles at the older couple, the man with a walker, the woman with an obligatory smile waiting to get in. Once she is clear of the doorway, two teens emerge, together yet sadly apart, not looking where they are going, both lost in thought with their fingers flying across their phones' keyboard. Unaware of my prey or of me, they walk their slow I'm-too-self-absorbed stroll down the aisle, the older couple glaring at them.

I wait but my prey hasn't emerged. The older couple start into the elevator then stop. I know he is still in there but for reasons only known to him he hasn't decided to come out into the open.

Like fate, prey can be fickle. I don't know whether, like fate, there is an element of erratic changeability or whether my prey is in fact stupid. I have given some thought to this but it remains a mystery to me that I doubt I will ever solve.

Cautiously he appears, scanning the terrain for his senses have also heightened. Whether out of fear or the excitement of being close to his quest, I do not know. However, it heightens my senses as well. I can smell his fear, although others could not detect that he exhibited any visible signs.

He heads towards his chosen path, to his false freedom. I wait, his mistake is my gain. He will walk in front of me; so close I could reach out and grab him but I will not for that would end the hunt and I crave to it.

My lovely prey is coming closer and closer to me as if I am the beacon and he is the storm-tossed ship racing in hope for shelter but that inevitably shipwrecks.

His scent, heightened with fear, exhilarates me. I see his eyes glistening with hope, the sheer pleasure of escape; for he is sure it is within his grasp. I will allow him this for the passing moment. Hope is to be cherished for its falseness. It leads people to a belief in fulfillment of an emotional desire that cannot be measured and is therefore the greatest falsehood of all. That is what makes prey so easy, their unrelenting vulnerability.

Walking toward the doors I see his reflection in the mirrored wall. His smirk amuses me. Only a fool would be so sure of himself, so self-confident that he cannot fail. Everyone fails at times and this is his time.

He steps forward, the doors open, fresh-air rushes at us. His step quickens with the joy of achieving his quest but, alas, he has failed. The hunt is mine. I step toward him, grasp his shoulder and say, "You're under arrest for shoplifting."

Hideaway

by Madona Skaff

Madona Skaff describes herself: After earning a degree in biology, I spent 20 years working in mining research. Now I've earned the opportunity to write full time. I started out in life as an SF writer with several short stories published in the small press. In the mystery field, I was assistant editor for "The Ladies' Killing Circle". My story Night Out *appears in their third anthology,* Menopause is Murder. *I am a member of Capital Crime Writers, an Ottawa mystery writing group and was past President for the Ottawa Chapter of Sisters in Crime. I have recently completed a mystery novel which is bravely out in the world looking for a home.*

All Yvette Brisebois wanted was a cottage by the sea. A quiet place to get away from everything—especially the law.

As soon as her flight instructor had signed her out for her first solo cross-country trip to Kingston, she tucked the flight charts under her arm, picked up her box-shaped flight bag and bounded up the stairs and out of the flying club. Yes, her dream was finally within reach. Breathless with excitement and eager to get into the air, she was glad that she'd already done the preflight inspection. She practically skipped onto the tarmac to her waiting Cessna 150.

And tripped to a stop, her heart pounding.

Richard.

He stood next to the club plane. Her getaway plane!

He must have gone into work early and discovered his empty safe. She tightened the grip on her case. For an instant he looked as startled to see her as she was him. He shoved his hands into his pockets and smiled brightly, as though nothing had changed. As though he hadn't ended their affair four months ago.

Good. He didn't suspect... Cautious, she went up to him.

She was prepared to hear him offer to split the half-million that he'd embezzled from the bank. Or ask how she'd got into his private safe and found the altered ledgers. Or maybe try to convince her that the diamond necklace in the safe, along with that insipid note, was actually meant for her not his wife. A wife he'd once promised to divorce. She was prepared to hear him say anything. Or so she thought.

"Yvette, my love," he reached for her hand.

She took a step back and glared at him till he reluctantly dropped his hand to his side. "Richard," she said, barely able to hear her own words through the blood rushing in her ears, "Why are you here?"

"I came to wish you luck. Everyone at the bank knows how nervous you've been about your first solo cross-country flight, so I just came to encourage you."

"Why are you really here?" She asked.

"I've been thinking that I made a mistake," he said. "You wouldn't slow me down on my way up the corporate ladder. As a matter of fact, I'm up for a VP position. Once that comes through, I'll divorce Brenda—she won't make any trouble—and then we can get married."

She forced her lips into a smile as she softly said, "Oh, Richard, you'll never know how that makes me feel." He couldn't possibly have expected her to fall for that old line again.

Waving him away, she climbed into the Cessna 150 and started up the engine, resisting the sudden urge to run him down as she taxied for takeoff.

She'd timed her departure for 8:00 am, rush hour at Ottawa International Airport. Air Traffic Control would have their hands full. Once airborne, she turned south on her planned course to Kingston. Twenty miles outside the control zone, she turned due east. After a few more minutes she switched off the transponder that might identify her on radar.

The calm air made it a smooth, effortless flight. But she couldn't relax and enjoy it. She had enough fuel for five hours of flight and had decided to risk flying through Montreal's large control zone, a busy airspace.

Forty minutes later, her heart pounded as she skirted the edge of Montreal's huge control zone, gave a false call sign and was cleared through with no problem. Everything always came easy for her and she knew it always would. Just the same, from now on, she'd avoid all control zones. She turned off the radio not interested in listening to all that inane chatter.

She sat back and admired the view of the Quebec hills all ablaze in radiant fall colours. Last week she'd driven out to an abandoned airfield, east of Sherbrooke, to hide a fuel supply and aircraft paint. It was still two hours away. A glance at the fuel gauge and her watch. A quick mental calculation. Four hours of fuel left.

She'd refuel, paint new call letters on the plane and by tomorrow she'd be on the east coast in her own private cottage, on her own private beach. Any trace of Yvette Brisebois and the aircraft identified as C-KJJ would be gone. She'd stay at the cottage until she got bored, then move on. She patted the case on the seat beside her. Thanks to the money inside, she could go anywhere.

She came to Sutton Mountain range and climbed to 5,000 feet to have plenty of clearance above the trees. From this height, the ground looked deceptively flat. A beautiful carpet of browns, golds and reds. Hard to believe some peaks stood over 3,000 feet.

A bump.

Air turbulence? Another bump then an odd sound. What...?

The engine was sputtering! She gasped at the sight of the propeller. She shouldn't be able to see it spinning. Another bump that she felt in her gut this time. Then, a terrifying new sound.

Wind.

Her single engine plane had become a glider!

She adjusted the gas mixture. Put carb heat full on. Switched the magnetos on and off. Tried the ignition.

God! The ground was still creeping towards her.

Why...? Her eyes locked on the gas gauge. Empty? Not twenty minutes ago she'd looked at it. Close to full. She turned the gas select off. Then on again. Switched fuel tanks. Nothing.

Damn! She wiped sweaty palms on her jeans. This was no time to fall apart. She barely had enough time to find a place to land.

She looked around. Mountains everywhere. A snaking river. 4,500 feet and descending. That gave her four and a half miles to glide. She grabbed her map. There had to be level ground nearby. The road five miles ahead looked promising. Slim chance of getting over the mountain range though. Better odds with the lake just behind.

A gentle turn. A small loss in altitude. Wing flaps at ten degrees for more lift. Now at 2,000 feet.

She tuned the radio to the emergency frequency making sure the analogue display read 121.50. She took a deep breath and spoke as calmly as she could.

"Mayday, mayday, mayday. This is Cessna 150, Kilo, Juliet, Juliet. I'm five miles south of Bolton Sud making an emergency landing near a lake." She repeated the message two more times. Let the microphone fall to the floor.. She concentrated on flying.

One thousand feet. The trees – too close. Damn! She'd forgotten that the altitude was above sea level, not ground level. Trees whipped beneath her, frighteningly close. Her path to the lake was clear. Not enough of a shore to try to land on. Trees were everywhere. She'd have to ditch in the lake. Get close to the shore. Minimize the swim. If she survived.

Don't panic. The lake was calm. Easy landing. Wispy tree tops slapped at the plane. A large branch hit the wing. But she kept the plane steady. Emergency procedures drilled into her brain guided her.

Clear. Over the lake. Full flaps down. Airspeed decreased fast. So did altitude. She waited for the double impact. The first came when the tail hit the water. She pulled back on the controls. Keep the nose up. Don't want to pitch over.

The shore approached.

The second impact came when the main wheels hit the water and the nose fell hard. In painstakingly slow motion, the plane pitched forward. Water filled her vision. Yvette sucked in her breath as she waited an eternity for the trees and sky to return.

Down and safe, but not for long.

Water lapped around her ankles. Horrified she watched the water rise as she fought to push the door open.

If she waited, the cabin would fill with water, equalizing the pressure. Not a pleasant thought. She unlatched the window, swung it open and crawled out.

She started to swim out from under the wing then remembered the money was still in the plane.

She turned back.

With an extra kick in the water, she heaved herself up to the window. Her weight shifted the plane suddenly and the canopy hit her on the head. The water grabbed hold and pulled her under.

Yvette gradually became aware of swimming furiously. She had to reach that patch of grey.

Strange. She could breathe. With each breath, the murky waters parted until she found herself lying on a narrow bed in a small room. She expected to see sterile hospital walls. Instead, she saw log walls and recognized the faint smell of a wood fire.

"My cottage by the sea," she said, smiling at the thought. But things didn't feel right.

She lifted the sheet covering her. No cuts. No bruises. She wore only a gigantic blue t-shirt and her own panties.

"I see you're still alive."

She dropped the sheet and found a large, muscular man looking at her. He had shoulder length dark hair badly in need of a trim and a slightly less ragged beard. His eyes, set in a deeply tanned face, were so dark she could barely distinguish the pupil from the surrounding colour. She guessed he was close to fifty.

"Where am I? What happened?"

"Why, you crashed into my lake, didn't you? You're safe now," he said with a heavy Newfie accent.

"Your lake?"

"Lucky for you, eh, I was out fishing when I saw your plane come down. You got out safe, why'd you go back?"

"I, uh, got disoriented I guess – I'm not sure. You pulled me from the plane before it went down?"

"You're welcome."

Maybe she should have thanked him. She wanted to ask about her flight bag, but how could she without raising his suspicions? She shut her eyes, fighting back tears of frustration.

"You're alive. That's all you should be caring about."

She opened her eyes to watch her saviour walking away. He closed the door quietly behind him, leaving her alone. Starting to sit up, she thought she heard him lock the door. It was probably the bed springs creaking. Yvette leaned back on her elbows. Enough for now, she decided when her head started to spin and lay down.

Just a short nap would bring her strength back. Drifting off to sleep, she wondered if she should tell him her name, or guard her new identity. Interesting that he hadn't told her his...

Yvette woke at the sound of the door being unlocked. She swung her legs over the edge of the bed. She went to the door and reached for the handle just as the door opened.

She shrank away involuntarily, as his huge bulk eclipsed the doorway. At five foot four, she barely reached the middle of his chest. He brought in a tray of food and put it on the night table.

"Good to see you're up. Hope you like fish." He smiled as he took her arm and guided her back to the bed. He fluffed the pillows behind her and lifted her legs up on the bed, pulling just the sheet over her bare legs. His impersonal manner relaxed Yvette. He put the tray on her lap.

71

"Wait," she called to him, as he turned to leave. She had to find out how much time she had to disappear before the authorities arrived. "I guess you phoned in my crash?"

"No phones here."

"Well, how far is the road, then?"

"It's a long climb down from the mountain."

"How long before help arrives?"

"You're safe now."

"Well, I know, but I sent out a Mayday with my position."

"Guess with all the hullabaloo over running out of fuel, you forgot your radio was off."

"That's impossible ..." she broke off remembering. No need for all that inane chatter she'd told herself. And she guessed that her landing hadn't been hard enough to activate the Emergency Locator Transmitter, or help would have already arrived. The last thing she wanted was the police finding her, so that was good. Right?

Looking at this man, she wasn't so sure.

"Besides," he turned and started for the door, "no one would be able to spot the wreck. The lake's very deep. This is a nice place to get away from things."

"One more thing," she said, stopping him at the door with her voice. "Where's the bathroom?"

"Only an outhouse here. But till you get strong, use this." He came back, reached under the bed and pulled out a bedpan and put it on the bed.

"Look, I feel fine. I want to go outside."

"Maybe tomorrow. Yes, I think tomorrow's the day."

She stared at the bedpan as he left. This time she heard the unmistakable sound of a key turning. She tried the door handle. Why save her just to lock her up? Yvette hugged herself with trembling arms as her imagination answered. No rescue parties were coming. Especially not here. They'd have to believe they were looking for a complete moron for them to look hundreds of miles off course.

She felt like a complete moron. Her plane and all her plans lay in a watery grave. Even if they didn't, a lot of good the money would do here.

She looked around the room. Other than the door, the only way in or out was a small window. She tried to open it, but the latch was rusted shut and wouldn't budge.

Only the view of the trees was perfect. She could see part of the lake and the beach. There were deep gouges in the sand but with the noon sun it was hard to tell what they were.

Yvette examined the door again. It opened in so no chance of knocking it down. The hinges however were on her side. She could pry them off she thought happily and rushed back to the tray.

"Stupid plastic knife." The fork and dish were also plastic. She sat on the bed with a frustrated sigh.

She reached for the grilled fish on the plate. It looked tasty. She couldn't bear the thought of eating, but it was a good idea to keep her strength up in case she needed it suddenly. It tasted fresh and flavourful, but considering her circumstance, she couldn't enjoy it.

His smile, when he'd said 'tomorrow' she could go out... It had a finality about it. She was convinced he'd make his move, whatever it was, tomorrow. So she had to make her move today.

Leaving the rest of the fish, she returned to the window and looked out as she jiggled the latch again. If only she had some WD-40 to loosen the rust. Wait!

She grabbed a piece of the fish skin. It wasn't WD-40, but it was oily. She rubbed it on the latch and worked back and forth until it finally moved. She pushed the window up and tried to open the storm window. It lifted a crack, then refused to budge.

At least the few extra centimetres increased her view around the cottage. There wasn't much to see, just a bit more of the lake and an endless supply of trees.

She leaned her head on the window sill as tears burned her eyes but refused to let them fall. Get away from it all? This was hell! Even if she escaped, the nearest road was down a three thousand-foot mountain. But that was by air. By foot, it was light years away.

She hadn't risked jail just to wind up as a pet for some mountain man.

She took a closer look at the shore and those gouges in the sand that looked a lot like tire tracks. The more she stared at them, the more she became convinced that they were her plane's tire marks as it was dragged out of the lake.

Damn! How many more times was she going to be lied to? Yvette grabbed the storm window and yanked upwards. She took a stronger hold and shook the window to vent her frustration. Another shake released her tears. No! She refused to be used anymore! She pulled up, drawing on the anger and frustration of two years wasted on a man who'd lied when he'd said he loved her. A man who had used her.

The window rose another centimetre. One more pull and it was open far enough to squeeze through. She landed in a crouch on the cold rocks outside the window. Barefoot, wearing only a t-shirt and panties, she wasn't exactly ready to make a cross-country trek. Her escape had to be more thought out or she risked rushing into the arms of the mountain man. First thing: find out where her alleged saviour was. She stood up and inched towards the front of the cottage. She sucked in several deep breaths looking for her inner courage. Holding the last breath, she peered around the corner. Her air rushed out with a groan at the sight.

Her plane sat on dry ground in front of the porch. How the hell did he pull it out from the bottom of the lake? Looking at the water, she realized that it remained shallow for quite a distance. Damn, her plane had never been in danger of sinking!

And on shore was a float plane with the man working on its engine. Her aircraft's cowling was gone as he used parts from her plane to fix his own. That's how he'd known about the radio and that she'd run out of fuel. So busy feeling stupid about the radio that she hadn't picked up on the clue. He'd said tomorrow would be the day. He'd be leaving. She had to do something. Find her clothes. Knock him out.

In that moment of indecision, the man looked up. She ducked back behind the cottage.

"Hello, there!" he shouted.

No chance of outrunning him barefoot through dense woods. She took another deep breath and stepped out into full view.

When he looked at her with a big toothy grin, she wanted to bolt for the nearest rabbit hole. Especially when he strolled towards her. Yet, she stood her ground.

"Good to see I was right about you." His voice was mellow, and good-natured. "You're tough. A survivor."

"I'm thrilled that you appreciate me." How could her voice sound so calm? Did he see her tremors? "Now I know why you kept me locked up. Didn't want me to see your plane." She paused a moment then added, "There's enough in that case for the two of us."

She flinched as he reached for her arm. But he didn't hurt her. He just guided her to the porch swing and pushed her down to sit. He turned his back to her as he looked out on the lake.

"Yes, we could split the money, but wouldn't do to give the cops a witness."

"I see," she forced a smile. "I know you won't turn me in."

"No, 'fraid you got that assbackwards." He laughed then added, "Can't be sure you won't turn me in. Well, you recognize me, don't you? The most famous man in Canada? Labrador City?"

She shook her head.

"Come on," he coaxed, "Gabriel Morgan."

It took a moment. It was three years ago. An orderly suspected of smothering five elderly patients. The last she'd heard the police were still looking for him.

"You remember me," he said with a satisfied nod. "Good. Hate to think the world forgot me. You know, just couldn't stand their suffering. Put them out of their misery, I did. Anyways, the hospital didn't see it like that and called the cops. Knew it was a matter of time before they would. Had all my supplies ready at my cottage at a lake outside Labrador City. That's where I kept my plane. Won it in a poker game, you know. At the first sight of trouble I loaded up the plane and came here. Took me several trips, but was long gone before they knew where to start looking for me."

He turned back to look at the lake as he continued, "Everything I need is here. Do you like the cabin? Cut down the trees and built it myself. Snow comes early here and stays forever. Didn't want to stay through a fourth winter. Was planning to leave, but as luck would be, blew a gasket on takeoff. Barely made it back safely. Got me stuck here this past year. Till you came along."

"Right. A ready-made companion who fell from the sky," Yvette said, her voice on edge.

"Don't need you. Only your plane and your money. You won't be needing it as I see it."

"What?" She jumped to her feet and grabbed his arm. "You can't kill me." She tried to shake him. Like trying to move a tree.

"No worries, now. I got all the parts I want. Hope you don't mind I took a few extra that were getting old on my plane. I sees it as a fair trade. I take your money and jewels and you get my cabin."

"I won't turn you in," she said. "How can I? The police want me too. Just drop me off anywhere near a road."

"Right. You heard of anonymous tip?" He never looked at her, just smiled gently as he continued. "No, you'll be safe here. You're young, strong and smart. You'll make it through the winter okay."

"Isolated? All alone? Never to be able to go home?"

He turned to look at her, openly surprised. "But I said you're safe here. So why do you want to be where someone tried to kill you?"

"Kill me?"

75

"The reason you ran out of fuel? A hole in the bottom of each wing tank. Gotta be more careful with your walk-around checks. The holes were filled with some kind of paraffin wax. Found some on the wing. Once the fuel ate through the wax...well, wouldn't be long before all the fuel ran out."

Her hands fell limp by her side. Then through clenched teeth she snarled, "Richard!" Now that odd look he'd given her at the airport made sense: guilt at almost getting caught sabotaging her plane. But why? Afraid she'd tell Brenda? He'd been caught cheating before and had managed to smooth things over with his wife. That couldn't be it, unless...

He must have opened his private safe at work on the weekend, probably to get the necklace, then discovered it, and the money missing. Not to mention the duplicate ledgers she'd grabbed on a whim. He was probably afraid she'd call the police once she was safely away. Too bad she hadn't thought of that herself. But what kind of a twisted mind would kill someone without a second thought? How had she missed seeing the potential killer in him?

She looked at Gabriel Morgan in a new light, any sense of fear gone now. He was just a mercy killer not a cold blooded murderer. Her voice was strong as she said, "I won't let you leave me here."

She grabbed his arm again. Wide eyed, she stared at the large knife at her throat and the transformed man brandishing it. She'd never seen him pull it. Barely breathing, she let him go and with hands held protectively in front of her, she took a step back.

"Don't want to start giving orders, do we? You got a choice. Keep out of my way, or I kill you now." He hadn't raised his voice, yet it seemed to reverberate through the woods. "Sit."

Afraid to move, she was more afraid not to obey him. She sat back down on the swing, her eyes locked on the knife. First she'd misjudged Richard. Now this man. Each error had almost cost her life.

He sat next to her, twirling the knife in his hands, the double edged blade glinting in the sun.

"Almost finished repairs, just a few more checks. It's such a beautiful day, so, I think you should just sit here and enjoy it." He looked deep into her eyes with an unspoken "or else" before he returned the knife to its sheath on his belt and went back to the float plane.

The man was insane. Unpredictable. One moment, kind and gentle, the next... She saw a small log near the porch steps. A good smack on the head and she'd be the one leaving. But if she missed, he'd kill her.

One option would be to wait for him to leave then walk out of here. But people got lost in shorter distances than that. One of her co-workers, an experienced hunter, had got lost while hunting with friends. They'd found his body the following spring.

She hugged her knees to her chest, as she pulled the t-shirt over her legs and feet for warmth. She considered asking him to let her go inside. But what if he decided to lock her up until he was ready to leave? A knot grew in her stomach as she forced herself to wait.

"All done," he said as he closed the cowling and jumped to the ground. With frightening strength, he dragged it further into the water. "It should fly." He gave a snort of a laugh, as he added, "At least I hope so. Now, how 'bout I give you a tour of your new home."

"Could I get my clothes first?" she asked, her teeth chattering now.

"Well, why didn't you speak up? I put 'em by the wood stove to dry." He led the way into the kitchen.

She eagerly pulled on her jeans first, never having appreciated the cliche, "toasty warm" before. She leaned against the small counter by the window and pulled on her socks. He started chatting about the food supply, fishing equipment, the wood shed and other things she'd need to survive. She only half listened as she tried to come up with some way to persuade him to take her with him. If she didn't handle it right, he'd probably kill her just to get her out of his hair.

Then, she remembered the radio. The knot in her chest relaxed as she came up with a new plan. Let Morgan leave. She'd radio for help once he was gone. She could say she'd lost her maps and ... what the hell, she had time to come up with a convincing story. The police would be so happy to have a lead on Morgan that they probably wouldn't give her own story a second thought. After she was rescued, she'd decide what to do about sweet, loving, murderous, Richard.

"By the way," he said, his voice cheerful, "I also took your radio."

"What?" The word came out as a half gasp, half cry.

"Mine is old, and well, don't want to hear you calling the cops after I leave, do I?"

Her head spun. She felt impotent as she finished dressing. She leaned against the counter to put on her runners. And then she saw it out of the corner of her eye. The glint of steel from behind the door. She turned her head slightly to look. An axe.

As Morgan droned on and on about the benefits of living in the woods, she added the occasional "oh really" or "how interesting" and moved closer to the axe. Morgan walked to the window to point at the pump house, telling her how, though insulated, the pump frequently froze in the winter. He sounded proud that he simply melted snow for water.

His back was to her. She picked up the axe with both hands. It was heavier than she'd thought. Panic was quickly replaced by cold resolve and it gave her the physical strength that she needed. Holding her breath, she heaved the axe up high above her head. And let its own weight drop it onto Morgan's head.

She closed her eyes against his death throes, before falling to her knees and throwing up until all that was left were dry heaves. She hadn't expected it to take so long. In all the movies, one knock on the head and the bad guy fell dead and still.

When Morgan's thrashing stopped, she opened her eyes, making sure she didn't look down at the body. Swallowing the bile that once again rose in her throat at the sight of the blood on her clothes, she pulled off the t-shirt and cleaned her arms. Luckily the shirt was long and had protected most of her jeans. She got her own t-shirt from the chair. Every time she blinked she could see Morgan writhing and twisting.

Heart pounding, she grabbed her jacket, pressed herself against the wall to squeeze past the spreading pool of blood, keeping her eyes averted from the body. Her head cleared once she was out in the crisp air. A few deep breaths and her pulse slowed to near normal. She got to his plane with a fleeting moment of apprehension. She'd never been in a float plane in her life, never mind trying to fly one. But it was just a Cessna 172 on floats, bigger and heavier than the plane she was training on. She remembered her flying instructor said that it took several hours of practice just to get a float plane off the water safely. Her instructor constantly told her that she was better than the other students and she knew he was right. She'd manage just fine.

Luckily Morgan had pulled it into the water. She double checked that the leather flight bag with her treasures was in the back seat. Then after a pre-flight inspection of the plane, she climbed in.

Killing Morgan had been hard. Things should get easier with practice. She smiled knowing Richard would help her find out if it was true.

She started up the engine.

Dying With Things Unsaid

by N. J. Lindquist

N. J. Lindquist is an award-winning author and international speaker. Her published work includes the Manziuk and Ryan mysteries, Shaded Light *and* Glitter of Diamonds, *which received rave reviews from Publishers Weekly and Library Journal. N. J. also has five coming-of-age novels, a fantasy, and a Christmas play, as well as numerous short stories, columns and articles. She edits and publishes the* Hot Apple Cider *anthologies. Her current works-in-progress are another mystery and a memoir. N. J.'s vision led to the founding of The Word Guild. She is a member of Sisters in Crime International, Crime Writers of Canada, and the Writers Union of Canada. N. J. lives in Markham, Ontario. www.njlindquist.com*

Many people die with their lives unfinished, important things unsaid.

Relaxing on the recliner in her small hospice suite, sipping her morning cup of Assam vanilla tea while she read the personal advice column in the morning paper, fifty-four-year-old Mary Kline nodded. Yes, she'd known quite a few people who'd died suddenly, with no chance of saying what needed to be said. Maybe just a few words—a simple "I love you" or "I'm proud of you." Or perhaps volumes of unspoken phrases: "I'm sorry," "I was wrong," "Please forgive me." Not to mention the long speeches they'd either never thought of delivering or chosen to keep to themselves.

And now here she was, knowing the medical establishment had done its best and all that remained was the wait for her body to give up the fight. Three months, give or take a few weeks.

She could choose to be in a drugged haze with little discomfort, or alert with ever-increasing pain.

A hint of a smile touched Mary's lips as she remembered her first labour. She'd been adamant about natural birth. After all, women had been having babies for centuries without all the medical foofaraw. But six hours into labour, she'd have climbed out of bed and wrestled the nurse to get an epidural. For the next two children, she hadn't given a moment's thought about whether or not to take advantage of all the ways to stave off pain.

Was there a charity that helped provide epidurals for neglected women in third world countries? If so, maybe she should send them some money...

But that wasn't what— Oh yes. Things unsaid.

She had time to say those unsaid things. But should she? "Ah, there's the rub," she muttered. "There are loose ends I ought to tie up. But what will happen if I do?"

Specifically, should she tell someone what she knew about Joan's death? Or should she allow the truth be buried with her?

"Mom?"

Mary jerked, spilling a little tea on the front of her sweater.

"Mom, are you okay?" Mary's eldest child came into the room, her face twisted in concern. "I'm sorry. I didn't mean to startle you."

"I'm fine, Deidre. I didn't hear you come in."

"I used my key. Thought you might still be sleeping. Would you like me to make you some fresh tea? I baked banana-pecan muffins this morning, too."

Mary absent-mindedly fingered the pink afghan that covered her knees. "I can try one. Yes, maybe some fresh tea. This is cold."

"Coming right up." Deidre stepped into the tiny kitchenette.

"Are the kids okay?" Mary asked, raising her voice slightly.

"Fine. I dropped them at school. I have to pick up some groceries and go to the police station, so I thought I'd check first to see if you need anything."

A cold hand of fear clutched Mary's chest. She willed her voice to stay steady, but heard it wobble as she asked, "The police station?"

"It's a drop-off center for the toy drive." A cupboard door banged.

Mary's heart thumped wildly in her chest. She waited until she could control her voice. "Oh, I see. I thought maybe something was—was wrong." She forced her lips to shape a smile in case Deidre looked over.

"Nope. We've never heard anything about the break-in at your house last month, and I don't expect we ever will."

Mary's heart did a flip. "Break-in?"

Deidre's head popped out of the kitchenette, her hand over her mouth. "Oh, no!"

"You didn't tell me," Mary whispered.

"You were in the hospital when it happened, and we didn't want to worry you. Besides, nothing was taken." Deidre came further inside the room, giving Mary the impression of energy held back. Her daughter's lithe, muscular body was clad in a black track suit with red piping and a red, scoop-neck T-shirt. Her long black hair was tied back in ponytail. At thirty-two, and despite having three active children and a part-time job as a social-worker, people often thought she was ten years younger.

"Nothing was taken?" Mary's voice broke slightly and she bit her bottom lip.

"No, Mom. It was all very strange. Broken window and stuff tossed around as though they were looking for something in particular, but nothing missing. At least that we know of. I mean, they could have taken some papers or something without our realizing it, but nothing of value was taken."

"My will?"

"In our bank deposit box with our important papers."

In a voice as casual as she could make it, Mary asked, "And my letters from Joan?"

"Why, those are—" Deidre's eyes rounded. "I put the box that contained all your letters and cards in the storage closet with other things we need to go through with you. I'm sure they're still there. Why on earth would anyone want to steal your—? Mother—? Mother—!"

Mary woke up in a hospital room. While being examined, first by a sympathetic nurse and then by a red-haired doctor who barely said a word, it occurred to her that she was a very foolish woman. "Over fifty years old, and I don't have the brains of a newborn," she muttered aloud. The doctor finally told her she'd fainted and that although she seemed fine now, he wanted to keep her a bit longer for observation.

Mary barely noticed the doctor leave the room. Her thoughts centered on the fact that while she'd been thinking she was the only person alive who knew Joan had been murdered, she'd completely forgotten that the murderer also knew. Could the murderer be worried that Mary would say something before she died?

The letters...

During Mary's second operation, which had followed the chemotherapy and only delayed her approaching death, her children had arranged for her to move into the small apartment in a hospice a few blocks from Deidre's house while they began the process of going though her belongings and packing up her house to sell it.

Mary had of course realized the letters were still in her house, but she hadn't been overly concerned about her children's reading them and seeing what they meant. Both the coroner and the police had decided that an inebriated Joan Hammerville had died as the result of an accidental fall down her stairs. At the time, no one had ever questioned that; not even Mary, who knew it couldn't possibly be true.

Mary and her cousin Joan had been the same age, and since their Ottawa homes were within a few blocks of each other, they'd been best friends since they were toddlers. They'd continued to be close after they married their high school sweethearts, and even after Joan and Peter moved to Kingston.

An avid mystery reader, Mary was well aware that to identify a murderer, you needed to look for a motive, means, and opportunity. After Joan's death, she'd determined there were really only three people who had motive and means, but only one with the opportunity.

Joan's husband Peter might have wanted her dead, but he had a rock-solid alibi. Mary's older sister Amanda might have had a motive, but she'd been at home alone in Ottawa while her son was at a sleepover with a friend only a few blocks away. Not an alibi exactly, but there'd been no reason to think she'd lied. Amanda, who was two years older than Mary and Joan, was a head-strong, lively creature who wore her heart on her sleeve. A single mother after a teenage romance, she'd never hidden the fact that she admired Peter, and no one was surprised when she made a dead-set at him after Joan died. But going after a widower was one thing; making him one was something else again.

Since the cancer had been diagnosed, Amanda and Peter had visited Mary often, usually bearing presents. Peter, who had always reminded Mary of the easy-going actor, Peter Lawford, was the one person who could always make her laugh.

Mary's third suspect was Steve Kline, the love of her life, and the source of pain more severe than that caused by the cancer. She'd divorced him nearly ten years ago, right after Todd, the youngest of their three children, graduated from high school. Neither had remarried.

Steve had come by the hospital after the first operation. Later, he sent flowers and candy. She refused the flowers when they were delivered and gave the chocolates to Deidre for her kids.

If there had been an intruder in her house, it had likely been Steve, looking for the letters. If he'd found them, maybe it was for the best.

But Mary knew that murderers—in fiction at least—were often inclined to paranoia. The logical next step was to get rid of her. She smiled. Yes, kill a dying woman; that made a lot of sense—not! And very risky unless you could make it look like suicide or an accident.

Of course, the powers that be had ruled Joan's death an accident. Only Mary knew Joan couldn't have been drunk—not by choice, at least. No matter how much alcohol was in Joan's blood, no one was ever going to convince Mary that Joan had fallen down the stairs in a drunken stupor.

Deidre walked into the hospital room. "I found them, Mom. The nurse said you started asking for 'Joan's letters' the moment you woke up, so Todd and I hunted them down. They were in a box at the back of your storage room, beneath a bunch of dishes." Deidre placed the small bundle of letters, tied with a mauve string, into Mary's open hand. "We left the house looking as if more intruders had been there." She laughed, then frowned. "But, Mom, I don't understand. Why are they so important? And why did you faint? The doctor said you'd had a shock."

"Yeah, Mom. What's up?" Mary's third child and only son, Todd, had followed Deidre into the room. "Susan is here, too. The nurse said two at a time, so Susan's waiting for one of us to leave." Todd smiled.

Mary smiled back. Todd reminded her so much of Steve when he was young. Dark hair, broad shoulders, and deep, brown eyes. So reliable and good-natured. A tower of strength. She wiped her eyes. She used to be able to hold the tears back, but the cancer seemed to have weakened her tear ducts.

"So what about the letters, Mom?" Deidre said. "Is there something you want to tell us, or will talking about them upset you?"

"Did you read them?" Mary asked.

"I glanced at them to make sure they were from Joan."

Mary clutched the bundle to her chest.

"What is it, Mom?" Todd leaned toward her, his face a picture

83

of concern. "Is this upsetting you? Do you want us to leave?"

Mary shook her head.

"I'd better go and let Susan come in." Deidre walked out of the room.

"Deidre read them," Todd said.

"I know."

"So, Mom, what's all the mystery?"

Tears began streaming down Mary's face.

"Mom! Should I—?"

Mary put her hand out and grabbed his arm. "I have to tell you. But it's just so horrible."

"I don't understand."

"I never wanted anyone to know," she whispered.

"Hi, Mom." Susan, Mary's middle child, slipped into the room, brown hair floating around her face, caressing the shoulders of her grey suit and the neck of the bright blue blouse—the picture of a well-dressed, young criminal lawyer.

Mary said, "I'm sorry you both had to leave work."

"As if that matters!" Susan kissed Mary on the cheek and sank into the chair next to the bed. "Work will always be there. You're my mother!"

"Sue," Todd said from his position at the foot of the bed, "Mom wants to tell us about the letters."

"I don't really want to," Mary said. "But I'm afraid I have to. Deidre needs to hear it too. But the doctors—"

"I'll get her in," Susan said, hurrying out.

Todd and Mary looked at each other and smiled.

"Todd, help me sit up."

Todd found the button to raise the top of the bed, and was positioning the pillows when Deidre and Susan walked in together.

"I talked to the doctor," Susan said. "We have fifteen minutes."

"All right," Mary said. "I don't want to do this, but I'm afraid I need to tell you." She paused, licking her dry lips. Then, pushing each word out as if it were alone and not part of a sentence, she said, "Joan. Was. Murdered."

As all three of her children stared at her, Mary raised her hand to keep them from speaking and continued, "I never wanted anyone to know." Her eyes filled with tears.

Susan grabbed a bunch of tissues from the stand near her mother's bed and placed them on Mary's lap.

Deidre began to comment, but Mary shook her head. "No, just let me get it out. You need to make copies of Joan's letters, and you'd better make notes of what I'm saying."

Susan reached into her purse and pulled out a digital recorder. As she did it, she seemed to morph from concerned daughter to competent lawyer. "Please speak slowly and clearly."

Mary cleared her throat and sat up straight. "This is Mary Kline. I am fifty-four years old, and I am of sound mind and—but not of sound body; I'm dying of cancer. But that hasn't impacted my mind, and I don't want to go to my grave without telling what I know. The death of my cousin, Joan Hammerville, was officially termed accidental. But I know it wasn't an accident. The autopsy showed she had high levels of alcohol in her bloodstream. But I know she didn't drink it of her own free will."

"Mom, how do you know that?" Todd asked, his eyebrows furrowed into a deep V that made him look exactly like Steve.

"It's in the letters," Deidre said. She blushed.

Mary smiled at her daughter. "You saw it?"

Deidre nodded. "Joan used to be an alcoholic. But when she and Peter moved to Kingston, she stopped drinking and started going to AA. She had started drinking in the first place because she hadn't been able to get pregnant. The doctor in Kingston did a new test that proved there was no reason she couldn't have a baby, so she suspected Peter was sterile. But Peter wouldn't go to the doctor to be tested, so Joan wrote Mom that she was just going to find another man and get pregnant and let Peter think the baby was his. She went to AA and stopped drinking so that when she got pregnant the baby wouldn't be harmed in any way."

"She told me she hadn't had a drink for eight months," Mary said. "And a week before she died, she wrote to tell me she was three months pregnant."

"Did she tell you who the baby's father was?" Todd asked.

Mary studied the covers of her bed for a long moment. Finally, she whispered, "Joan didn't tell me. But I found out. The night Joan was murdered, Peter was here in Ottawa, in my living room, telling me that my husband, Steve—your father—was the father of Joan's baby. Peter thought it had happened when they visited us during Christmas and New Year's. The timing was right."

There was a long moment of silence.

"What did Daddy say when you confronted him?" Deidre asked.

Another awkward silence.

"Mom?" prodded Susan. "We don't have long."

"I've never said a word to him," Mary whispered. "He has no idea I know."

Todd jumped up and turned to the window. "I can't believe you never talked to him about it!"

"Mom," Deidre said, "how could you not say something?"

"It's simple," Mary said. "I was thirty years old, a homemaker with no job skills, and I had three kids aged eight, six, and three. I had no source of income and no one else to help me. If I'd said anything, what would happen to you? If your father killed Joan, he'd likely kill me. And even if he didn't kill her, he still fathered her baby. There was no way I could see us coming out of it intact. So I didn't say anything, and neither did he."

"Was Dad the only one you suspected?" Deidre asked.

"The only other person I ever wondered about was your Aunt Amanda. I always knew she was jealous of Joan. When we were teenagers, even though she was a couple of years older than Peter, she was crazy about him. And look what happened. A year after Joan died, Peter married Amanda."

"I sort of remember Joan," Deidre said thoughtfully. "She laughed a lot, but it was kind of a funny laugh. I used to stay away from her."

"She brought candies," Susan said. "The kind kids like. Sour things and licorice and jaw breakers."

"She was my best friend," Mary said simply. "We told each other everything."

A grey-haired nurse walked in and shooed them out. "Time for some rest," she announced. "You can visit your mother again tonight."

Each of her children gave Mary a hug and told her not to worry. Susan took the letters so she could make copies.

When Mary woke up two hours later, she realized with a start that someone was in the room. The perfume was unmistakable. "Amanda," she said, struggling to sit up.

"Here, let me get that." Amanda rushed over and took the pillow from Mary's hands. "You ought to be up sitting in a chair instead of in bed. Or going for a walk. You start lying around all day and you'll lose whatever muscle you have left."

"Not sure it's worth the effort," Mary said.

"Just because you've been told the grim reaper's coming doesn't mean you have to rush to meet him." Amanda lifted Mary up. Her perfume was overwhelming and Mary suddenly felt dizzy and afraid. The pillow was near her face and for one brief, terrifying moment she thought Amanda was going to smother her. The next minute she found herself sitting up comfortably with a glass of water in her hand.

"Drink it all," Amanda said. "You don't want to get dehydrated."

Mary drank. Then, realizing this might be her only chance, she said, "Amanda, what did you think of Joan?"

Amanda raised her eyebrows. "Well, I know you liked her, but I always thought she was a wicked liar who liked to make people squirm."

Mary frowned. "I don't know what you mean."

"She made things up. But whenever I tried to warn you, you went off in a huff. Never would listen." Amanda walked toward the window. "I always thought Joan was jealous of you."

"Joan? Jealous of me?"

Amanda turned back to Mary and smiled. "Why not? You had a great family and a happy home. And what did she have? A philandering husband, no children, and not much of a career."

"A philandering husband?"

"Oh, come on, Mary. You must realize that Peter was no more faithful to Joan than he's been to me."

"Peter?"

"Oh, I don't go running around telling everyone. Peter's got enough money to look after us in style, and he always comes running back saying he's sorry. But he has his little fling every few months. I told him he can have them provided he uses protection, he isn't with someone I know, and they take place elsewhere. So he goes to St. Moritz or Paris or to the Bahamas. And I don't exactly stay here by myself." She laughed. "It may not be the ideal marriage, but it suffices."

"Oh, Amanda! I'm so sorry. I never realized—"

"You needn't be sorry. At least I managed to keep my husband. Look at you. Throwing away the best man any of us ever knew."

Mary looked down. "I didn't throw Steve away."

"He didn't go of his own accord."

"He wanted the divorce as much as I did."

"Like fun he did! Why has he never married? Or shown any interest in another woman? Why do his eyes light up whenever your name is mentioned?"

White-hot anger engulfed Mary. "You talked about your philandering husband. Well, Joan was pregnant when she died—with Steve's baby!"

Amanda stood still. Then she smiled. "Joan? Pregnant? No way."

"She wanted a baby and Peter was sterile, so she got Steve

to—to help her out."

Amanda frowned. "What do you mean Peter was sterile?"

"What do you think I mean?"

"Joan didn't want children. Think she was going to spoil her figure? She pretended she did so everyone would feel sorry for her. It's how she got attention. Meanwhile, she made Peter get a vasectomy."

"But she—"

"And what did Steve say?"

"I—I—" Mary looked down at her hands.

Amanda stared at her. "Don't tell me you never asked him?"

Lips tightly compressed, Mary shook her head.

"Wait a minute. Are you saying that you lived in the same house with Steve, as his wife, until Todd graduated high school—fifteen or sixteen years—believing Steve was unfaithful, and you never once asked him about Joan?"

"No. I mean yes. I never asked him."

"Why on earth not?"

"Because if I'd said anything, I thought he might murder me."

Amanda stood with her mouth open for several minutes. "You think Steve—your husband—murdered Joan?"

Mary nodded.

"And why exactly do you think that?"

Mary whispered, "Because Joan had stopped drinking, but she was drunk when she died. Someone must have forced her to drink."

"Joan had stopped drinking? Are you positive?"

"Yes. Because she was pregnant."

"But she can't have been pregnant."

"She said she was," Mary whispered. "With Steve's baby."

Amanda tilted her head to one side. "And did Joan tell you Peter was divorcing her?"

Mary's heart flipped. "Peter was what?"

"A few weeks before she died, Peter asked her for a divorce so he could marry me."

Mary put her hand to her throat. "But then—then you had no reason to want her dead?"

"Me?" Amanda laughed. "So you think I killed her, too?"

"I thought—if Steve didn't—that perhaps—"

"And all this time, you've never said anything to anyone?"

"I had my children to think about. I was so afraid."

"Well, let me ask Peter. He'd know if she was pregnant or not."

"Oh, Amanda, should you?"

"I'll go outside. We're not supposed to use cell phones in here. Be right back."

Mary sank back onto the pillows, her mind whirling. Had Joan lied to her? If she had— No, it was too horrible to contemplate.

Amanda returned in a few minutes. "Peter says there was nothing in the autopsy results about Joan being pregnant. And that she never wanted to be pregnant."

After a moment of silence, Mary said, "But you told me just a few minutes ago that you thought Joan was jealous of me."

"I said she was jealous of you: I didn't say she wanted to be you."

"I don't understand."

"Of the bunch of us, you and Steve were happy. Peter wanted to be with me. I was a single parent watching my cousin Joan being unkind to the man I loved."

"But you ended up with Peter."

"And you and Steve divorced."

There was another long silence. Finally, Amanda said, "If Joan wasn't pregnant, does that change things?"

"Aside from her lying to me? Oh, yes. It means— Oh, Amanda, I don't know what to believe any more!"

"Hi, Mom. Oh, Hi, Aunt Amanda." Deidre walked in and set a few magazines on the foot of her mother's bed. "How you are doing?"

"Hi, dear." Amanda gave Deidre a quick hug. "I know it's late. I'm just leaving. Your mother and I've been talking about old times."

"About Joan? I found some letters from her. She seemed to lead an interesting life."

Amanda paused in picking up her purse. "Do you think so?"

"I think she thought so." Deidre held the letters out to Mary. "Mom, here are your letters. You look exhausted. I'll come back in the morning. I'll walk Aunt Amanda out to her car."

The two of them left and a few minutes later, a nurse came in with a sedative. Soon, Mary was fast asleep.

The next morning, Mary was untying the string around the bundle of letters when Susan walked in. "What are you doing?" Susan asked.

"I thought I'd reread these to see if I can understand what really happened."

"No need. Those are fake. I gave the real letters to the police."

"I don't understand."

"You were right, Mom. Joan was pregnant when she died. I read the autopsy results."

Mary felt the world spinning again. Had she dreamed it? "But Amanda was here last night. She said—she called Peter, and he said Joan wasn't pregnant."

"Really? Well, that will help."

"Help what?"

"Build a case against them. You were right, Mom. Joan was murdered. Aunt Amanda and Peter were in it together. That way, Peter could marry Amanda and still keep Joan's money. Dad always thought it was fishy."

"You talked about it to your dad?"

"He's here. He wants to see you."

"But—"

"Come in, Dad. I'll be just outside." And then Susan was gone and Steve Kline was walking through the door.

Mary stared at him, her mind whirling.

"The kids called me," Steve said. "Asked me if I'd an affair with Joan. I told them I'd never had an affair with her or anyone else. Since I met you in grade seven, I've never wanted anyone but you. They said I needed to come and talk to you."

Mary swallowed hard. "But—Joan—"

"I read the letter where Joan said she was going to get another man to father her child, but it sure wasn't me."

"But—"

"Apparently, at the time, the police suspected Peter had something to do with her death. But he had a rock-solid alibi. He was here in Ottawa with you."

Mary swallowed hard and covered her mouth with her hands.

Steve cleared his throat. "Mary, the day before Joan died, Amanda told me you and Peter were having an affair. And then you were his alibi. He was here with you. I didn't want to believe it, but you were so cold to me...."

Mary buried her face in her hands. "I thought you'd murdered Joan."

Steve stood there shaking his head. "Amanda told me you and Peter were having an affair, so I drove down to Kingston that night to confront him. Amanda had told me that Joan would be at the theatre because of some play she was involved with, and Peter would be home alone. But there was no answer at the door, so I left.

"I found out later that Joan died not long after the time I was there. I was just lucky a neighbour saw me on the porch and told the police I never went inside."

Mary's eyes filled with tears.

"So, why were you with Peter?" Steve said gruffly.

"He drove over here to ask me if it was true about you and Joan having an affair."

Steve's eyes bulged. "He what?"

"He said Joan had confessed to him that she was having your baby." Mary's voice trailed off. "Oh, Steve, I'm so confused."

Susan walked into the room. "Both of you can relax. Deidre kept Aunt Amanda busy while Todd and I paid a visit to Uncle Peter. We confronted him with the letters and he broke down. He's sterile all right. Something to do with an injury he had when he was young. And Joan was desperate to have a child. She got pregnant, but it was with a friend of Peter's—at Peter's suggestion. But then Peter got cold feet. Aunt Amanda was insisting he get a divorce to marry her, but he kind of liked Joan's money.

"So Aunt Amanda sent Peter over to visit you while she killed Joan. They hoped Daddy would get blamed, but that didn't happen. When the police decided it was an accident, they thought they were in the clear. But, apparently, Deidre said something to them about finding your old letters from Joan while we were going though your house, and that got them worried. So they broke in and tried to find the letters and, well, here we are."

"Here we are," Steve said.

Tears were streaming down Mary's cheeks. "I've been such a fool."

Steve took her hand. "So have I. All this time, I believed what Amanda told me, and I couldn't get up the nerve to ask you about Peter." He hung his head. "I even wondered if Todd was really my child."

Susan stared at her father. "Todd is the image of you!"

"I know. My brain knew. But once you start getting suspicious, it's so easy to trick yourself."

Mary shook her head. "Such a waste. Such a horrible waste. And now it's too late."

Steve took her hand. "Mary, do you still have your wedding ring?"

"It's in my jewelry case."

"Well, I'll get a license and a preacher, and we can get our marriage back to where it ought to have been all along."

"But Steve, I only have a few months."

"They'll be the best months of your life."

"I'll be in pain."

"They have painkillers, don't they?"

"I'm not taking anything that makes me a zombie." Mary wiped away some of the tears. "Oh, Steve, just this morning, I was thinking it would be a terrible thing to die and leave things unsaid. But there's something so much worse—what we've been doing: living with things unsaid."

Amber Free Annie

by Helen Nelson

There was no AMBER Alert for Annie.

Ron, her mother's latest boyfriend, had walked into her room the evening she took off. "Hey kid, your Mom says its time you started earning your keep." He unzipped his pants as he said, "So I might as well get first crack before the paying customers start lining up." Annie grabbed the scissors she had been using for a school project, stabbed him and was already throwing her few prized possessions into her pack as he ran screaming from her room.

As Annie tore through the kitchen on her way out the door, her mother tended to Ron's wounds. She paused to scream, "What did you expect you bitch? He's just tried to be a good dad to you, but you're always fucking coming on to him and you expect he isn't going to take your offer? If anyone is looking for you I'll tell them you've gone to hell."

Annie suspected Ron was just glad to see her go. As for her Mom, Annie had overheard her mother's musings about pimping her out so she suspected that when her Mom calmed down a bit she would just regret the potential loss of income.

So no AMBER Alert. Annie slipped out the door and through the cracks into the world of young, homeless Toronto.

Annie held on to her little radio long enough to realize her Mom and Ron hadn't reported the stabbing. She guessed they just didn't want to answer any questions about why her Mom's boyfriend had been attacked by a twelve year old.

Within a week, Annie had almost nothing left. Her radio and iPod were gone. What little money she had was gone. Her clothes—gone. All taken by bigger, rougher kids.

Panhandling was hard. She couldn't get a decent spot, those were already claimed. She slept under the Gardiner Expressway or in the Don Valley, but often she'd be roused and sent on her way by older tougher kids. She counted herself lucky when she didn't get roughed up in the process. She knew to say no to the constant offers of help from the pimps; through her Mom she'd had enough of them to last a lifetime.

She thought about calling Ms. Loannie, who was just the best teacher ever. But what would she say? "Hey Ms. L. I tried to murder my step dad, so I ran away from home. I'm never going near my Mom again and I'm trying to stay clear of the cops." Maybe not.

When Annie found the small, yellowish stray dog, she adopted him and called him Sandy.

In a drug induced haze Annie's Mom had named her Myrtle. After watching the movie *Annie*, when she was six, Annie changed her own name. She wanted to be like Annie. No, she wanted to BE Annie. Being Annie would be so much better. She wanted to be an orphan. Annie's mother never gave up on the name though. Every time she brought home a new man she would still chortle "Myrtle the Turtle, funny, right?"

They were a pair. The small girl and her small yellow dog. Sandy was her love, and she was his. Sandy always ate. Annie? No. Most days she had something—but if there was only food for one it went to Sandy. In return when someone would try to steal Annie's food or rough her up, Sandy protected her with growls, snarls and bared teeth.

Life with Sandy was better. No menacing step dads. No stoned or drunken mother. No johns floating in and out. She did miss school. But she could go to the library and read and use the internet to stay in touch with the world around her. No email and no facebook, nothing that could be traced directly to her. A few generous donors while she was panhandling had allowed her to buy a couple of books about that other well-known orphan—Harry Potter.

Then she met Eddie.

The day she met him, she had been panhandling by the Eaton Centre and scored well; there was going to be enough for food for both her and Sandy, with some left for laundry and maybe even another Harry Potter book.

When the thug attacked, the first thing he did was kick Sandy in the stomach. That sent poor Sandy whimpering and Annie scrambling to make sure he was okay. It was enough to distract Annie and the thug attacked while her guard was down.

And there was Eddie. Like so many bullies, the thug backed off when confronted with resistance. The small blade in Eddie's hand didn't hurt either.

Annie smelled pimp. "Thanks and fuck off!" she snarled at Eddie. And he did. That surprised her, but she was glad. To Sandy she said "Alone is best."

That night, among the trees in the Don Valley, she cuddled Sandy and fed him a special treat. It meant no book that day, but Sandy had earned it.

Eddie just kept showing up.

When she needed it most, he'd have a bit of food for her and Sandy. With a cheery "Hi," he'd sit beside her on the sidewalk, offering up a burger for her and some kibble for Sandy. Sandy would gobble the kibble and she'd eat the burger. Her response seldom varied. "Thanks and fuck off".

After a few weeks she realized he definitely wasn't after her body so the response became, "Thanks and fuck off, faggot." Or, "Thanks and fuck off, pervert." Almost personal.

Eddie persisted.

In early December, on a cold rainy day, Eddie showed up with kibble, a burger, fries and hot chocolate. It was late in the day, she was cold and wet and her panhandling efforts had resulted in almost nothing. The hot chocolate tasted and felt good and, best of all, warm. "Thanks," she said. "What the fuck's with you? Why do you keep coming back?"

Eddie paused for a few seconds "You make me think of my sister. If she were out here, I'd want someone looking out for her."

"Right. So not only are you a faggot—you're a pimp, too. Jesus."

"No." He sighed and told her his story. Eddie was sixteen. His parents had kicked him out when they found out he was gay. Told him he'd be welcome home when he "changed his mind". He had a small room, and because he was in school, some of the time anyway, received social assistance—not really enough to live on, but he got by. Annie cried. She thought being gay was pretty disgusting but somehow she found herself warming to Eddie.

He seemed so lonely. He needed a friend. So did she.

By early January, when the city issued the first extreme cold alert of the season, Annie and Sandy were sleeping on the floor in Eddie's room. "Just for a few days," she said when he asked her. "Just till the weather gets a bit warmer."

In February Eddie had an idea. Between them Annie and Eddie hatched a plan. With so many pimps after Annie they realized there must be a market for young girls, maybe even especially ones who looked younger than their age. So, why not take advantage—pretend to be a hooker? Those jerks who want young girls—get them in a compromising position and take them. Or their stuff anyway. Their cash.

And it worked. Annie would pick up some old dude. They'd go to his hotel room but before any action could begin, there would be Eddie. Pounding on the door. Playing the older brother. Grabbing cash in exchange for silence, for not calling the cops or the hotel staff.

And who would report them? What would they say? "Hey I got robbed while trying to seduce (rape? molest? fuck?) a twelve year old." Right. Or maybe they had a choice— "Hey I got robbed while trying to fuck a sixteen year old boy."

No one reported them.

Oh yeah, they were living well. Sandy got real bones, good kibble and a little jacket so he didn't shiver so much. Annie got the rest of the Harry Potter books. She had never owned books while living with her Mother. She was in heaven. Both Annie and Eddie got an iPod. Did regular laundry. Bought a few new clothes. Real food. They got an upgrade on Eddie's phone to include data and the internet. They contemplated getting an apartment.

They didn't feel they were being greedy. They'd only run the scam once a week or so, less if they made a particularly good score. "And who are we hurting?" Eddie would ask when Annie would worry about it. "Just sick old fucks who want to screw a twelve year old."

In early March Annie had her thirteenth birthday. Eddie turned seventeen. They went out and spent sixty bucks on dinner. Gave the waitress a ten dollar tip. They felt like millionaires. Over desert, they vowed to be 12 and 16 forever—to keep the scam going for as long as they could get away with it.

During March break, Annie ran into Ms. Loannie on Yonge Street.

"Annie, uuuh Myrtle, Annie, is that you?"

Annie turned, stunned. Ms. Loannie was right behind her.

"It's great to see you. I guess you're visiting from Vancouver."

After Annie had been absent from school for a few days, her teacher, Ms. Loannie, had phoned her Mom. But when Annie's Mom said Annie had gone to live with an aunt in Vancouver, Ms. Loannie thought Annie would be better off away from her mother. She let it slide. If she had stopped and thought about it, she might not have, but with more than 30 kids in her Grade 7 class she wasn't altogether displeased to have the class shrink by one, even if the one was one of her best students.

Vancouver? Annie blinked. Playing it safe she said, "Yes."

"You left so suddenly, I'm so pleased you're back. Are you here for spring break? How are you?"

Annie's mind raced. WTF, she thought. "Well, I'm fine, how about you?" she asked.

"I'm fine. I miss you, you know. You are one of my favourite students ever—you have such a fire in you to learn. How long are you here for? I have to meet someone right now, but can we do lunch? What about tomorrow? My treat. Should I call your mother?"

Annie felt both flattered and flustered. She answered "Oh, I'm leaving tonight, so I guess not."

Ms. Loannie was perplexed. Something seemed off. She fumbled a bit and found a business card in her purse. Handing it to Annie she said, "Oh, well, next time you visit, please email me or call before you come. I would really love a chance to talk with you about how you are doing. Well, even if you aren't coming—email me."

Annie was almost half a block away when she saw that Ms. Loannie was at her shoulder again. "Listen Annie, really..." Ms. Loannie was hesitant. "If you ever need, ummm, any help with anything at all, please call." And she gave Annie a hug.

This time Annie watched her as she disappeared north on Yonge Street. She decided it was a good thing Ms. Loannie thought she lived in Vancouver. She was glad Sandy was locked in the room while she trolled for a creep. And she was glad she hadn't found anyone yet. She didn't know how she would have explained Sandy or the creep.

Early in April Annie picked up an older, uptight looking guy. He said his name was Ron. That spooked her more than a little bit. But a creep is a creep. And she knew that Eddie would be right there. This Ron had her meet him at his hotel. That was okay to Annie, meant he didn't want to be seen with a kid. It likely made him a better mark.

After Ron strode off in the direction of his hotel Eddie had approached her. "Maybe we should forget this one. I really don't like the look of him. He makes me nervous."

Annie just looked at him. "Fuck Eddie, they all give me the creeps. What's so different about this one?" Eddie had no reply.

They weren't in Ron's room more than two or three minutes when, right on schedule, Eddie was there, pounding at the door. Eddie pushed his way in as Ron opened the door. "What are you doing with my sister you motherfucker?"

Ron just laughed. "Aren't you the same little punk who was pimping some other 'sister' to me six or eight months back? You are. I remember you. What's your game now?"

Annie was stunned. Eddie? A pimp? She looked at Eddie's eyes and knew it was true. She was sick, wondering now if Eddie had just been biding his time.

"What are you talking about, you sick asshole? This is the only sister I've got. And you aren't going to fuck her over. I should just call the cops. You can explain to them how you want to fuck a twelve year old girl. Or maybe you'd prefer I told them it was a sixteen year old boy you were interested in." He paused and pulled out his phone and pointed it at Ron. "Or, wait, you can just give us your cash and we'll go away."

Every other mark had caved at this point and given them money, sometimes, with extra prodding, a lot of money. Not this time. For a split second Annie and Eddie both thought he was getting them money but when Ron reached into his briefcase he pulled out a huge black gun. The world slowed down—it ran in slow motion. "No," he said, "I don't think so. I think this is going to be a freebie. And, big brother, you're going to watch. We're in for some fun tonight. Maybe before the night is out we'll teach you how to fuck a girl. Come on, she's not really your sister is she, you little punk?"

Dear, brave Eddie pulled his little knife. "Come on Annie!" he said "We're out of here." And he lunged, grabbing Annie by the arm.

"I don't think so." The shot was just a little pop—the gun had a silencer. Annie froze in horrified silence as she watched Eddie topple and his gut blossom with blood

Ron kicked Eddie hard in the ribs and heaved him into a chair. "Now, you're going to watch and learn. But I guess you won't be in on the fun now—bleeding all over like that—will you?"

Tears ran down Eddie's face as he clutched his gut. He closed his eyes. Ron backhanded him across the face. "Keep watching, you little prick. You and little sister here are going to die. But not before I have a lot of fun."

He turned his back on Eddie, set the gun on the bedside table and grabbed Annie. Then, as Annie's knee flew toward Ron's groin, somehow, with strength that came from his depths, Eddie lunged at Ron, knocking him off balance. Ron spun and quickly had Eddie pinned in the chair again, his knee on Eddie's chest

Annie never knew how she moved so fast. In a moment the big

gun was in her hands, pointed at Ron. "Stop!" she sobbed, as the tears streamed down her face. "Stop! Let him go! You can have me, but let him go." She held the gun tightly as she backed away.

Ron stood, then whirled to face her. And he laughed. Laughed. "A little girl like you can't handle that gun. It would knock you on your can to shoot that bugger. You won't shoot me. You're just a child, you wouldn't shoot me." He stepped toward her, beckoning with his hand for Annie to hand over the gun. And crumpled as she pulled the trigger.

The gun's kick sent Annie flying backwards and she landed with a thump on the floor.

"Eddie, Eddie. We gotta get you out of here..." Frantically she scrambled to Eddie and tried to help him out of the chair.

Eddie's breaths were shallow and ragged. "No. You, you have to get out of here. Go to the room and get your stuff and Sandy and run. Give me the gun. Take the phone. With luck they will blame me. I can't make it out of here anyway."

"What do you mean? You'll be okay. Maybe we should just call the cops. It'll be okay, we'll explain. You'll be fine, you will!" Tears streamed down Annie's face and she shook with fear and panic.

"No, no I won't. I can't. No cops. That's just trouble. Get the fuck out of here." He paused, trying to catch his breath. "It's true. At first I did want to pimp you. But I couldn't. I don't really have a sister. Just you. And I...love you...little...sister..." He stopped breathing.

"Please, don't die!" screamed Annie. "Please!" But Eddie was perfectly still; the light faded from his eyes.

Terrified, tears streaming down her face, Annie pressed the gun to his hand. She picked up the phone and ran all the way to Eddie's room. There, she saw the blood on her hands and her shirt, Eddie's blood. She washed it off her hands, changed her shirt and stuffed the bloodied one in her bag.

With Sandy and a few possessions thrown in her backpack, she headed to the Don Valley. For the trees. For the water.

Within hours she read on the internet about the discovery of the bodies—two unidentified victims, a youth and an older man. Police were on the lookout for a young girl, thought to be between the age of ten and twelve, often seen in the company of the unidentified youth. That, she realized, would be her. They know and they are after me, she thought.

Among the rustling trees she sat, wide awake, sleeping bag

wrapped around her body, shaking, tears streaming down her face, checking the internet for more news till the phone died. How many tears? For herself. For the life she could never have. For Eddie who gave up his life to save hers. And now she had killed a man. Could she ever forget his look of shock as she pulled the trigger?

As she searched her backpack for a tissue to wipe away more tears, she came across something else, something she had forgotten about. She knew what she had to do. Tomorrow.

Finally, toward morning, Annie slept. The moon cast an amber glow on Ms. Loannie's card, clutched tightly in the hand that held Sandy to her. Sandy gently licked away Annie's tears.

In the distance a coyote howled.

The Job

by Steve Shrott

Steve Shrott's mystery short stories have appeared online and in print publications such as 5minutemystery.com, Futures Mystery Magazine, *and various anthologies such as* The Gift of Murder. *His story,* Clean *will be appearing in the upcoming* Fishnets *anthology from Sister's in Crime (The Guppies). He was also one of five winners in The Joe Konrath Short Story Contest. In one of his other lives (unlike a cat, he has forty-two) he has crafted material for well-known comedy stars, and written a 'how to' book on humor writing. Some of his jokes are in The Smithsonian Institute and he has received the Robert Benchley Society Award for Humor.*

When the man with the steak knife exited the alley, Tony slid behind the liquor store. The man didn't pay him any mind and slithered away.

He had killed the blonde girl and Tony could easily describe him—bald, heavy-set, a long scar carved into his cheek.

Someone else might have gone to the police. Not Tony. He wasn't any damn hero. Not that he didn't have the courage. He had more guts than most. He also had a past and a present and couldn't get involved.

Besides, the game he played had rules. Like the one his first grade teacher gave him. Don't tattle. In his world, tattling caused problems.

Tony knew he had to scram before some big-nosed cop saw him and started asking questions. But his curiosity got the better of him and he stepped into the alley, stared at the woman's body spread-eagle on the ground—the blood spitting out of her chest like a plugged-up sprinkler. Reminded him of the way you found road kill.

She lay motionless, yet her iridescent sea-blue eyes made her seem alive. Tony yearned to touch her. Not in a sexual way, gently like a loving father might have touched his daughter. Not that he would know anything about loving fathers. Tony knelt beside the woman, plucked up her purse, curious. He found her name, Anne Firestone. She wrote for a newspaper and taught art at a school for slow kids.

In her wallet, he saw a picture of the proud teacher laughing with a group of different-looking children.

Just being near her beauty, her youth, made Tony feel good. Maybe youth and beauty always did that to men, no matter what evil haunted their insides. He placed his hand on hers. It was soft, small, sweet.

A tear slipped down his cheek. It surprised him. He thought all his emotions had been sucked dry.

He decided he'd hung around the girl long enough. He knew the cops would eventually find her and he couldn't be there when they did.

Tony headed toward the bright lights of the street. On his second step he heard something.

The girl was alive.

He knew, in her condition, she wouldn't last long and he felt tempted to turn back.

That would be a mistake

He heard another sound, or had it been the words, "Help me"? He couldn't be sure.

Maybe he'd go back—just for a minute.

When he got close, he kneeled, whispered, "Can you hear me?"

No sound, no movement.

Maybe he had imagined it. Sometimes things happened in the dark that you couldn't explain. He stood up to leave.

"Help me," she said in a breathy voice.

Tony swallowed hard, felt his throat constrict. "I gotta go."

Her eyes looked at Tony, pleading.

"I'll get someone to help. I promise."

Tony needed air, time. The dark had made his thinking fuzzy, off kilter. He raced out of the alley.

What would stop him from walking away, forgetting all of this? He could go on with his life as if nothing had happened. Yeah, he could do that.

However, when several people walked by, Tony tried to stop

one. "Listen I need your help, see..."

The man stared at Tony, his eyes widening as he moved away, like Tony was the devil. Tony looked at his hand, saw the girl's blood. "This isn't mine. This is..."

The man fled down the street.

Tony wiped his hand, tried again. No other passers-by would help.

A siren sounded in the distance.

Tony had no choice. The paramedics were on some kind of strike this week. Sure, if he called, they'd come. But when?

He sprang down a side street to his parked car and drove to the mouth of the alley. He noticed the weathered No Parking sign, but figured, what the hell. He opened the back door, about to get the girl.

"Sir."

He heard the voice.

Hated to turn around.

Had to.

The cop glared at him. "There's no parking here."

"Yeah, I know. Won't be a minute."

"Move your car now or I'm going to give you a ticket."

Tony didn't care about the damn ticket. He only cared about not giving the cop any kind of information. He also knew he had to get this woman to the hospital now or she'd die.

He looked around, saw no one in the immediate area, then punched the cop. He dropped to the ground, hit the concrete hard. Tony raced to the alley.

Now, the woman's eyes were closed.

He pulled them open with his fingers.

"Anne, it's me, Tony. I'm going to take you to a hospital." He could have sworn she attempted to nod.

He put his hands under her back; they felt sticky from blood. He gently lifted her up. He knew how to lift dead weight. He'd carried bodies before.

Tony made sure the cop was still out and the streets deserted. Then he lumbered over to the car, slid Anne into the back seat.

He sped to the hospital.

The nurses took charge of her and Tony vanished. He didn't want to have to answer any dumb questions.

The vinyl couch in his living room was not overly comfortable, but it gave him an opportunity to reflect on things. He didn't understand what had possessed him today.

He didn't know the girl. Hadn't cared about another person in a long time.

Yet he had tried to help her. Why?

For a moment, Tony thought that maybe age had crept up on him, that the time had come for him to retire. But he knew when he got the next call he would be ready.

That night the call came.

"Tony, I need you to do something," Edward said in a voice that asked and told at the same time.

"Uh huh."

"You know Freddie Seville?

"No."

"He's from Minneapolis. I hired him to kill this bimbo. He screwed up. I told Seville, make it look accidental. The moron stabs her in an alley with a steak knife. You believe that? Then the next crap thing I hear, she's in St. Agnes Hospital. Alive!"

Tony swallowed hard.

"I need you to finish her off. Room 503."

"What she done?"

Edward paused on the other end of the phone. "You having trouble doing a lady, Tone?"

"No, no problem."

"Just you usually don't ask no questions other than where and when. What's up?"

"Getting curious in my old age, that's all."

"Sure, sure. Anyhow, she's a reporter for the newspaper. We found out she's been checkin' us out, got hold of some documents she shouldn't have. So we wanna send a message to everyone at that moron paper." Edward inhaled a long breath. "So you do it?"

"Uh..."

"Well if you don't wanna, I'll give the job to Rawley."

"No, no. I'll take it."

"Make it look like the injuries got the best of her, okay?"

"You don't have to tell me how to do my job."

"Awful snippy, aren't ya? You sure...?"

"I said I'd do it." Tony slammed down the receiver, headed out the door.

He didn't want to do the job. He also knew he would.

He got into his four year old Hummer, a symbol of better times, and headed to the hospital.

On the way, he stopped off and got what he needed from Hoag.

"This stuff'll do her good," Hoag laughed.

Tony handed him the cash, took the bag.

Hoag smiled, showing a dentist's nightmare. "She pretty?"

Tony ignored the creep and headed to St. Agnes. He made his way inside and rode the elevator to Anne's room. He wanted to get this over with as soon as possible.

When he swung the door open, he saw her lying on the bed, asleep. She had bandages on her chest, but looked a hell of a lot better than the last time he'd seen her.

He removed the bag from his pocket, took out the hypodermic needle filled with potassium chloride.

He pulled the cap off the needle, about to inject it into the IV bag when his hand slipped and the cap toppled onto the floor. Stupid! Stupid! Stupid! Anne's eyes fluttered and she awoke.

Fear, confusion filled her face. Then she noticed Tony and a smile replaced it. Her lips quivered. "Tony."

No one had ever said his name with a smile before.

"You remembered."

"You saved...me." She dragged her arm out from under the covers and grabbed his hand.

Tony felt that soft, small, sweet hand and knew he couldn't go through with the plan. He picked up the cap, replaced it on the hypodermic, and stuffed it back into his pocket.

He smiled at Anne and whispered, "Bye."

He dashed into the hall, headed to the elevator, when he noticed Edward approaching him. At first he thought it strange, then all at once it hit him. He had come as backup in case Tony didn't do the job.

He knew one thing. He wouldn't let Edward in Anne's room no matter what.

"Hey Tone, what's up?"

"What the hell you doing here, Ed?"

"Figured I'd pay a call. Make sure you do what you're s'posed to do."

"You know my work."

"Yeah, but somethin's different this time, Tone." He rubbed his nose. "You asked too many questions."

"Go back home, Ed."

"Just tell me. Is it done?"

Tony inhaled, bit his lip. "Not yet."

Rage flashed across Edward's face. "Why the hell not?"

Tony bit harder on his lip, put his hand in his pocket. "She's just a kid."

Edward yanked out his gun. A shot exploded, the body

105

slammed to the ground.

Tony looked at his own gun, still smoking in his hand. He stared at the blood coursing out of Edward's chest and whispered, "Now it's done, Ed. And so am I."

He threw his gun down, walked back into Anne's room. Hands clasped, they waited for the police.

A Ring For Jenny

by Tracy L. Ward

*A former journalist and graduate from Humber College's School for Writers, **Tracy L. Ward** has been hard at work developing her favourite protagonist, Peter Ainsley, and chronicling his adventures as a young surgeon in Victorian England. Her first book featuring Peter Ainsley titled, Chorus of the Dead, is slated for publishing in late 2012. Her website can be found at www.gothicmysterywriter.blogspot.com. Tracy is currently working on the second book in the Peter Ainsley mystery series. She lives near Barrie, Ontario with her husband and two kids.*

London, 1868

"She was found like this, Detective?" Peter Ainsley asked, approaching the body. Careful not to disturb the scene, he stepped purposely, examining her with his hands deep in his pockets. He doubted his sense of caution was shared by the throng of constables and detectives at the scene long before he was summoned. He noticed ruts from a coal cart, narrowly missing the dead girl. The scene had already been compromised.

"Yes, Dr. Ainsley," answered Abe Simms, the Scotland Yard Detective who had greeted him when he arrived.

They stood in a slim alley amidst one of the poorest neighbourhoods in London, where prostitutes pulled their men into the shadows and drunks slept off their inebriate state. The stone walls of the tenement buildings close on either side of them were slick with rain water draining from rooftops three storeys high. The dead girl was lying mostly in a pool of black, muddy water and other unknown filth at the base of a rickety wooden staircase. Her body was contorted, though not terribly so. She rested on her hips, her legs to one side while her shoulders lay flat on the ground. Her neck was snapped, or so it seemed by its unusual angle, inconsistent with a normal range of motion.

Ainsley glanced at the sliver of sky above them, and surveyed the half rotten wood that comprised the staircase to the tenements on the second and third floors. She could have fallen, from either the second or third floor landing, though Ainsley expected more contortion to her limbs and broken bones if that were true.

"No one has touched her except Constable Barker."

Ainsley raised an eyebrow. Forensic investigations were still in their infancy and it seemed certain members of the force were slow to accept the new ways of policing. Five years ago a surgeon would never have been summoned to the scene of the crime. Ainsley would first meet the victim on the wooden slab of his examination table in the hospital morgue. In recent years though Ainsley had received a certain amount of notoriety, and for some cases it became beneficial for him to see the victims where they were found. Det. Simms seemed to rely on him almost weekly and benefited greatly from the expertise Ainsley provided.

"He was checking to see if she was breathing," Det. Simms explained.

Ainsley nodded and crouched down at her side. He knew any footprint evidence was lost. There were over twenty officers loitering around them, weaving through the alleyway to control the curious crowds that gathered at both the front and the back of the buildings. At the front pedestrians craned their necks to see beyond the strategically placed police carriage and horses that marred their view. In the back, tenants hung out of windows and off stairwells to take in the scene.

"And no one saw anything..." Ainsley said to himself as he lifted a tendril of the girl's hair from her neck and brushed it back. There were faint markings there but in the grey light Ainsley could not decipher them.

"One neighbour said they heard screaming, and they alerted the patrolling constable." Det. Simms explained. "How old would you place her Dr. Ainsley?"

Ainsley shrugged. "By examining the skull and teeth I could know for sure, but for now I'd venture she is young. Eighteen, maybe younger." Ainsley surveyed her face trying to ignore the mud splashes and spatters on her pale skin. "She hasn't a single grey hair on her head, nor any wrinkles whatsoever." Ainsley turned to the Detective. "Have your men taken a picture yet?"

"Yes sir."

Ainsley gingerly grabbed a hand and pulled it away from the girl's body. "She had a ring on this finger. A slim one, but by the way her skin is indented I'd say she had it on for a while." Ainsley pointed to the girl's ring finger on her left hand and Det. Simms bent down to take a closer look. "She was engaged...at one point."

The detective scribbled something on his notepad.

"She hasn't been here long," Ainsley explained. "Three hours, perhaps a little more. I can tell by her rigidity."

Ainsley pulled the girl's other arm away from her body and examined the hand before placing it gently on the ground. She was a seamstress of some sort, or an assistant to a tailor, he concluded. Her finger tips were scratched and cracked, especially on the thumb and index finger but her nails and cuticles were not dry, which helped exclude washer woman from the possibilities.

"How do we know she didn't fall?" asked an unfamiliar voice.

Pulled from deep concentration, Ainsley looked up and saw another detective standing beside Simms. Ainsley recognized the man as Det. Cooper. "Because she didn't fall," Ainsley explained. "She wasn't pushed either." Ainsley stood up and stepped away from the body. "Whoever did this wanted you to believe she fell."

A sorrowful moan erupted from the crowd that was loitering at the mouth of the alley. Ainsley looked up and saw a man breaking through the barricade of officers. He charged towards them.

"No!" he cried. The man had almost reached the body when the three men, Ainsley, Simms and Cooper formed a wall. He pushed against them, colliding squarely with Ainsley who used all the forced he could muster to halt the inconsolable man. He smelled of fresh laundry soap and shaving cream.

The longer he stared over Ainsley's shoulder at the body, the more the man's strength disappeared. Ainsley soon needed to hold the man up instead of holding him back.

"She said she would marry me!" he cried while clinging to Ainsley and pulling his eyes from the scene.

More officers appeared, one with handcuffs at the ready. They attempted to pull the man from Ainsley. "Gentlemen, it's fine," he said in a tone that commanded them to obey.

Ainsley led the man away from the body. He protested slightly but soon gave in under Ainsley's steady grasp. Ainsley sat the man at the base of another stairwell far enough away from the scene but still within view of the body. The man threw his hands up to his face and cried.

"What is your name?" Det. Simms asked, appearing behind Ainsley.

"How could this happen?" the man asked, ignoring the detective's question.

"Give the Detective your name," Ainsley commanded. "Or he will be forced to arrest you."

The man swallowed. "It's Jeremiah. Jeremiah Scott."

"Well Mr. Scott, what is your relation to this young woman?" Det. Simms asked.

"We are engaged," he said plainly.

"Do you know if anyone had a grudge against her?"

Jeremiah raised his gaze, his eyes wide as if realization struck him. "It was that rogue, John Waters! He killed her."

Jeremiah stood but Ainsley pushed him back down into his seat. Det. Simms poised his pencil over his notepad. "Who's John Waters?"

"He had a fancy for her but she turned him down. It was his temper. She told me he kept coming around and pestering her. I said I could teach him a lesson but she defended him." Jeremiah's hands balled into fists and he clenched his jaw at the memory. "I'll kill him!"

"I'll pretend I didn't hear that, Mr. Scott." Det. Simms wrote something down on his notepad.

Ainsley gestured toward the stairs. "Did she live around here?"

"Third floor. She roomed with two other women from the shop."

"Shop?"

"Mr. Adelaide's Tailors on Tottenham Road. I work there too." He buried his face in his hands. "Oh good Lord, why?"

Ainsley rolled his eyes. A religious man he was not.

"Mr. Scott, where can we find this John Waters?" Det. Simms asked.

"He works at the docks."

"Very well." Det. Simms nodded. "Cooper!" Det. Simms looked over his shoulder. Officer Cooper came and stood in front of the detective. "Take this man to the station. Get him a cup of tea and take an official statement in writing."

Officer Cooper nodded. "Come with me."

Ainsley helped the man get to his feet and gave him a reassuring pat on the shoulders as he walked away.

"Sad business, this." Det. Simms shook his head.

Ainsley sighed, and shoved his hands deep in his pockets. "Sad business but it's our business, Detective." He gave one last glance to the stairwell before looking at Simms. "Send the body to the hospital and come see me in two hours."

Dr. Peter Ainsley's workspace was a rather large room in the very back of St. Thomas hospital with floor to ceiling frosted windows, and high timber frame ceilings. His main workspace was a long desk with a meticulously organized treasure trove of metal implements and tools. The temperature was kept cold, as per his instructions, to keep the handful of bodies from decomposing before he had a chance to examine them. Some of the bodies came from the hospital and Ainsley examined their corpses in an effort to understand more about what had ailed them. Some bodies were gathered from the overcrowded streets of London, abandoned babies, and malnourished children who were never claimed. Ainsley was often asked to determine age, and perhaps a cause of death, though finding any definitive cause was difficult, if not impossible in those cases.

Peter Ainsley's real name was Marshall, second son and heir to Lord Abraham Marshall, who forbade Ainsley to enter medicine. He only conceded, once Ainsley agreed to use his mother's maiden name professionally. This arrangement kept his identities separate and allowed him the freedom to do the work he enjoyed while his father could pretend his son had not disappointed him entirely.

The girl arrived at his examination room shortly after Ainsley. Despite having a dozen other bodies requiring attention, he made her his priority.

"Will you be needing someone to take notes, sir?" asked a young porter. Ben Catch, a fifteen year old orphan from the workhouse, just recently started on at the hospital in the hopes he could learn a decent trade. He stood before Ainsley with square shoulders and an eager look on his boyish face.

"I assume you know how to write then?" Ainsley asked, as he slipped on his leather apron.

"Yes, sir," Ben answered, "I have been studying some of the anatomy books and—"

"Don't let Dr. Crawford see you doing that," Ainsley warned. Dr. Crawford was the head medical examiner, a cantankerous old man without charity in the slightest measurement. He despised Ainsley who was proving to be everything the old man was not; admired, sought after and incredibly intelligent.

"No sir," Ben answered quickly.

"He will send you back in a heartbeat and then what would I do?" Ainsley asked with a smile and a wink.

Within seconds Ben was perched on the high square stool behind the tall writing desk that overlooked the examination table. He posed, fountain pen in hand ready to take Dr. Ainsley's dictation.

"Woman, approximate age 18. Body found in alley behind Fullerton Street at approximately 8:45 a.m." Ainsley stood over the woman, at first examining her with his eyes. "Appears in good health prior to death, though slightly underweight." He pulled her hair back from her shoulders and attempted to hide the mass of curls beneath her head. With the neck exposed, he saw the purple bruising that circled her throat and collar bone. "Suspect bruising on neck and throat. Not clearly witnessed at crime scene." Ainsley leaned in and used his own hands to confirm his suspicion. Without touching her, he positioned his hands as if he was choking her from the front. "Bruising resembles that of two hands used to constrict airflow."

Ben's pen scratched furiously and Ainsley made sure he paused often to allow the boy time to catch up. "Approximate size to my own." Ainsley glanced up and waited until Ben's hand paused before continuing.

Ainsley made the first few cuts, making a Y-shaped incision in the woman's torso before systematically removing each organ and placing them on the table behind him. He would eventually weigh them all and survey them for damage or disease. He focused mainly on the neck wound and cut into her throat. Her oesophagus was crushed. As Ainsley looked over the damage he imagined the crunch her throat would have made when her murderer was choking the life out of her. The struggle for breath would have been excruciatingly painful. Her eyes wide, she would have been pounding her attacker with all her strength but with little effect given her slight stature. She was strangled from the front, facing the devil who did it to her.

"Dr. Ainsley?"

Ainsley looked up and saw Det. Simms standing next to Ben, who remained at the writing desk. "Dr. Ainsley, the Detective is here to see you," Ben spoke with hesitation, his hand remaining poised for further dictation.

"Do not let me disturb you," Det. Simms said, gesturing with his hand to insist they continue.

"Very well." Ainsley looked back to the woman. "Crushed oesophagus and a cracked vertebra. In my opinion, the victim died from strangulation, not from a fall."

Ben left shortly after the dissection ended. Ainsley replaced the woman's organs, finding no illness though there was slight visible damage to the liver, and then he stitched her closed. He covered her with a sheet, then dealt with his bloodied bare hands at the wash basin.

"You will get my official report tomorrow," Ainsley explained to Det. Simms as he washed.

"We have her name," Det. Simms said.

"I don't care for the names, if it's all the same," Ainsley answered, turning to face the detective. "In my line of work, it is best to avoid attachment. I am sure you understand." Ainsley could scarcely believe his own words. As much as he wanted to remain detached, he found it increasingly difficult. The stress of his profession wore him down, drove him to drink, and sometimes he became too personally involved. He was determined to maintain the aloofness required to retain his sanity.

Det. Simms nodded in agreement but said nothing.

"In the meantime, it is my opinion that she was murdered by someone she knows."

"How do you conclude that?" Det. Simms asked.

Ainsley turned, towel in hand, drying his fingers thoroughly. "She was attacked from the front. But no sign of struggle exists to indicate a prolonged ordeal. She knew the person before her and had no reason to fear him."

"Very well," Det. Simms agreed. "Did she fall?"

"No," Ainsley nearly laughed. "She has no broken bones to support that theory. She was placed there, like I said at the scene." Ainsley removed his leather apron and hung it over a hook in the corner before returning to the victim. "Look here. Bruising, like a hand. I can almost make out each finger."

Ainsley pointed to the purple-black marking on the neck. "It was a person with somewhat larger hands, like mine." Ainsley positioned his hand above the marks and hovered there until Det. Simms nodded his acknowledgement.

"Good work Dr. Ainsley. I am impressed."

Ainsley covered her again with the white sheet. "Have you found John Waters?"

Simms shook his head. "No. He did not show up to work in the morning. We have all our patrols looking for him."

Ainsley nodded and gave an assured smile. "Running is an admission of guilt."

"Very true." Simms looked to the sheet-covered body, folded up his notepad and placed it in his left breast pocket. He glanced around the room at the half dozen other corpses waiting for their turn on the examination table. "I will leave you to it then. Seems there is no shortage of dead bodies in London."

Ainsley worked well into the night. It was too dark to properly dissect so he reverted to the mountain of paperwork that seemed to multiply when he was not looking. He had promised Simms his official report by morning. Ainsley preferred to work in the examination room rather than the morgue office down the hall. He remained undisturbed in the solitude. He huddled at the small table, with two lanterns poised strategically around him, illuminating the immediate darkness and nothing much beyond.

He could have fallen asleep, and perhaps he had, when he heard the jarring sound of the distant door opening. Straining against the contrasted darkness, Ainsley looked but saw no one.

He pulled his watch from an inside pocket. It was two in the morning.

"Hello?" he asked, expecting to see another doctor or porter enter and identify himself. He could also believe it to be a nurse and her lover looking for a hideaway. "Is anyone there?" He heard a faint step and a breath but nothing more. Reluctantly, Ainsley stood up and took one of the lanterns with him into the darkness.

The bodies were covered in sheets of dingy white, some with blood seeping onto them. He rounded each one, looking for whoever had entered. When he reached the door, he had seen no one. The shadowy hall revealed only the empty porter's reception desk. He slipped back into the room. Something crashed near his examination table.

He weaved through the bodies quickly to get back to his desk. There was the distinct sound of weeping near the corpse found in the alley. When he rounded the table he saw a man, lying on the stone floor with medical tools scattered around him.

"Who the hell are you?" Ainsley asked.

"I loved her." The man gulped and gasped for breath as he tried to stand. Drunk, this task was laborious. The man reached for Ainsley, pulling on the doctor's clothes as he tried to stand.

Ainsley helped the man to his feet and held him steady while he swaggered slightly, leaning into the sheet covered table.

"They say I pushed her, but I didn't. It wasn't me, I swear! She loved me, even after the accident." The man lifted his left hand revealing three stubs and only an index finger and thumb. "Please Doc, I have to see her, one last time."

Ainsley hesitated. He didn't want to expose this man to her

post-mortem image, stitched from neck to sternum to pelvis. In the morning she would be fully clothed, smelling sweetly from fragrant oils rubbed into her skin. But now she was hardly prepared for a viewing.

The broad shouldered man reeked of salt and ale. His clothing was dingy with permanent discolouration worked into the woven fabric. He wore a white shirt, sleeves rolled to the elbows, the collar and cuffs a permanent shade of grey from years of wear. A bushy beard hid the man's face but not the raw pain in his eyes. The grieving man was a far cry from well-kept Jeremiah Scott.

"I'm sorry, Waters, that is not possible." He glanced towards the body beneath the sheet and then quickly looked away. It was an error the doctor hoped the man hadn't seen.

But Waters caught his shift in gaze. He inched toward the head of the sheet-covered mound, reaching out a trembling hand. Swiftly making a fist, he pulled the sheet from her. "Oh Jenny!"

Waters slumped, with faint, shallow breaths before he unleashed a deep throaty moan. Ainsley could see his gaze surveying the cuts over her body and the numerous stitches required to pull the skin back together. With his hand hovering over her, he outlined the Y that marked the front of her before reaching for the girl's shoulders, as if to lift her. Ainsley stopped him.

"Don't touch her," he commanded, taking a step closer to the grieving man.

Waters rounded on him, his jaw clenched, teeth bared. "You!" he groaned, "You did this to her!"

Ainsley saw tight fists at the man's side and took a step back, but found his table of tools blocking any chance of escape. Waters took a step forward, swinging widely, missing. Ainsley blocked a second blow and used Waters' own momentum to push him to the side while he slid out of the way. The man staggered. He noticed the array of tools and grabbed a small saw, used to raze through the sternum and rib cage.

Ainsley grabbed the closest thing and when Waters cut through the air with the saw, Ainsley smashed him over the head with a jar of formaldehyde and preserved human lungs.

Det. Simms eyed Ainsley, his notebook poised, his expression doubtful. "So he just waltzed in here in the middle of the night?"

"Yes."

"And what were you doing here so late?"

"I was working on your report for the girl." Ainsley thrust a few pages at Simms.

Det. Simms accepted the pages and glanced to the newly stitched up man in the cot beside them. A nurse lingered to administer some bandages but it was Ainsley who had sutured him while he was unconscious.

"He said he needed to see her one last time," Ainsley explained. Waters stirred slightly, moaning.

Simms cocked his head to the side, motioning for Ainsley to follow him into the hall. "Did he say anything else?"

"Only that he didn't kill her."

Ainsley saw a slight smile touch Simms' lips. "And do you believe him?" he asked.

"Yes."

Simms shook his head and jotted something down on his notepad.

Ainsley could feel the muscles in his face tightening as he watched Simms almost laugh at his suggestion. "I'll prove he didn't," Ainsley said sternly.

The doctor walked back into the room and approached Waters. He was lucid, moving against the pain and pushing the nurse's hand away.

"Oh sit still you cow!" the nurse chided him.

"Doctor, was I in a fight?" he asked, clearly not remembering the night before.

"Not exactly," Ainsley answered. Simms approached the bed.

"Sir, can I see your hands?" Ainsley asked, "Raise them."

Waters outstretched his hands and Ainsley took them in his own. "Look here, Detective Simms." Ainsley waited while Simms drew closer. "This man is missing three fingers." Ainsley presented the mangled hand to the detective. "Physically incapable of applying the force needed to choke someone to death. You'll recall the bruises did not show a two fingered hand."

"Oh good God! Is this about Jenny? " The man sat up in the bed, startled to sobriety. "She was strangled? Oh Jenny, Jenny!" The man hid his face in his hands and cried while Ainsley and Simms left the room.

"So if he's not the one who killed her, who is?"

Ainsley smiled. "I have my suspicions."

Within the hour, Ainsley and Simms were approaching Mr. Adelaide's Tailors, on Tottenham Rd. It was a small, corner shop with two ready-made suits displayed in the windows and an assortment of bolted cloth arranged to one side of them. "That colour would look good on you," Ainsley suggested, pointing to a bolt of blue cloth "Something a bit more dapper than brown."

Simms shrugged and followed Ainsley inside.

Jeremiah Scott, behind a counter, spoke with a customer. Beyond him, Ainsley could see two women, through a doorway. He saw the black Singer sewing machines turning as the women pressed the treadle at their feet. The cloth the women held seemed to slip past the quick moving needle with ease.

"How can I help you gentlemen?" Jeremiah Scott's words rang out in a sing-song voice. Ainsley knew he recognized them but Jeremiah did not let on.

"Hello, Mr. Scott," Ainsley began.

Jeremiah nodded and leaned over the counter. "Have you found him?"

"In a matter of speaking, he found us," Simms explained.

"We have some more questions, if you don't mind," Ainsley pressed. "You said Jenny had meant to marry you, correct?"

Jeremiah looked around him nervously. "Yes."

"Will anyone here confirm that?" Ainsley asked, "I mean, since you both worked here."

Jeremiah hesitated, biting his lower lip before speaking. "She had wanted to keep it a secret," he explained.

"Truly?" Simms laughed and glanced to Ainsley. "Most women I know are quite excited to announce an engagement. I wonder why Jenny would want to keep it quiet then?"

Jeremiah shrugged. "I can't say I know the hows and whys of women, gentlemen."

"Certainly not, such a talent would render you a magician," Ainsley quipped. Simms chuckled.

Aisnley grabbed a sheet of brown kraft paper from a nearby shelf and slipped it onto the counter in front of Jeremiah. "Place your hands on the paper please, Jeremiah," he commanded.

"Why?"

"Just do as the doctor ordered," Simms raised his eyebrow and leaned on the counter to watch. Jeremiah placed his hands on top of the paper and shifted his gaze from Ainsley to Simms.

"Spread your fingers," Ainsley instructed. He pulled a pencil from his pocket and began tracing around the edge of Jeremiah's hands. "You may take your hands back," Ainsley said, once he finished. When Jeremiah pulled away Ainsley placed his own hands on the outlines and looked to Simms.

117

"A perfect match," Simms said.

"Wait a minute," Jeremiah backed away from the table, realization coming over him. "It was an accident. I swear, she fell. What could I do? I was scared."

"You're wrong," Ainsley answered, drawing in and placing a hand under Jeremiah's upper arm. "She didn't fall. No other bones were broken. She was strangled by your four-fingered hands." Jeremiah tried to jerk his arm free but Simms flanked him on the other side. Looking from Simms to Ainsley, Jeremiah's face fell.

"A confession and show of remorse can go a long way, unless you want to see the gallows," Simms explained. Jeremiah hesitated, pressing his lips together. Ainsley imaged the gears turning in his head as he tried to manoeuvre his way out of it.

"She wasn't going to marry you," Ainsley pressed. "She was engaged to John Waters, wasn't she? It was you she refused."

Jeremiah let out a deep breath and looked as if he could cry. "He wasn't good enough for her, him and that claw of his."

"So you told her this?" Simms asked.

"Many times. She wouldn't listen. You know how stubborn women are—"

"So you went there to kill her?" Simms asked.

"No, I went to talk to her, again, before work. I cornered her on the stairs but she wouldn't listen so I... I grabbed her hand and took her ring. She came after me, and tried to get it back but... I dropped it. She was so enraged. She was hitting me again and again, crying."

"So you strangled her?" Ainsley asked.

"It was the only way to get her to stop hitting me. I didn't mean to kill her, I swear."

Simms shook his head, as he led Jeremiah from the store.

Ainsley kept his eyes to the dirt, his hands in his pockets as he walked the alley where Jenny had been found the day before. It was not as wet as it had been. Ainsley began a grid pattern, pacing back and forth between the walls of the surrounding buildings.

"You think you can find it?" Simms asked, coming down the alley towards him. "After all and sundry have been walking this lane?"

Ainsley didn't look up. "Worth a try."

Simms watched from a distance. "What's the difference? I mean suppose you find it, then what? She's dead. Who will care?"

"I will."

Simms let out an exhale of breath and shook his head. "A fool's errand, Doctor Ainsley." Simms moved away, then turned back. Ainsley kept his gaze to the ground. "I'll see you again, Doctor, before long."

"That is our way, Detective."

Simms remained for one more moment, perhaps hoping he could witness Ainsley finding the ring, before finally giving up. With Simms gone, Ainsley saw a shiny object in the gravel beneath the stairs. He rinsed it in a nearby puddle. It was the thinnest of gold rings with no adornment. In his examination room, Ainsley pulled the sheet from Jenny's left hand. Gingerly, onto the still-dented finger, he slid the ring.

It was just a symbol, but one that cost Jenny her life.

An Unexpected Christmas Gift

by A.J. Richards

A.J. Richards is a former text book editor and a retired high school English teacher. She's had a lifelong interest in writing. She's published non-fiction, but as a fan of mystery, she's delighted to be working on stories.

Although the bumpy roads were making her carsick, Helene asked the cab driver to go faster.

She was anxious to get home before her husband. She wanted to array herself in her new dress and perfume, so she could seduce Gerard into telling her what was on his mind. Had he discovered that the series of articles on this godforsaken country that had appeared in Le Devoir were written by her?

As the French Ambassador here, she knew he would be unhappy about the articles, but she felt compelled to tell the stories of these people whom she both admired and pitied.

Gerard always said he loved Helene's dark eyes and hair. But it had been months since they had slept together or even shared a decent conversation. Had his interest in her waned because he thought he knew everything about her? Perhaps some other beautiful woman had bewitched him. His assistant Liane was gorgeous, although he had always insisted she was not his type.

Not long into their marriage she realized he was ruthless. People became disposable when they were no longer useful. Had she moved more quickly than his previous two wives into the disposable category? His long hours at the office and the dinners to which she had not been invited added to her suspicions.

When they married, Gerard had insisted he wanted no more children. He had three with his previous wives, one with Isabelle and two with Genevieve. He was twenty years older than her, so she understood. Swept off her feet, besotted with him, and with his appointment as Ambassador she thought she hadn't wanted children either.

But now all these months of volunteer work at the orphanage had made her long for her own child. She would love to adopt little Adeena whose eyes lit up whenever Helene appeared.

When she raised the subject, pointing out that such an adoption would encourage the goodwill of the local government, Gerard had sneered. France did not need the good will of so poor a country. They would be leaving soon enough and did not need to bring home any souvenirs.

The cab sped up to the guardhouse, jolting her stomach as it stopped. She waved through the window to Carlo who opened the gate to the compound of embassy and ex-pat houses. For a moment she thought about lowering the window to ask if Gerard had come home, but the heat was still so intense she knew the cab driver would be upset at hot air invading his cool taxi.

The torrid air stunned her as she punched in the door code and staggered into the chilly foyer. The house was dark and quiet except for the hum of the old fashioned air conditioning. Good. Gerard wasn't home yet and the staff had left for the day. Helene inspected her face in the hall mirror, frowning at her smudged eye make-up and the wisps of dark hair that had escaped their clip. She had a lot of repair work to do before Gerard arrived. She hoped to persuade him to talk before they went over to the Christmas party hosted by one of the ex-pat entrepreneurs.

Leaving her parcels in the little sitting room, Helene went straight into her bathroom. An hour later she emerged, pink and relaxed, her hair clean and dry and pinned in an attractive chignon.

She unwrapped the new dress and the perfume, then carried them through the folding doors into her unlit bedroom.

She flicked on the bedroom light and saw Gerard asleep on her bed, his left arm flung back above his head, the right by his side. He was dressed in his office clothes, his usually crisp shirt and trousers rumpled. His jacket hung on the door of her closet. His phone and wallet were on the night table to the right of the bed and the drawer table was open. She had a moment of panic. This was the drawer where she kept the pistol she had bought before they had come here. She put down her dress and perfume and closed it. The movement activated the phone. Liane, his assistant had texted that he should meet her at midnight at the casino.

Helene inhaled sharply. It seemed her suspicions about Gerard were confirmed. He was romancing his assistant.

The whole scene puzzled Helene, as Gerard never came into her bedroom. The times they slept together, he insisted on his bed. She moved to wake him up. Then she saw the small Beretta from her bedside table dangling from the middle finger of his left hand behind the pillow. How could that be? He didn't know she owned a pistol. Then she saw the bullet hole in his left temple. She screamed.

Trembling, she called Carlo at the gate. He would know how to contact the police and an ambulance. While waiting for help, she paced. Had he really killed himself? She checked the pockets of his jacket for a note, then gingerly felt the front pockets of his pants. There was no slip of paper in any of them. She looked in his wallet. Plenty of cash and the usual cards, but no odd pieces of paper. She decided to wait for the police to check his back pockets. Would he have left something in his room? She walked down the hall to Gerard's room on the other side of the large bungalow. It was clean and tidy. No notes were visible and none were in his bed table drawers.

It looked as though Gerard had shot himself. It was true that he was left handed and would have used that hand, but Helene was certain that he hadn't killed himself.

First of all, Gerard saw himself as a rare valuable human being. He'd regularly told her that no one else could have pulled off the various coups he'd managed in his work as an ambassador. He argued that he was relegated to this backwater because of his skill in dealing with unstable regimes.

Second, she was positive he didn't know about the pistol in her bed table drawer. When they were posted here, he had insisted that the security measures were excellent and that he would take whatever other precautions she felt were necessary. He didn't want her worrying her pretty head about anything. She bought the pistol anyway because she had learned growing up to look out for herself. No one else would guard her as carefully.

Third, he wouldn't use her gun, even if he did know about it. He'd use his own fancy Browning.

Alphonse Barousse, the chief of police arrived with his deputy and the medical attendants. After viewing the body, he quickly decided the death was a suicide and asked the medical attendants to remove it. Then just to be sure he was right, the chief asked if Helene would answer a few questions. The chief, his deputy, and Helene moved into the dining room.

Chief Barousse was short and thick set, with heavy brows and thick lips. Beautiful women like Helene irked him. He thought they were stupid. Their vacant brains were incapable of appreciating the qualities of a real man, such as himself. While Helene and his deputy sat at the oval teak table in the dining room, he stood at one end. Patting his forehead he barked, "Do you know any reason, Madame, why Monsieur, the ambassador would kill himself?"

Helene stuttered, "We weren't very— He didn't talk to me much in the last few months."

"Hm," Chief Barousse muttered and made a note. He could not imagine the ambassador killing himself over a woman. Perhaps he was involved with something else that became too difficult. And it was not surprising that he did not confide in his wife. It was unusual that he had not left a note, but perhaps he didn't have time.

"Carlo said the ambassador arrived home around 3:30 pm. Was that a usual time for him to come home?"

"No. He often worked quite late. But today was the last day before the Christmas break and we were going to a party."

"Would there have been any other person in the house when he got here?"

"Possibly our maid Tamra. But she would have left around four."

That information fit with what Carlo had told him. Tamra had left at ten minutes after four. Staff from some of the other houses had trickled out in the next two hours. He could have them all questioned, but the only one who was likely to have heard anything was Tamra. And surely if she had, she would have called for help.

"What do you know about this Liane whom he was supposed to meet?"

"She's his assistant. I don't really know why she wanted to meet him at the casino."

"But you have a good idea?" Barousse sneered.

"I do not. Gerard did not discuss his work with me. It was confidential." Helene bristled. "I don't think he killed himself. It just wasn't like him. Besides he didn't know about my pistol."

"But madame, you just said that you and your husband were

not confiding in one another. So how could you know what was going on in his brain? As for the pistol, Madame, he could have easily discovered it. There is no sign of a struggle. Unless there is some compelling evidence to the contrary, it looks as though your husband has killed himself. To be sure we'll test his hand for gunshot residue. As you know there's a lot of criminal activity in this town. We do not have the resources to go chasing after reasons a person might want to die." Barousse stood and closed his notebook. "I'm sorry for your loss madame." With that he turned on his heel and left. His deputy who trailed after him nodded sympathetically to Helene.

When the host of the party, called at 10 p.m. to find out if they were coming, Helene said that unfortunately Gerard was indisposed, so they were unlikely to make it. She wanted to delay the news of Gerard's death as long as possible. That way she would have a few hours to check into his affairs without having to be the publicly grieving widow. She decided her first step would be to go to the casino to find out why Gerard was planning to meet Liane.

Casino Versailles tried to live up to its namesake. The floors were marble, the walls hung with tapestries depicting scenes of hunting and love, and the roulette tables were trimmed with gilt. At first glance, the impression was stunning opulence. Then one noticed the faded colours and chipped paint.

Liane, dressed in a slender black sheathe and dangling crystal earrings, her copper hair piled high, was at the end of the long room watching a game of baccarat. Helene walked up behind her and touched her elbow. Liane turned to Helene, blushed then turned white. "Where's Gerard?" she asked.

"I need to speak to you about him. He won't be meeting you," Helene replied staring into Liane's eyes. "Where can we talk?"

"We can go to the hotel room," Liane hesitated. The casino was part of a mid range American chain, which had seen better days.

I was right, Helene thought bitterly. "Alright, let's go."

They were silent during the elevator ride. Unlike Gerard to carry on an affair here, Helene thought, remembering his courting of her.

When they arrived at the room, Liane went straight to the mini-bar, poured herself a shot of whiskey and held the bottle out to Helene who declined.

"What's happened to Gerard?" Liane murmured as she sipped her drink.

"He's dead," Helene told her.

Liane's eyes widened, "My god, how can that be?"

Helene described how she had found him. "But I don't think he shot himself. Do you know anyone who would want him dead?"

"You mean aside from me?" Liane spluttered.

Helene stared at her, "Did you shoot him?"

"No, I was at the hairdresser's when you found him. Helene, I can't tell you how relieved I feel. He was blackmailing me - for sex. I made a bad mistake. I borrowed some money from the embassy's discretionary fund to send to my mother. Anyway Gerard found out and said I'd lose my job and go to jail unless I did him some favours. I had to go along with him. I need this job, although I'm looking for another one."

Helene believed her. Liane had always been polite and helpful and interested in how Helene was doing. In the past few months, Liane had been accommodating, but no more, turning away from Helene's friendly inquiries with mutters about her workload.

"Who would have wanted him dead, aside from you?" Helene inquired.

"Well none of the staff really liked him, because he was so arrogant. But he knew how to do his job and he was good at it. I don't know if he had any under the counter business with the development companies, but the government officials here will be very sorry to hear he died."

"Well, the police believe he shot himself. They're not going to pursue an investigation, because they're too busy with other cases."

"That's typical. Not only are they lazy, they're incompetent," Liane said. "I don't actually care. I'm just glad he's dead."

"Well I want to know why," Helene responded.

The next day, Christmas Eve, Helene began to receive calls of condolence from people with whom Gerard had worked. The president of the country was particularly solicitous, telling her that she had only to tell him what she needed and it would be hers.

In the afternoon she went to the orphanage with gifts of candy for the children and a doll for little Adeena. The child put her soft brown arms around Helene's neck and said, "I your girl."

Maria, the matron, watching the two said, "It will be very hard for her, when you don't come any more."

"Yes, so you have heard about my husband." Helene smiled then, as she understood she was free to pursue her heart's desire. "Maria, I would like to adopt Adeena. What do I have to do?"

One of the requirements, aside from income statements, was that Helene needed the support of a local person who was also a parent, someone who could vouch for her character. The only person she could think of was Tamra, their maid, who had two children. Helene and Tamra didn't know one another very well. They were polite and friendly, while maintaining the employer/employee barrier. Helene had sent Christmas gifts with Tamra for her children and given her a bonus as well.

Two days after Christmas, a junior police officer called to say there had been traces of gunshot residue on Gerard's left hand. As far as the police were concerned his suicide was confirmed.

When Tamra arrived shortly afterward to clean the house, she glanced at Helene, as she put away her bag and headed to the cleaning closet, "I am very sorry about Mr. Gerard, Madame. The police spoke to me but I didn't hear anything. I was working in his bedroom and the door to yours was shut when I left."

There was something so hasty and dismissive in her manner that Helene paused. Then she said, "Could I speak with you when you are finished working, Tamra? There's something I want to ask you."

"Could we make it another day? I don't have a lot of time today," Tamra responded, her eyes sliding away.

"Well, this is important to me, so let's talk now. I don't care if all the cleaning gets done."

"Alright, Madame, what is it?" Tamra's manner was so defiant, that Helene was quiet for a moment.

"Tamra, what's the matter? Are you upset about the ambassador?"

Tamra looked away, her tall, thin body slumping. "Anyone's death is always hard."

"That's mostly true, but I'm only half sad about it," Helene responded. She explained her desire to adopt Adeena and Gerard's opposition to it. "I need your help with this, Tamra. Will you vouch for my good character? That you think I'd make a good mother."

Tamra hesitated a moment, "You've always been kind to me, Madame. I can do this. What do I have to do?"

Helene explained that the orphanage wanted to interview her, and that she hoped Tamra could go to see the officials in the next few days. She would arrange a taxi to take her. She would soon have to fly Gerard's body home to France and she would like to take Adeena with her. The government had been very helpful so far and she thought that she could get most of the paperwork done in the next week. Gerard's deputy would expedite permission from France.

Tamra cocked her head to one side, stray black curls framing her brown face. She was quiet, then said, "You aren't sorry that the ambassador is dead." When Helene gave her a half smile and a nod, she continued, "I'm not either. You see, he tried to rape me that afternoon. I was in your room when he came in and pushed me on to the bed. I knew about your pistol in the drawer. I pulled it out while he was tearing at my clothes. I told him to stop, but he didn't. He grabbed at my hand and I shot him. Then I arranged his body." Tamra looked down, her arms folded across her chest.

Helene sat on the hall chair. She hesitated. "How frightening, how terrible for you, Tamra. Thank you for telling me. I never believed he shot himself, but I'll never tell anyone what you've said. You have given me a new life." Helene smiled as she touched Tamra's arm and marveled at her unexpected Christmas gifts: freedom from Gerard and a lovely child.

Crossing Over

by Rosemary McCracken

Rosemary McCracken's mystery novel, Safe Harbor, *is published by Imajin Books, and was shortlisted for Britain's Debut Dagger award in 2010. Born and raised in Montreal, Rosemary has worked on newspapers across Canada as a reporter, arts reviewer, editorial writer and editor. She is currently a freelance journalist who specializes in personal finance and the financial services industry. She lives in Toronto with her husband, and is a member of Sisters in Crime Toronto, and Sisters in Crime International.*

I walked on water tonight.

Well, not quite. The river was frozen. Even so, it was pretty scary. Sophie was scared to death.

At noon today, the teachers had left for a convention downtown, and the cool chicks of Holy Angels High headed for the washroom to get ready for the afternoon off. They crowded in to gel their hair and glitter their faces. I don't go for all that hair and face crap, but Sophie liked hanging with the gang in there.

Zoë Lawson shoved her aside. "Out of the way, Sophie. You're blocking the mirror."

Poor Soph, with her acne, her frizzy hair and those braces on her teeth. Awesome boobs, though, 36C to my 28AA.

I tugged at Sophie's sleeve. "C'mon, let's go."

She followed me out of the washroom. We got our gear from our lockers, bundled up and put the school behind us.

We ate burgers and fries at McDonald's, across the room from Zoë and her friends. When the cool kids had drifted out, we walked over to Sophie's house. We each had a slug of her mom's gin, and made sure to top up the bottle with water. Then we watched *Pretty Woman* for maybe the zillionth time.

"This stinks," Sophie said, shutting off the TV when the video ended. "Like, it's totally unreal."

"Yeah." We weren't going to live happily ever after like Julia Roberts.

She sighed. "We need guys in our lives."

We put on our jackets and boots, and went back outside. We've had some pretty warm weather for early March so we walked down to the park. Sophie stuffed her toque in her pocket.

I plopped down on a bench and turned my face up to the sky. The sun was sinking behind the bare treetops.

"I can hardly wait for summer," Sophie said. "No school for two whole months. We'll go to the pool, work on our tans."

I braced myself for a discussion of boys. That was all Sophie was interested in. Me, I don't care if I never have a boyfriend.

"Yeah, we can try out our new bikinis on the lifeguards. Wouldn't it be awesome to date a hottie lifeguard?"

I tried to sound interested. "If we had boyfriends...we could go to movies on Saturday nights."

She heaved a great sigh. "Kyla, there's more to having a boyfriend than going to movies."

Sophie'd told me she had a boyfriend when she was in Connecticut last summer. Pretty amazing, considering. But she hadn't said much when I probed her for details. She just pouted her lips and looked at me through half-closed eyes. "You'll find out someday," she said. I decided to get to the bottom of it.

"Got a cig, Soph?" I'd started smoking Sophie's cigarettes from time to time. I don't really like smoking, but the cool girls all smoke.

"Inhale, Kyla," she told me when I lit up. "You're not smoking if you don't inhale. You're just wasting my cigs."

I tried to inhale and coughed. "What do you mean there's more to guys than going to movies?" I asked when I recovered.

"Well, there's things you do on the way home. Things guys expect."

"Like what? What things?" As if I didn't know.

"Well." She drew out the word. "First of all, you gotta be a good kisser."

I suddenly felt queasy. "You're a good kisser?"

She looked at me out of the corner of one eye. "Maybe."

I swallowed the bile that rose in my throat and did my best to flash her a smile. "I'm good at keeping secrets." And I am.

Sophie tossed her head. "Sorry, Kyla. I don't kiss and tell."

It was starting to get dark and the temperature had dropped. We stood up to shake some warmth into our arms and legs.

"Let's walk a bit," I said.

Two blocks below the park, the street runs down to the river. Where the pavement ends, six steps lead to the water. I headed down them.

Behind me, Sophie squealed. "There's ice on these steps, Kyla. We could break our necks."

I pretended I didn't hear.

Darkness had fallen and there were no streetlights, but the sky was studded with stars. We stood in a soft, grey world, with a vast swath of snow-covered ice in front of us. Beyond it, lights beckoned on the far shore.

"The river's frozen solid," I said. "It won't break up for weeks. Even in May, you can still see big chunks of ice floating down it. Let's walk out a bit."

Sophie joined me on the bottom step, looking doubtful. "What if it cracks open? We'll be sucked under."

One afternoon last fall, Daddy and I sat on these steps throwing sticks into the water. I remember how quickly the angry, black water whisked the wood downstream.

But I pushed the thought away. "The ice won't break. C'mon, Soph. Don't tell me you're scared?"

"Well, just for a little way. But I'm not crossing to the other side."

I stepped onto the snow-covered ice, and thought of the river rushing beneath my feet.

"Wait up!"

I looked back, and watched Sophie dig her toque out of her pocket and pull it down over her frizz. Then she stepped on the ice as if she was walking on eggshells.

"Follow me," I told her. "If the ice breaks under me, you can run back."

A tingle ran down my spine, but I wasn't scared. I felt a sudden surge of energy. I'd never felt so alive.

Sophie was puffing behind me. "This snow is soft and wet. We're going too far, Kyla."

"Go back if you want."

"Come back with me. I don't want to be by myself out here."

"We're more than halfway across. I'm going on."

She howled. "Kyla! You're crazy! We're completely alone out here. No one would see us if we fell through the ice. And I left my cell back at the house."

I smiled. Sophie didn't have her precious cell phone with her so she couldn't tell the world where we were. Okay, I was jealous. I don't have a cell because Daddy doesn't like them.

I turned and looked at her. She'd never go back on her own. She'd have to follow me to the other side.

Her howls became whimpers. "My feet are wet. My new boots are wrecked."

My boots are waterproof plastic. Daddy won't buy me expensive leather boots. "C'mon, Soph. It's still pretty warm out. Your feet can't be cold."

"Kyla," she wailed, "I lost a glove. It must be back there somewhere. I took them off when I put on my toque. I bought those gloves with my Christmas money."

"We gotta keep going, Soph. The other side is closer now. We'll be across in no time."

"It must be way past six. Mom will be home by now and I didn't leave a note to say where I was going. She'll be throwing a fit."

"Did she know where you were when you stayed out all night with that guy last summer?"

"I was visiting my dad. He doesn't care when I come in."

"How can you be afraid of a little walk across the ice when you did all that stuff with that guy? Weren't you scared?"

"Not as scared as I am now."

"You could have got pregnant."

She started to sob.

"Personally, Soph, I'd rather be dead than pregnant."

In a flash, I knew it was true. Being pregnant would be the end of the world.

Sophie let out another howl. "You don't know what you're talking about."

I smiled to myself. "You weren't out with anyone at all. You made all that stuff up."

Sophie wailed, then started to sob. "Kyla, how can you be so mean? I'm fourteen years old and I've never had a date. Never been kissed. Doesn't it bother you that you've never been kissed?"

I walked ahead. She'd finally admitted it. She'd never been out with a guy.

"I'd give anything to have a boyfriend." She panted behind me, trying to keep up. "You don't understand, do you? You're not interested in guys."

"Shut up," I said.

But she wouldn't let it go. "A guy like Jason..."

132

"Shut up."

"Or Zoë's Rickie..."

I wanted to stick my fingers in my ears. "Shut up, Sophie!"

"You want to be Daddy's little girl forever?"

I froze, fear gripping my heart.

"Daddy's girl! Daddy's girl!" she sang.

Furious, I wheeled around. "Shut the fuck up!"

"That's your problem, isn't it, Kyla? You like being Daddy's little girl."

I turned my back to her and plunged ahead, my heart pounding. She knew. Sophie knew!

"Kyla, wait. Please."

I hurried on.

"Kyla, why are you so mad?"

Ahead of us was a big, brick house. Curtains were drawn over its windows, but I could see the rooms were lit behind them. And several outdoor lamps lit up the grounds. My eyes followed the white sweep of lawn down to the river. With a jolt, I saw a ribbon of black running along the shoreline. I looked down, suddenly afraid that the ice under my feet might break.

Sophie came up beside me and grabbed my arm. "That's water over there. What're we going to do?"

I shook off her arm. "We could go back." I inched forward on the ice. The ribbon of black in front of us wasn't very wide but I could see the water was moving swiftly. Daddy said the current was really strong on this side of the river and the water was deep. We couldn't risk falling in.

Sophie whimpered behind me. "I'm too cold to walk all the way back."

I had an idea. "See that block?" A white concrete square with a metal ring in its centre sat between us and the bare stones at the edge of the water. "We're going to jump onto that, then jump to land."

Sophie was shaking. "What if we miss? I can't swim."

"We can't miss," I told her. "It's just a small jump."

"Help!" she cried, raising her voice.

I put my hand over her mouth. "Quiet, Sophie. They'll call our parents and then we'll be in big trouble. We'll get across, then we'll walk to the bridge. No one will know where we've been."

Sophie's sobs had turned into hiccups.

"Come on, Soph. Watch me."

I jumped and landed on the block. "Come on. You can do it."

She gave a little shriek and landed beside me, nearly knocking me into the water.

She wrapped her arms around me. "Kyla, I just peed my pants."

She was such a wimp, but wimps can be dangerous if they have big mouths. I took hold of her wrists and pulled her arms off me. "One more jump, Sophie, and we'll be across."

"I'll find a phone and call my Mom. She'll come and get us."

I put my hands on her shoulders, and gave her a push. It was just a little push, but she fell backwards into the rushing water.

"Kyla!" Her hand came up once before she disappeared.

It took longer to walk back than I'd thought it would. By the time I reached the bridge, the stars had vanished from the sky. Daddy had said there'd be snow tonight. Thinking of Daddy, I was relieved he wouldn't know I'd been out on the ice. But what made me feel really relieved was that I wouldn't have to worry about Sophie's big mouth.

I returned to the steps we'd walked down and went back out on the ice. I found Soph's glove a little ways out. I took it with me and stashed it in a dumpster at the end of the block.

Snow had started to fall when I reached my street. I turned my face up to it, knowing it would cover our footprints on the ice.

"Where've you been, Kyla?" Daddy called down as I let myself in the front door. "I called Sophie's house and her mother said she wasn't back either."

"I was at the library," I said, pulling off my boots in the hall. "I wasn't with Sophie. She's got a boyfriend. Guess I won't be seeing much of her anymore."

"Well, you know your Daddy loves you. Come on up here, honey."

I shrugged off my jacket, swallowed hard and slowly climbed the stairs.

Stress!

by Steve Shrott

Harry Freedman pulled the torn half-map out of his pocket and stared at the forest in front of him.

"Screwed again."

The instructions on the map indicated he should turn in the direction of the elm tree. Great, just great! Which damn elm tree? There were two.

Harry shook his head in disgust. He took a deep breath, turned left. He trudged through the high grass, hoping to come to the winding stream shown on his map. But all he saw in front of him was even more dense forest. It seemed to go on forever. "Crap."

As he stumbled through the flora, all Harry could think about was how badly his divorce had gone—beginning with his stupid lawyer, Janice Robbins. "You have to calm down, Mr. Freedman," she would always say in that irritating nasal voice of hers. How could he be calm? It was because of her idiotic mistakes that the divorce took sixteen months.

Harry's marriage had been no picnic either. Mona hadn't cooked, cleaned or given him any action in the last seven years. Plus she cheated on him with that creepy grease-monkey, Ricardo.

Yet, for all her evil deeds, she still got the house, the Jag, the motorboat, even his nutty dog, Ralph. It's not that he loved the slobbering mutt so much, he just didn't want HER to have him.

The only good news was that he had the map. Or at least half of it. It had come from Mona's ex-con brother, Mike Dixon.

He had croaked and willed it to them. At first, Harry thought it was the last act of a sick mind. But then Harry realized it was Mike's way of paying him back for all he'd done for him.

The police hadn't recovered all the money from Mike's robberies and Harry believed the map showed where the rest had been buried. At first, he wondered why half a map? Then he figured that out as well. Mike hated Mona. He must have thought I'd kill Mona to get the rest of it!

Of course, Harry knew he couldn't kill her.

Just last night, he had gone over to Mona's place, all friendly-like, to ask for her section of the map. He said he just wanted it as a memento of Mike. But apparently, she had figured out it led to money as well.

He explained in his kindest voice that there probably wasn't anything actually buried there, knowing what a loser Mike had been. Mona's eyebrows shot up like a rocket and she started screaming. Harry couldn't understand what the problem was. He was just trying to save her some trouble. She suddenly lunged at him with a knife. Harry was lucky to escape with his life.

What a crazy!

Harry stared at the hugeness of the forest in front of him and realized he couldn't walk any further. He had arthritis in one leg and decided he had to rest for a bit. He sat down on a large rock and pulled out a cigarette from his shirt pocket. He'd started the habit about seven years ago when his marriage had begun unravelling. He smiled as he realized that part of his life was over now. He had already met someone new—Francesca. She was a dream, a beauty. Plus he was going to be a rich man very soon.

Of course, being a greedy bitch, Harry knew his ex would try and steal what was rightfully his. So last evening when Mona left for Ricardo's love-nest, Harry got in touch with Francesca's cousin—Raul. He was a small time crook and would do anything for cash.

He had Raul sneak into the house and mix rat poison into the container of ice tea in Mona's fridge. He knew she drank it every day. Harry laughed when he thought of her lying dead on the ground.

Lucky, he had Raul. Harry knew he couldn't have done it himself. He wasn't good with cloak and dagger stuff.

Harry's leg felt better so he stood up to continue his trek to find the money.

Suddenly he felt something hit the back of his head. He teetered back and forth for a moment, then collapsed onto the ground screaming, "Owwww."

A moment later, he lay unconscious.

"Owwww!" yelled Mona as she adjusted her backpack. It really hurt. Maybe she had stuffed too much into it. Still, she was going to need the rubber gloves, garden trowel and all the other knick-knacks when she found the cash.

She stared at the half-map in her hand. Then looked at the stream that lay before her. She turned the map this way, then that. The stream veers to the left, she thought. But do I follow it or go the other way? She shook her head and decided to go right.

She was in such a rush this morning she hadn't gotten a chance to have her morning ice tea. So she packed the bottle into her knapsack for later. Maybe, she'd have it as a celebration when she found the money.

As she walked forward, she thought about her divorce. That Collins was one stupid lawyer. Always saying, "Take it easy, Mrs. Freedman," in that pip-squeak voice of his. The guy seemed totally confused. That's why the trial lasted so damn long.

She didn't understand her miserable jerk of a husband either. How could Harry want a divorce when she'd been such a great wife—cooking all those gourmet meals, cleaning every day, giving the animal sex, whenever he wanted it. She even ignored the fact that he was having an affair. What was that slut's name again? Oh yeah, Francesca. What a dumb-ass name.

God knows why Harry forced the car, house and boat on her. She couldn't possibly make those payments. Plus she got seasick when she went sailing. Did he really have to insist that she take Ralph? That mutt would royally mess up her hand-woven, Indian carpet.

The only good news was that she had the map. At least half of it. It must have been Mike's way of paying her back for all the things she'd done for him.

At the same time, he obviously wanted her to kill Harry so she'd have the complete map. Mike never did like him.

Mona, of course, knew she could never do that.

She actually thought that when Harry came over last night, he was going to be civil. She tried to gently explain that she was keeping the map and that by rights she should have the other half as well. After all, it came from HER brother.

But then Harry got this wild look on his face and came at her with the knife. What a psycho! She would have phoned the police but fortunately for him, he ran out before she did.

Mona knew the greedy freak would try to go after her money. So last night, she had Ricardo go to Harry's place and cut the brake lines on his Lexus. She hated to wreck a great car like that, but Mona smiled at the thought of Harry screaming as he drove down a steep hill. Once she got the money, she'd have one terrific life.

Luckily, she had Ricardo. She didn't know a brake from a carburetor.

Mona saw two elm trees in the distance. She looked at the map, twisted it this way and that. Which elm tree was it? She picked the one on the left. But as she walked toward it, she felt something hit the back of her head. She fell onto the ground unconscious.

Harry awoke, slowly remembering that he had fallen. He felt his neck and noticed a little blood on his hand. He wondered if perhaps someone had thrown a rock at him. He could only think of Mona, but she'd be fast asleep 'til—forever. He couldn't stop himself from giggling.

Maybe he just tripped on some dirt on the ground. His body seemed to be in good working order. Even his arthritis wasn't quite as bad now. That's the reason he took a cab way out here instead of driving. He knew it would be a bastard when he had to push the accelerator with his bad leg.

Harry looked down at the map wadded tightly in his hand and tried to get his bearings. He saw a stream in front of him that veered to the left. He examined the map but couldn't tell which way he should go. Harry decided to turn right.

Mona awoke feeling dazed. She examined the rock on the ground, positive someone had thrown it at her. But who? Normally, she'd say Harry, but right now he was probably on a fatality list somewhere. She smiled to herself. With him gone, once she got the cash, her life would be perfect.

She gazed at the X on the map indicating the location of the money. She'd probably reach it in about ten minutes.

Harry looked at the map and at the muddy area in front of him. The X indicated that this was the location of the cash. Harry's breath quickened. He ran over and started clawing at the earth with his fingers, like a starving man searching for food.

He dug for thirty-five minutes, but to Harry, the time went by in a flash. His leg seized several times, but he didn't notice the pain.

Finally he uncovered a large wooden crate. A wide grin lit up his face. He cleaned off the dirt lying on top of the crate and slowly opened the lid. As he gazed at the insides, a tear dribbled down his cheek.

There were rows and rows of money.

Mona stood in front of a muddy area of land. She snatched the garden trowel from her bag and began scooping out mud.

Some time later, exhausted, but elated, she uncovered a large wooden crate. She licked her lips as she slowly opened it up. A moment later, a big smile appeared on her face, as she stared at rows and rows of money.

After the gunshots, lawyers Janice Robbins and Paul Collins jumped down from the giant elm. They scooped out the money from the crate and buried Mona's body just like they had done with Harry, moments earlier. Then they buried the gun.

"Thank goodness it's over," said Janice as she threw the shovels into the car.

"Yeah. Although, I hated to do it," replied Paul.

"We had to. They were miserable, stupid, jerks. He was the worst client I ever had. Always complaining. Then when I told him what to do, he'd scream at me. He said he had other jobs for me too. I was scared it would never end."

"Ditto her. She wanted me to sue the postman 'cause her mail was late one day. I don't know why they wanted a divorce; they were made for one another." Paul laughed.

"I told you we'd need the gun."

"Yeah," nodded Paul. "I thought the rocks would knock them out and we could get the maps. But both of them had such tight grips, even unconscious, I was afraid the maps would rip. I figured it would be better if we waited till they found the money and then we could just grab it." Paul gave Janice a toothy smile. "You were right about the stress too. I feel great!"

"Dr. Abrams said he didn't know how we sucked it up for eighteen months. He told me that if we didn't do something to ease the tension, we'd explode."

Paul moved close to Janice. "There was one good thing about working for them."

"What's that?"

"It brought us together."

Janice smiled, then kissed Paul on the lips.

When they broke away, Paul patted Janice on the shoulder. "I'm so glad you convinced me we should go after the money ourselves."

"I heard that Dixon had a pang of conscience about his criminal past and sent the half-maps of where he buried the money to Mona and Harry. Apparently, he wanted to do one good thing for his only living relatives before he died. But when he left a note telling them both to get the money the next morning, as he heard the cops were investigating, I was a little suspicious about his motives."

Paul nodded. "He must have hated them as much as we do and meant for them to kill each other."

"I certainly can't blame him."

"Me neither," said Paul as he picked up a large leather bag. "Anyway, now the hundred grand is all ours."

Janice smiled, wiped the sweat off her forehead. Then she reached for the glass container sitting on the ground. "I found some ice tea in her backpack. I'm gonna have it. Want any?"

"Nah. But I think I'm gonna go." Paul jingled the car keys he removed from the dead man's pocket. "I thought I'd head over to Harry's and take his precious Lexus for a victory spin."

"Okay. See you later, honey."

Jackie's Girls

by Linda Wiken

A former broadcaster and journalist, **Linda Wiken** *also worked for the local public school board as a community worker before making the monumental purchase of Prime Crime Mystery Bookstore (along with Mary Jane Maffini) in Ottawa. For 15 years, she happily sold books, hob-nobbed with customers and authors, and attended to business until it closed in March, 2010. Along the way, she wrote short stories and has been published in the seven Ladies' Killing Circle anthologies (of which she is a member) and several mystery magazines. She was short-listed for a Best Short Story Arthur Ellis award. Now, with a three-book contract from Berkley Prime Crime in hand, she's writing as Erika Chase. The first in the series,* A Killer Read, *hit the bookshelves in April, 2012, featuring a mystery book reading club in the southern U.S.*

"Jackie always knew how to look after his girls."

"What do you mean, Chrissie...knew?" asked Barbara. "I'd say he hasn't lost his touch. Look at this. We may be out in the middle of the boonies, but this place looks like he picked it up and moved it from Point Grey."

All four women nodded as they moved around the living room, a hand grazing the Bose sound system; a lingering look at the Lawren Harris, a Dale Chihuli glass vase, a brown saddle leather archer chair that matched the three-seater sofa. Jackie Montana had always treated his girls to the best but in the sixties, he'd had a different appreciation of just what that might be.

"He's definitely classed-up," she added.

"So, does anyone know...is he coming up here, too?" That was Judith of the "don't call me Judes" line. Barbara was Babs,

Christine was Chrissie, Claudia was Claudie. And then there was Judith. Straight up. In all things.

Claudia shrugged into the thickness of a white wicker chair lined with pillows, three-deep, brocade-covered. Eclectic, as always. "He might. He says he wants to tie up some loose ends."

"Oh, Jackie and his loose ends. Even after 25 years, he's all business. I used to wonder, how a fella like that was going to cope behind bars." Christine looked from one to the other although who could answer?

None of the girls had visited him, at his request. He hadn't kept in touch, not until the silver-embossed-on-white invitation had arrived, asking for an RSVP to a long weekend at the Montana summerhouse in the Okanagan. The phone number listed hooked into an answering machine. Instructions had followed by mail and the white stretch limo had picked them all up, starting with Barbara, ending with Judith, for the five-hour drive to Pickett Lake.

Barbara stopped her wandering in front of the gilt-edged mirror that covered a quarter of the wall, the one opposite French doors that led to a multi-terraced patio.

She tucked a strand of her once-black hair, now more salt than pepper, behind her right ear. The pewter Celtic cross now dangling in full view had been a gift from Jackie, in his Irish phase. "I'd say, girls, that Jackie had a lot more going for him than just the service."

Christine giggled. "I haven't been called `girl' for eons. Oh, those were the good old days, weren't they? Nothing but the classiest restaurants."

"The nightclubs," added Judith. "Remember The Living Room—all those sleek couches, orange wasn't it...yes, they were orange leather and the glass coffee tables? Dancing on the second floor. I loved that place."

"The hours at the hair salon." Christine again. "I'll have the total package today, Janice. Colour, style, manicure," she added in a rich, middle-aged tons-of-breeding voice.

Barbara turned to face them and waggled her eyebrows. "The hotels."

"The stars," Christine grinned. "Remember we all went back stage to meet Neil Diamond and then out on the harbour cruise for dinner?"

"Personally, I loved the party that bigwig threw at his house in Shaughnessy after the Grey Cup game. Lots of out-of-town movers and shakers at that one," said Barbara.

"Let's not forget the money. I managed to set myself up in a new line of business as an antique dealer." They all looked at Claudia.

"Wow. Do you have a shop, Claudie? Do you travel a lot?" Christine bounced onto the sofa and leaned towards Claudia.

"You never change, Chrissie," said Judith. "A dyed-blonde, now sixty-something twit."

"That's not fair, Judith. You're always saying mean things to me."

"Always? I haven't seen you for almost thirty years, Chrissie."

"O.K., so you're still calling me names." Christine's eager smile had turned into a pout.

"I need a drink. There's got to be a bar around here." Judith scanned the room and walked over to a sideboard of inlaid marquetry next to the door. She pulled open the doors until she found what she was looking for. "Aha...well-stocked, as always. Anyone want anything?" she asked as she poured a generous McCallum, straight up.

Barbara joined her at the sideboard. "I hope you two aren't going to go at each other all weekend. We're here for a good time and we'll only talk about the fun we had. Got it? What can I get you Chrissie?"

She sniffed before answering. "G&T, please."

"Claudie?"

"I'd like some of that Scotch before it's all gone."

Judith whirled and glared. "What's that supposed to mean?"

"Oh, Judith. Always able to dish it out but not take it." Claudia smiled, a friendly smile, no malice in it, none intended.

Judith stared at her a few minutes. The tinkle of ice being dropped into a glass, the only sound. Finally, she took a sip and smiled back. "You're right. I do apologise to one and all, especially you, Chrissie. I promise to be on my best behaviour for the rest of this reunion."

"Oh, Judith. Thanks." Christine launched herself off the couch and threw her arms around Judith, who barely managed to save her drink from landing on the rug.

She glanced heavenward and shrugged out of the embrace. "I'm not the touchy-feely type, Chrissie."

Barbara snorted. "That's not what the guys used to say."

Judith stiffened then started to laugh. "I do think they appreciated my talents." She gave one side of her draping silver cardigan a swirl.

Christine sipped the drink Barbara handed to her. "You were

143

always in demand, Judith. Wasn't she Babs?"

Barbara hooked her arm through Christine's free one and led her back to the sofa. "We all were, honey. That's why Jackie kept us on." She eased away from Christine and sat at the end closest to Claudia. "But Claudia was special, weren't you, hon? All those trips. You were the only one Jackie sent out of town. I always wondered about that. In fact, I was even a bit jealous."

Claudia gave a small laugh. "No need to be. And it had nothing to do with being special. I just branched out a bit."

"That's right," Christine agreed. "You used to go around and buy him antiques and stuff, didn't you?"

"Yes. Now, I, for one, want to hear what everyone's been up to. You start, Chrissie."

"Oh, wow. Nothing very exciting, I'm afraid. Of course, it would've been hard to match what we had with Jackie." She sighed. "I found a guy, he owned his own club and he didn't ask me any questions and he didn't want me to work there. He brought in some good acts – the Animals before they took off on the charts, Lighthouse, I even met Burton Cummings." Her sigh came out louder than her words. "He was kind of cute, my Gary that is, not Burton. Well, he was cute, for sure. But Gary – well, he was kind of balding and in his late thirties. Anyway, he asked me to marry him and I said yes. We had a good enough life. Nothing as exciting as it had been though." Tears pushed at the edges of her eyes and she downed the remainder of her drink. "We had two kids, a boy and a girl, both married with kids, living out east. I don't get to see them near enough."

"What about Gary, Chrissie?" asked Barbara.

"He died, five years ago. Heart attack. I...I try to keep busy. I have lots of girlfriends and we go out shopping and things. But I sure do miss him."

Judith cleared her throat. "I never married. I'm not sure why."

"So what did you do, Judith? Where did you work?" Christine wanted to know.

"I took some secretarial training and then got a job with a law firm. That's a laugh, isn't it? Worked myself up to office manager and then I retired, seven years ago. Now I do volunteer work most days."

"You do?" Christine couldn't keep the surprise out of her voice.

Judith frowned. "That so hard for you to imagine?"

"No. No, I guess not."

"I go in three afternoons a week, to a hospice." She glanced at the others. "For men." She grinned.

Barbara roared with laughter and the others joined in. When she'd caught her breath she asked if anyone wanted a refill. As she poured drinks all around, she added her own story. "I spent several years living the good life, buying clothes, going to parties and then, before the money ran out, I went to university and got a degree in social work."

"I can see where this is going," Claudia said.

"Uh-huh. I got a job counseling teens on the street and I'm still doing it. Plan to keep going until they kick me out but they won't because I'm the mother figure around there. This hair and this waistline make it easy for some 15-year-old who's just been kicked around by her pimp to listen to what I have to say."

"Wow. That's so noble and...and..." Christine stopped talked and stared in awe.

"Altruistic," Claudia offered.

"Yeah. You've got a big heart, Babs."

"Yeah, along with my big butt, as you may have noticed. I lost that sweet, curvy figure many decades ago. Speaking of which, I'm hungry and I want to get out of these clothes into something more comfy."

"Are we entertaining tonight?" Judith asked, eyebrows arched.

"Only ourselves, honey. Only ourselves." She pushed herself off the couch and walked to the door. "I'll find out where the driver parked my bags, get changed and see you all in the kitchen."

"Wow, escargot, steaks, champagne...Jackie's thought of everything. I only wish he'd come join us," Christine added.

Barbara half-turned from the Jenn-Air grill she was starting. "Think of him as being here in spirit."

"Or, spirits." Judith waved one of two bottles of Pol Roger Brut in the air.

"Oh boy, everybody duck when that thing gets opened," Claudia said.

"I wonder why he isn't here," said Barbara. "Has anyone actually seen him since he got out?"

The other three shook their heads.

"And no one visited him in jail?"

Again, three dissenting heads.

"You know," Barbara continued, "I thought he might have wanted to talk to us, individual like, and try to find out what went wrong."

"What do you mean?" asked Judith.

"Well, like how the cops knew where to find the gun he'd supposedly tossed after shooting that Copland guy."

"You're right," Christine added. "I've been wondering that myself. And also, how'd they know where he kept all those books? His whole friggin' business, they found out about. The girls, the numbers, the dope."

"I always thought it was one of his boys who squealed," Judith said. "I doubt it was Frankie or Mike. Those guys took being his bodyguard way too seriously. But how about that bookkeeper he had? Isn't it always the accountant or bookkeeper who turns the goods over to the feds?"

"Only in the movies." Barbara relieved Judith of the bottle and started removing the dark protective foil from the cage.

"No, Judith could be right," Claudia said. "But if it's not one of the boys, then it has to be one of the girls."

They looked at each other. It took a few minutes before anyone said anything.

Christine was the first. "Well, it wasn't one of us. Was it? I mean, sure we knew what all he was into and I guess we'd seen him working on the books at one time or another. And we all knew where the wall safe was. Gee, it could've been one of us. But it wasn't, was it? I mean, why would we? We had it all. Lots of glamour, lots of cash. And, Jackie...he took real good care of us, didn't he?" A sob escaped her lips. "I mean, I was so friggin' happy back then." She grabbed at a dishtowel as the tears started flowing.

Barbara set the bottle on the counter and wrapped her arms around Christine. "No, honey. It wasn't one of us. You're right, nobody had a motive. We all loved Jackie and he knew it. That's why he thought he'd do something special for us, like this weekend. Loyalty was always important to him."

Judith grabbed the bottle. "Babs is right so let's get on with enjoying all this." She pulled the remaining foil off and twisted off the wire. "Bombs away." Aiming the bottle at the far side of the room, she popped out the cork and dashed to the sink as the froth showered over her arms.

They all filled their champagne flutes and toasted Jackie. Christine swallowed a mouthful of drink then asked, "So, what do you think happened, Claudie?"

Claudia eyed them all in turn over the rim of her glass. "I think that time will tell."

"Ohhh, how mysterious," giggled Christine. "Look, how about we go skinny dipping before we turn in, just like old times? We've got lots of privacy, there's nobody within miles of us out here."

"Then we could all sit around the campfire in our pj's and toast smores," Judith finished the last of her drink. "I for one am too tired to play pajama party. Besides, I'll bet you never got around to taking those swimming lessons, did you Claudia?"

"Actually, I didn't. I had better things to do."

"Like Ken, Pete, Tommy...." The well-aimed pillow caught Judith in the face.

"Oh, my head hurts. I haven't tied on one like that in a long, long time," Judith croaked as she eased herself into one of the ten green wicker chairs on the patio. "I could take that swim this morning." She squinted towards the west. "However, that's a marathon walk to get down to the lake. Maybe I'll just have a quiet morning right in this spot."

Claudia laughed. "You're definitely out of practice, Judith. Everyone else still asleep?"

"No, I think the twit went out walking much too early this morning." She groaned as she moved over to the cushioned comfort of a chaise lounge. "So, tell me Claudie, what do you really think happened about Jackie? Plots aside and all that."

Claudia stared straight ahead at the lake. "How would I know? We can keep on guessing until we're blue in the face and never really know." She paused. "Unless Jackie knows and wants to tell us."

"Hmmm."

"Chrissie is still out, you say?"

"Far as I know."

"I think I'll just go have a quick lie-down before breakfast. It's still too early for me." Claudia barely stifled a yawn.

"And I don't plan to move a muscle until I smell some bacon. Thanks for putting on the coffee, by the way. I do assume it was you?"

"You're welcome. Nighty-night."

Claudia re-filled her mug as she passed through the kitchen. She locked the front door so that Christine would have to go around back and encounter Judith when she came back. That would be good for several minutes of chatter, all on Christine's part. She hurried up to her room, dialed a number on her cell phone. "Pick me up in ten minutes," was all she said.

She checked that she'd packed everything, moved her bag to the top of the stairs, then carefully walked the hall to Barbara's room. She glanced at her reflection in the array of mirrors that lined the hall, about a dozen in all, different sizes, shapes and frames. She was ready for this. She'd been up early doing last minute preparations. It had been a long time since she'd done anything like this for Jackie but she knew she could still do it. Just took some psyching up. The business never quite leaves the soul.

The door opened easily and quietly. She breathed out then took a deep breath in, moving silently into the room. Barbara lay in the bed, on her side, back to the door. The pale green Egyptian cotton thread sheets matched those in her room. The colour looked better for Barbara.

Claudia took a couple of steps to the right, then aimed the gun at the head on the pillow. A slight squeeze of the trigger would do it.

The door burst open. "Hold it right there, Claudie."

She almost dropped the gun in surprise. Judith ran over and grabbed it from her hand, keeping it pointed at the floor. Barbara sat up in bed as Christine moved over to her side.

"Jackie sends his best, Claudie," Barbara said.

"Jackie? What do you mean? Jackie's the one who set this all up."

"You're right there, kiddo. Jackie set you up to kill me. He told you I was the one who had ratted him out and he was re-instating you in your hit man or rather, hit woman capacity, to take me out. Right? But he knew all the time it was you, Claudie. You're the one who turned him in. And that's how you really got the cash to start your business. A nice big pay-off from the cops."

"After all he'd done for us...how could you, Claudie?" Christine whined.

Judith answered. "It was always the money with you, wasn't it, Claudie? You weren't making enough being a whore so you branched out into doing hits for Jackie. For big bucks, too, I'll bet. But you went through it all pretty fast, too, didn't you?"

Claudia backed up a few steps. "So? I worked out better taking people out with a gun. I had a natural talent for it and who would suspect a woman? Jackie got a lot for his money. But why this scam? Why didn't he just hire someone to do me?"

Barbara got out of bed, fully clothed. "My guess is he's lost touch with the boys or couldn't trust any of them to do this one last job. But he knew once we realized you'd be willing to kill any one of us, we'd have no hesitation in doing this job for him. Besides, we owe him big time. We all do." She glared at Claudia.

"You can't be serious. You're not going to shoot me? None of

148

you have the guts to do that." She sneered but her mouth quivered.

"You're right about that, Claudie," said Judith, giving Claudia a slight shove towards the door. "But you see, Jackie's a detail man. So, we're going to go for a short boat ride instead."

Barbara reached for the door handle. "Time for that swim you missed out on last night."

The Bouquet

by Madona Skaff

Present day

Blake sat on his sofa, in his penthouse, staring out at a cumulus cloud in the blue sky. He wore comfortable grey trousers and a white golf shirt. A deafening roar came from somewhere. He tried to focus. He wanted to move away from it. Soon he realized it was coming from inside his head. He returned the receiver to his ear to listen to that insidious voice.

"Uncle Blake? Hello?"

He cleared his throat and feigning joy said, "Jennifer! What a wonderful surprise. How are you?"

"I've had it with Toronto. I've come home."

"Home?"

"To Ottawa. I'd love to come by to visit you. It's been ten years."

"You're in Ottawa? Now?" He felt that all too familiar knot in his stomach twist.

"I never thought of Toronto as home, and well, I..." Her voice faltered. "If you're busy, I don't want to bother you..."

"No, no. You're no bother." Blake took a deep breath before he continued. "You just surprised me, that's all." Blake ran his fingers through his short graying hair. "I'll clear my schedule and wait for you here."

Oh, God! Jennifer, after ten years. Why? Why now? A few years into the new millennium, he'd thought he was finally free. His business was better than ever. He was well on his way to making yet another million. He'd even gone to his father's grave just last month to tell the drunk bastard in person.

151

Twenty years ago

"Blake Farrell, you'll always be a loser."

Blake ignored the echo of his father's words in his head. Some loser. He began life as a slum kid from Eastview and now owned a penthouse.

He quickly swapped his business suit for black, casual trousers and a black t-shirt. He caressed the fabric of his Versace blazer before he slipped it on, then looked at himself in the full length mirror. Guess the salesman was right. He did look good in black, especially with his dark shoulder length hair and dark eyes. Maybe it was time he started pampering himself, acted like a millionaire and hired a fashion consultant.

A great aunt's inheritance had allowed Blake to buy a house with a friend. They sold it for a profit after a few months, bought two more houses and did it again. Eventually, as business partners, they moved on to commercial real estate where obscene profits were the norm. Blake's keen understanding of the market and his talent of finding investors meant constantly increasing profits.

Barely twenty-five, he'd made his first million. After he closed the deal tomorrow, he'd be on his way to his second million.

A prodigy they called him.

A failure, his father had called him.

Too bad the old drunk hadn't lived long enough to see his son's success.

Blake came around the bedroom partition and stopped to admire his new home.

When he'd bought the high-rise two months ago, the open concept of the penthouse had appealed to him. Rather than go for the bright colours and overdone ultra-modern decor of the eighties, he chose a simple look. A plain opaque glass wall concealed the bedroom area. A brown leather sofa and armchair sat in the centre of the living room area, near a state-of-the-art record player and sound system. Blake planned to buy one of those new large rear projection models, having never really watched TV growing up. Only his father had the privilege to watch their twelve-inch black and white set. A mahogany dining table designated the dining area, with the oak cabinets of the kitchen visible just beyond.

His favourite part, and the main reason he'd decided to move in, was the balcony. It ran the full length of the penthouse, overlooking Ottawa and the river thirty stories below. A glass patio table and cushioned, white metal chairs provided a comfortable respite for early morning coffee or late night cocktails with Claire.

Present day

A couple of months after Claire's death, he'd felt strangely driven to check on Angie and her daughter. Before he knew it, he'd taken over for Claire, pinch-hitting for an absent babysitter on more than one occasion. He'd made sure that the little girl never wanted for anything. He'd lavished toys and clothes on her, until Angie had protested. The occasional babysitting was more than enough, she'd insisted.

At first when she'd see him, her big round green eyes tainted with fear, she seemed to be judging him. With time he recognized her gaze as adoration. Despite that, he felt his self-imposed life sentence would never end. Those green eyes reminding him of his guilt every single day, until finally, ten years ago when Angie and Jennifer had moved to Toronto.

Twenty years ago

Claire would be waiting for him. They were supposed to go out this evening, but his business meeting dragged on and on, so he'd left her a message saying that he would pick her up at 10:00 pm. He checked his watch. Just on time.

Blake grabbed the flowers from the table and ruffled the stems to perk up the bouquet. He would have bought roses, but Claire loved carnations. Pink ones. He took the elevator down to the 25th floor.

He smoothed his hair and ruffled the flowers once more before knocking on the door. As he waited he fiddled with the gold bracelet Claire had given him last week on the anniversary of their first date. He'd never cared for male jewellery, but this one was special, refusing to take it off, even to shower.

After a moment the door opened to reveal Claire, her straight raven hair loose about her shoulders. Even without makeup her smile illuminated her natural beauty. She wore a blue silk robe.

Eyebrows raised in anticipation, Blake gave her a wolfish grin. "I take it we're staying in." He wrapped an arm around her tiny waist as he drew her in for a deep lingering kiss. Reluctantly, his lips left hers.

Though she smiled up at him, she hadn't molded her body to his during the embrace. She seemed distant. Damn, he hadn't thought that she might have an early court time tomorrow. She'd been defending some burglary punk all week. He should have spoken with her, not just left a message on her answering machine.

"Come in," she said, taking the flowers in one hand, holding the door for him as he followed.

He stopped short at the sight of the toddler's toys strewn on the floor near a Jolly Jumper.

"Let me guess why we're staying in. Babysitting duty." He didn't try to conceal his frustration.

"Blake, I'm sorry. I tried to call you. I left several messages with your secretary who wouldn't stop apologizing that she couldn't reach you."

"I was in meetings all day," he snapped. Softening, he added, "I'm sorry. I haven't seen much of you this week and I missed you." He nuzzled in her neck for a moment. "That's why I snuck away from my clients."

"If you have to get back to the meeting..."

"Some meeting – all those Texans want to do is party. It eventually degenerated into a trip to a strip club." He snorted. "Besides, everyone's so drunk, I don't think they'll even notice I'm gone. I left them stuffing tips into any g-string that moved. I was really looking forward to being alone with you."

"I'm sorry ..."

"Look, I know you like to help, but she's just a neighbour..."

"Angie's a friend." She cut him off. "She rarely asks me for anything. A single mother, raising a two year old girl on her own. She phoned me in a panic because the sitter cancelled at the last minute and it was too late to find someone to cover her shift at the hospital." She gave him a strained smile as she added, "How about we order something in? Angie's shift ends at midnight, that's only two hours. After that, we have the whole night to look forward to."

He realized he was being selfish. He loved Claire for her heart and generosity, not just her beauty. "So," Blake kissed Claire's forehead, "where is the munchkin?"

Present day

There were many letters at first, for Angie and Jennifer. Eventually they dwindled down to cards at Christmas and birthdays.

He had finally felt paroled.

Until Jennifer's call.

The doorbell on the penthouse chimed. He glanced at his

watch. Two hours. Had he been sitting here all this time?

If he didn't answer the door, maybe she'd go away. Reluctantly he got up from the sofa to open the door.

The rush of memories hit him as he stared into her eyes, the eyes of the baby looking at him. Accusing him. Fearing him. Before he could react, she lunged at him.

She hugged his neck. "Oh, Uncle Blake! It's so great to see you!"

"Jennifer!" he held her at arm's length to look at her cheerful face and green eyes that sparkled with tears of happiness.

He smiled back mechanically. He blinked to get that toddler out of his mind and focused on the young woman before him. Genuinely he said, "My God, you were a twelve year old kid just yesterday. Now you're a beautiful woman."

He ushered her in, closing the door behind her.

Twenty years ago

"In here." Claire held a finger to her lips and motioned for him to follow her to the bedroom. She pointed through the open door at the child asleep in the playpen, hugging a giant stuffed white rabbit.

They moved away as Claire said, "She won't be any trouble at all. She never is." She arranged the carnations in a vase, and placed it on the coffee table.

"You're such a softy," he murmured, stroking at an unreadable expression on her face. "Hard day?"

"Hmm." She nodded. "It's a beautiful night. Let's go out on the balcony."

"Will it be okay..." He nodded towards the bedroom door.

"Sure, we have a clear view of the bedroom from the balcony. I'll leave the door open, so that if she wakes up we'll be able to hear her." She took his arm, as they stepped out into the warm summer air.

He side-stepped around an open bag of soil and newly planted flowers.

"This one's for your balcony," she said, pointing at the large pot of bluebells.

"Thank you," he said. He looked around the balcony, cluttered with pots of flowers, and several hanging baskets of plants, almost forming a curtain. A white metal table and two chairs completed the menagerie. "But are you sure you can spare this one?" He laughed.

155

She chuckled. "You need some colour on your balcony." Letting go of his arm, she leaned against the railing, in the only clear corner, placing one foot on a white footstool that she used to water the hanging plants. She continued. "How was your day? Did you woo the Americans into investing in the shopping mall?"

"Who knows? It would have been easier if Jeffrey had been there. But, if they don't die from their hangovers, I hope to get them to sign in the morning." Tenderly he asked, "How about you? You look like you had a rough day."

"Rough client." She turned to gaze at the view. "It's hard to defend someone I know is guilty."

"Then don't."

"It's my job. And after a lot of plea bargaining, I managed to get him a reduced sentence. One year. Not bad for burglary. But," she turned back to Blake, "He did tell me something that was very disturbing."

"What?" He prompted after she'd been silently watching him for a while as though sizing him up.

Present day

Jennifer looked around the apartment, smiling widely. Remembering, he was sure, the times she and her mom had spent here. As he looked around, he realized with a sinking feeling that the place hadn't changed at all since the eighties. The same sofa faced the balcony door. The same stereo system with turntable. He kept planning to update it. And every now and then he thought of getting a flat screen TV.

"I see you still don't like clutter." She laughed as she went to the dining table to smell the pink carnations on the table. "Beautiful."

"Well, I've never been much for interior design, other than the occasional toy under the sofa." He forced a laugh, surprised at how natural he'd managed to make it sound. Perhaps, he was actually relaxing. "And I don't babysit anymore. You were my one and only client." His smile faded. "I'm sorry I missed your mother's funeral last month. Work and travel, you know." The truth was he just hadn't wanted to risk opening old wounds.

"I understand," She said, her smile slipping a bit. "I hope you don't mind that I just barged in on you. I just wanted to connect with my youth ..."

"Your youth?" He laughed, "You're barely 22 years old."

"What I mean, is," she spoke seriously, "I wanted to go back to

156

a simpler time." She looked away for a moment. "It wasn't easy for my mom raising me on her own – well, you know that. But she was never happy in Ottawa, too many memories I guess. My dad and then Claire."

"Did she talk a lot about Claire?" Blake asked, his heart pounding in his chest.

"Not much. Wish I'd known her." She broke off, as though embarrassed. "Oh, Uncle Blake, I didn't mean to bring up bad memories."

"I'm all right," he said with a wistful smile. There'd never been anyone since Claire. No one could ever come close. His voice hoarse, he added, "You would have loved her."

"Everyone did." She kissed him on the cheek. "But you took over watching me when mom worked those weird shifts at the hospital. If it wasn't for you, I think we would have left for Toronto sooner. I always hated it there. I don't know, if we'd stayed in Ottawa, she wouldn't have got into that collision ...." She broke off as a tear fell.

Twenty years ago

"A house he broke into," Claire breathed deeply, "belonged to your business partner, Jeffrey. I don't remember you mentioning anything about a break-in."

Blake felt his face flush. They hadn't reported it. How could they?

She continued as though not expecting him to answer. "Among the valuables my client stole, were some notes. It's amazing that he was smart enough to figure out the records, but too dumb to do anything but steal." She inhaled as though summoning up strength to continue. "There were two sets of books for a deal you'd made. A very big deal."

"Claire..." He started to go back inside to continue the conversation away from possible eavesdroppers when he remembered the sleeping toddler. Better to whisper than try to deal with a screaming two year old woken from a sound sleep. Keeping his voice low, he asked, "Did he tell the police?"

"He's hardly going to confess to a crime the police haven't tied him to. He was angry about his sentence and was trying to make a point. That the law helps to make the rich richer and the poor into criminals."

"So, he didn't tell the police." Blake sighed. He was safe. God, he loved this woman.

"No, I told you." She repeated stiffly. "He asked how fair was it for him to go to jail for a thousand dollars in scrap, while the rich got away with stealing millions."

Relieved, Blake pulled her into his arms. She stiffened, leaving him no choice but to release her.

"How could you do it?" she asked, eyes filling with tears.

"It's all right," he said, taking her hand to draw her to him. She pulled it away. Genuinely perplexed he insisted, "Honey, if no one else knows, everything's fine."

"Fine?" Though her voice quivered with suppressed fury, she spoke quietly. "I'm a lawyer. You've committed a felony. Do you have any idea of the position you've put me in?"

He contemplated the city lights beyond her. Of all the buildings he owned, he'd always liked this one best because of the view. So calming. And when Claire had moved into the building it had become perfect. He'd hoped that she'd join him in the penthouse one day.

"It'll be okay, I promise." He just wanted her to be happy.

"You have to turn yourself in," she pleaded. Holding his arm, she added, "I'll represent you. It's your first offence. I can get you off with a minimal sentence or even probation."

"Jail!" He'd do anything for her, except that. "My career is on the rise. I'm not throwing it all away because of an insignificant shortcut just to get the business going. We'll never need to do it again. Besides, the money was a drop in the bucket for those investors. They never even missed it."

"You embezzled money from people who trusted you. You have to come clean. Or you'll be looking over your shoulder for the rest of your life."

"No one knows, right? And your thief probably got rid of the books by now. So, there's no problem." He reached for her again. She backed away. "Claire, listen. Everything's going to be fine."

She shook her head. "I can't be with a... a..." She pushed him away and took a half step back.

"With what?" He was hurt.

"A criminal?" Anger punctuated each word. He thought she loved him.

"Are you going to turn me in?" A step forward.

She stepped back. He continued talking and advancing. "Are you trying to tell me you've never done anything wrong in your entire life? That you are so perfect? That you could never make a mistake? That you never took advantage of an opportunity?"

"Stop it!" Fear twisted her beautiful face. She shoved hard

against his chest.

He paused. What the hell was he doing?

He reached for her to apologize. The foot stool trapping her, she hopped onto it, while shoving him back with a panicked grunt. Still off balance, she reached for the railing.

In slow motion he saw her feet lift up.

"No!" he cried out as he regained his balance in time to grab her, but tripped on his pot of bluebells. His hands grabbed empty air.

Present day

"Traffic accidents happen everywhere. Even here," he said, his voice still rough.

"I know, I'm being silly. That's what my therapist tells me. Not in those words of course."

"I hadn't realized your mother's death affected you so strongly. I wish I'd been there for you." Yes, he could already feel his parole being repealed and he could almost hear those prison doors close again. Guilt was once again turning the key.

"Not so strongly. I've been having really bad nightmares for years. Bad enough I wake up screaming. They became even worse after mom died so I got help. It was my therapist's suggestion to return here, because it's the only place that feels like home. She believes I can find my answers here. Regression therapy didn't work, but she thought a trip down memory lane would help. It's only a matter of time she said, before we can unlock all the secrets my mind has hidden.

"I hope you're not paying a lot of money for this alleged 'therapy'," he said, taking on a fatherly tone.

"She's not a crackpot." Jennifer insisted. "She's worked with famous people and unlocked their early childhood memories. She's got quite a reputation. You've heard of her—Melinda Meynard."

His smile froze. His heart thumped. Who hadn't heard of Melinda Meynard? She'd been a media darling, helping victims remember important details of their attackers that led to several arrests. Now Jennifer was working with Melinda to unlock what she'd witnessed at two years of age. Why should he pay for a minor indiscretion he'd made twenty years ago? His entire business career had been spotless since then.

And Claire—was an accident.

Twenty years ago

How could she fall over the high railing? The foot stool. If he hadn't scared her...

"No." He pushed himself to his feet and stared down at her crumpled body on the grass below. "No!" He collapsed to his knees, gasping. He had to get help. Then he heard a scream from a lower balcony.

His head cleared as he realized the police would be here soon. How could he ever explain? He lurched to his feet and stumbled into the apartment. He had to get out.

Blake stopped short at the sight of the baby girl standing up in the playpen, staring at him with round green eyes, as she clutched her toy rabbit protectively in front of her. Maybe she hadn't seen anything. Through his tears, he tried to give her a smile of reassurance, but she started to cry.

He grabbed his coat and left. She'd be okay. The police would find her.

Present day

He looked at Jennifer and sucked in a shallow breath. She was two years old again, looking at him with those eyes that didn't understand, yet still accused him. Eyes that feared him. He blinked several times. No, no! The child disappeared. A young woman sat in her place.

He breathed slowly, calming himself. He smiled as he took Jennifer's hand and said, "Let's step outside, it's a beautiful day and the view is great."

Twenty years ago

He made it back to the strip club before the clients had even missed him. The police found him there and a young beat cop, Patrick O'Shaunnessy, gave him the news.

Present day

The trust was so clearly written on her face.

He opened the door for her and Jennifer stepped onto the balcony. About to follow, he started at the sight of Claire, peacefully standing near the railing. Suddenly, her face contorted with fear and she fell off the balcony. He blinked. No. Not real. Go back inside. But seeing two year old Jennifer on the balcony

160

stopped him. Big round green eyes. Staring at him. Fearing. Accusing. Witnessing.

He blinked, then blinked again. No, it was Jennifer the young woman that had greeted him with open trust. She didn't remember.

Yet.

As Jennifer looked out at the view of the city and river, Blake's father's voice drifted to him from inside the apartment, taunting him. "You'll always be a loser."

Blake looked over his shoulder at his father, wearing those same torn sweat pants, drinking beer as he slumped in the faded armchair.

No, he was successful. He wouldn't lose everything now because of an accident.

In a smooth movement, with no chance to hesitate, and too fast for Jennifer to react, he boosted her up and over the railing. She barely had time to try to reach out to him.

Clamping his hands over his ears failing to block out the high pitched cry, Blake stepped back so he wouldn't see her hit the ground. He imagined her green eyes wide, filling with fear once she realized what had happened.

He slowly became aware of his surroundings and clutched at his chest, sobs coming out in great heaves. Stumbling back inside he made his way to the phone, collapsing on the floor leaning his head on the sofa. He called 911.

"I need help," he rasped into the phone. "She jumped off the balcony. She kept talking about missing her mother..."

The police would believe an upstanding, successful businessman like him. A young girl, distraught at her mother's death last month in a car accident. Jennifer had been in therapy. She'd come home to the place her life had begun and chosen to end it here.

So tragic. So believable.

"I'm not a loser, dad," he whispered through the gasps for breath.

He let the phone drop from his hand as he curled up in a fetal position on the floor. Tears burned. He didn't need to feign the agony he felt.

The next day dawned dark and grim. The police had allowed him to return to his apartment sometime after midnight, their investigation complete. He avoided looking at the "DO NOT

CROSS" yellow tape across the balcony door. He'd never go out to see that hideous view, ever again.

He took a long drink of his coffee. It was sickly sweet. He'd put in extra sugar without thinking. He didn't have the strength to get up and get a new cup. The newspaper had been delivered and lay folded on the table before him. He hesitated to open it. Would it have made the front page? She was a nice kid. She deserved the front page.

Finally, the urge to find out, outweighed the fear of the headline.

YOUNG WOMAN PLUNGES TO DEATH IN WEST END HIGH RISE CONDO

He started to read the article, hoping they spelt her name right, his eyes glossing over most of the words. Then part way down the article, a name caught his eye. Patrick O'Shaunnessy. The investigating detective.

Blake remembered him.

Twenty years ago, O'Shaunnessy was the young, curly red-haired beat cop that had told him about Claire's death. The rookie cop had asked a lot of questions. He wondered why would a woman about to commit suicide agree to babysit? And the cop just couldn't get over the pink carnations on her coffee table. Why would someone suicidal buy a fresh bouquet of flowers?

Blake looked at the bouquet of pink carnations on his dining room table. They made him feel closer to Claire. As though she might walk in the door any minute.

Blake rubbed his eyes. He'd been terrified that O'Shaunnessy had suspected him in Claire's death. But there was no evidence and eventually the cop offered his condolences and left.

He scanned further down and stopped at the name Melinda Meynard, Jennifer's therapist. Shivering, he swallowed the hard lump in his throat as he read. The police were investigating her! Melinda had been under suspicion for some time for several shady treatments, bogus memory regressions. True she'd helped a few witnesses remember long forgotten details, but nothing more than a good police investigator could have done with properly placed questions.

Melinda Meynard was a fake.

The paper trembled in his hands as the words floated off the page to slap him in the face. He'd murdered an innocent. Murdered! A roar filled his ears. The room spun.

The roar faded. Awareness returned with a knock at the door. Still clutching the front page, he wiped his eyes with the back of his hand. That's when he noticed.

His gold bracelet was gone! The bracelet Claire had given him – engraved with her vow of eternal love. In its place were scratches. He lowered his shirt sleeve to cover the marks and stood up on shaky legs as he stepped on the fallen newspaper and limped to the door.

Claire had been an accident. He'd have to learn to live with Jennifer's...

Pulling himself together, he opened the door. The face of the young red-haired cop swam before him. He blinked several times, fighting to find reality. The beat cop was replaced by a middle aged red-haired man. Blake noticed him looking into the apartment and grinning. Blake started to turn to see what had attracted the other man's attention but his visitor's voice stopped him.

"I see you still like pink carnations." The man pulled out a badge. He looked Blake straight in the eye and said, "Mr. Farrell, I'm Detective O'Shaunnessy. May I come in, please?"

Big Brother

by Elizabeth Hosang

Elizabeth Hosang is a Computer Engineer by day, but wants to be a professional writer when she grows up. She joined Sisters in Crime as part of her on-going quest to polish her skills. She has been writing stories for fun, if not for profit, for over ten years. While she has several unpublished novels in various stages of development, she is working on building her collection of rejection letters for short stories. She enjoys mysteries and urban fantasy and is working on stories in both fields. In 2012 she was honoured to receive an Honourable Mention for the Audrey Jessup short story award.

He watched as the Corvette pulled to the curb in front of the house, the streetlights muting the cherry red finish. He could just make out the shape of her head in the passenger seat. He couldn't see details at this distance, but as the shadows of the two figures in the car merged into one he could imagine her golden hair, the curve of her smile, and he shifted restlessly in his seat. Several long, painful minutes later she got out of the car, and he realized his knuckles had gone white gripping the steering wheel. When she was finally in the house he allowed himself to look at the car again, but he was unable to see anything of the driver. As the Corvette pulled away he started his own engine and crept down the dark street.

A week later the midday sun streamed down on the crowds filling the amusement park. Andrea relaxed, listening to the chatter of her friends, her mind drifting. A tug on her hand brought her out of her reverie.

"Earth to Andrea. I said, do you want me to win you a prize?"

She turned to find Greg staring at her expectantly.

"A prize?" she repeated doubtfully.

"Sure." He nodded at the booth to their left, where the greasy looking operator offered three balls for two dollars to knock down a pile of milk jugs.

"I don't know. Aren't those games rigged?"

"Nah. Not for the pitcher from this year's championship fast ball team. C'mon, I'll win you one of those big bears up there." Andrea laughed, and the hint of a boyish pout marred his handsome features. "You don't think I can do this?"

"No, it's not that. It just seems so corny, my boyfriend winning me a teddy bear." The pout turned into a frown, and she relented. Throwing her arms around him and pressing close, she pursed her lips and batted her eyelashes. "Won't you please win me a great big stuffed teddy bear?"

Greg ran his hands up and down her back, and his face softened into a smile. "See? Was that so hard?" He kissed her before turning to address the man running the booth.

"Get a room you two." Andrea rolled her eyes at her best friend Sarah, as the other boys in their group grinned knowingly. They gathered around as Greg warmed up, standing back just far enough so as not to crowd his pitching arm.

Despite the warmth of the summer day Andrea felt a chill run down her back. She smiled at Greg as he went through the motions of warming up, but the feeling of unease grew. Glancing around the crowd, she spotted a man watching her from several booths down. One moment he was staring pointedly at her; the next he turned to examine the game in front of him. Something about his profile struck her as familiar, but she couldn't place him.

At a cheer from the crowd she turned to find that Greg had knocked down half the bottles on his first try. She smiled at him as he turned to flex for the group, who were cheering him on. Andrea glanced back down the midway to find the strange man staring at her again. This time when their eyes met he turned and walked the other way. It wasn't until she watched his retreating gait that recognition sank in. "Chris?"

The next evening she was still wondering if she had really seen him as she set the table for supper. Laying out the plates, she realized she had taken five out of the cupboard instead of the three required for herself and her parents. Rolling her eyes at her own stupidity, she put the other two back in the cupboard. Her big brother Jeff was away at University, and Chris, well, it had been a long time since Chris had eaten here.

She glanced at her mother, who was working at the sink. "Do you ever run into Mrs. Malone?" she asked, hoping she sounded casual.

She saw her mom's hands pause for a moment before resuming shredding lettuce. "No. I think she moved after Chris was sent to jail."

"You mean she didn't visit him?"

This time her mother stopped outright. "No. That poor boy. I guess I shouldn't be surprised." She turned her head and glanced at the corner of the table. Chris' spot, Andrea thought.

Chris had been Jeff's best friend since Andrea could remember. He had always been around, hanging out after school, usually staying for dinner. He'd been one more big brother, which meant twice the teasing. When she was eight Andrea had stomped her foot and insisted her parents stop letting him stay for supper. Supper was for family. Her mother had tried to explain that family wasn't just the people you were related to, but Andrea hadn't cared. The next morning Andrea decided if her parents wouldn't listen, then maybe Chris' parents would. She got up early and stormed out of her house.

Full of eight-year-old indignation, she stomped up the steps in front of Chris' house and rang the bell. She stood there, hands on hips, waiting.

She would never forget the sour smell of cigarettes and stale food that burst from the house when Mrs. Malone finally threw open the door. Red eyes glared down at her. "Yeah?"

She'd never seen anyone so angry. She wanted to run away, but she couldn't move. Finally she found her voice. "Mrs. Malone? I'm looking for Chris. Is he here?"

The woman with the bleary eyes bellowed for Chris. "You might as well come in." She stumbled into the house, leaving Andrea standing just inside the front door. Discarded coats and shoes lay on the hall floor. In the living room to her right Andrea could see a coffee table covered with empty beer bottles and take out containers. Old newspapers were piled on the dingy couch, and full ash trays were scattered around the room.

Loud voices came from down the hall. Mrs. Malone was yelling at Chris for his friend making so much noise so early in the morning. After a moment of silence Andrea heard her say, "Go on, get out," and footsteps came toward her.

Andrea never forgot the look on his face when Chris saw her.

All of her resentment died as she finally understood some of the things she had heard other people say about Chris' family.

"Whaddya want?" Chris asked. Andrea tried to speak, but her mind was blank. "Well?"

"Did, did you hide my Barbie again? 'Cause I can't find her."

After that Andrea never begrudged his visits. The corner chair was Chris' spot. Candid photos of the family over the years traced the growth of two boys, and Andrea got used to seeing him in photos on the mantle.

Neither of her parents had ever asked her about that morning, but an understanding grew between Andrea and her mother. Now that she was older Andrea realized that her mother could not have done anything else but include Chris in the family, giving him chores and checking his homework. Andrea suspected that Chris ate more regularly at the Gordon residence than he did at home.

Chris had been in his early teens when his father left and his mother moved to an apartment several neighborhoods away. Chris had visited the Gordon home less often, and when he did the boys often fought.

Andrea still remembered the day when the boys finally fell out. They were doing homework in the kitchen, with Chris goofing off while Jeff talked about the college recruiters who were coming next week. Jeff and Chris were still a year away from finishing high school, but already Jeff was talking about where he was going to apply. He was in the middle of rhyming off the merits of the various University sports teams when Andrea had walked in to get a drink. Leaning into the fridge she felt something hit her in the head. She turned around just in time to duck another wadded up paper ball thrown by Chris.

"Quit it," she said.

"Make me, Rug Rat," he replied.

"Forget her," Jeff said. "So which universities are you going to apply to?"

"University? Why would I want more school? I'm gonna get a real job, not some fancy piece of paper that says I spent four years studying poetry. Man, after all the complaining you do about homework I can't believe you're gonna do four more years. How stupid can you get?"

The argument quickly got ugly, and Andrea had fled the kitchen. After that day Chris stopped coming around. He took shop when Jeff took advanced science. Jeff stopped talking about his old friend, inviting new ones to the house instead. Chris began to get into trouble, spending more and more time in the principal's office. Andrea even noticed that her mother stopped asking Jeff about Chris after a time.

Finally news came that Chris had been arrested. He had been joyriding with some friends in a stolen car. While his status as a minor meant he ended up in juvenile court, it also increased the significance of the fact that he had been drinking.

After that Andrea had expected her mother to take down the pictures with Chris in them. Instead, she'd found out later, her mother had visited him, taking him cookies. The photos with Chris were shuffled to the back of the mantle, but never quite put away.

Standing by Chris' chair at the kitchen table, Andrea fidgeted with the glasses as she tried to word her next question. Her mother cut into her thoughts by handing her the napkins. "It's too bad Mrs. Malone isn't around, really. He seems to be doing well these days."

"You've seen him?" This surprised Andrea.

"Not in a while. But I did hear that he was working down at Jordan's Autobody. He was pretty good with cars, as I remember."

"But you haven't seen him around here."

Andrea followed her mother's gaze looking out the kitchen window, seeing for a moment two boys playing with action figures in the back yard. "No, not for a long time."

Two weeks later Andrea rolled her eyes as her mother handed her an umbrella. "It's supposed to rain," Rachel said by way of explanation.

"Yes, mother." Despite the tone Andrea was smiling. She handed the umbrella and her coat to Greg as she reached for her purse.

"You have your keys?" Rachel asked for the third time. "By the time you get home from the game your dad and I will be half-way to Aunt Becky's house, and I'd hate for you to be locked out."

This time Andrea's look was more exasperated. "Yes, mother. And I'll ask the nice hot dog vendor if he can bring me some broccoli and I'll be sure to wash behind my ears when I go to bed."

Rachel held up her hands in defeat. "Okay, okay, I know when I'm overdoing it. Just have a nice time, you two."

"Yes, Mrs. Gordon." Greg smiled at Rachel as he opened the front door and gestured to Andrea to precede him out of the house. "Don't worry about a thing. And have a good trip."

As they headed down the front walk Greg wrapped his arm around Andrea's waist. "I think we can manage a little better than a nice time, don't you?" he murmured in her ear. Andrea pulled away from him and blew out an exasperated breath as she reached for the car door handle. Greg put a hand on her forearm to stop her. "Don't tell me you're still saying no? Come on, it's perfect. We'll have two whole nights before they get back. They probably even expect it."

Andrea shook him off. "Not my parents, they don't."

Greg pulled her around to face him. "Don't you think they'd feel safer knowing you weren't here alone? Especially with that weirdo watching you."

"Chris isn't a weirdo. At least, he didn't used to be, and I haven't seen him in weeks, and I am not having this conversation again. You are not staying over while my parents are away. Now are we going, or do you want to miss the warm-up?"

Greg held up his hands in a sign of mock defeat. "Ok, ok, you win. Let's just go to the game and have a nice time."

"Fine." She yanked the car door open, ignoring his emphasis.

"Fine."

Despite the fact that their local triple A team were leading the league, Andrea was unable to concentrate on the game. She kept looking around the stands, but she failed to see the face she was looking for. Lots of males glanced at her, and a few tried to get her to smile at them, but no one ducked his head or started walking the other way.

"Unbelievable!" Greg exploded.

"What?" Andrea tried to scan the crowd on the other side of him.

"That call! The umpire must be legally blind. Didn't you see that?"

"Sorry, wasn't watching."

Greg turned fully to stare at her. "You're not watching? What are you looking at?"

Andrea glanced down and played with her program.

"You're looking for him, aren't you? That guy, the one your brother used to hang with." Greg glanced around the crowd. "Have you seen him?"

"No."

"So stop worrying. You're with me. If you do see him you just point him out and I'll have a little chat with him." Greg smacked his fist into the palm of his hand.

Andrea laughed in spite of herself. "Why Greg, you're such a Neanderthal. Thanks." She turned her attention back to the game, glancing at the scoreboard. "Yeesh. Maybe I'm better off not watching. Are we really playing this badly?"

Greg filled her in on the poor quality of officiating plaguing their team.

Despite her best efforts to focus, Andrea was still deep in thought by the time Greg pulled into her driveway. Greg brushed the hair back behind her ear and leaned close, determination showing in his eyes. "You know, if you're so worried, maybe I should come in and keep you company." Andrea looked warily at him as he continued. "C'mon Andie, your parents are going to be away until Sunday. When are we going to get another opportunity like this?"

Andrea fought back her annoyance. They had already had this conversation. "I told you, I'm not ready. Besides, my brother Jeff may be coming home from university tonight. He was finishing up exams this week."

Greg sat back and ran his hands through his hair. "Fine. Be that way. I thought we had something here, but if you don't agree..."

Andrea sighed. "Just have a little patience, okay?" She leaned across to kiss him, but he refused to turn to face her. "Well, fine." She got out and slammed the car door. She stomped all the way to the front step, shoved the key into the lock, and slammed the house door behind her. It didn't make her feel better, but it helped a little.

Outside she heard Greg squeal out of the driveway. "Dumb jock," she thought as she threw her coat into the closet. Sure, he was hot, and he had a great fastball, but he wanted a personal cheerleader more than a girlfriend. She sighed and turned away from the closet.

Farther down the street, Chris checked his watch. He had seen Andrea storm out of the car and Greg drive off. He was more careful these days about how close he got, but he had been watching them during the entire game. Now he glanced around the darkened street. A few lights were still on. It would be a while before all the neighbors went to bed. He checked his watch and settled more comfortably in his seat.

The light breeze tickled the wind chime on the house across the street from the Gordon residence, but otherwise the quiet of the night was undisturbed. There was no moon, and darkness wrapped itself around the figure creeping across the empty yard. All lights were off in the Gordon household, but he knew which

171

window was hers, knew exactly where he was going. The thrill of the hunt ran through him, anticipation heightening every sense. He approached the back door, his eyes straining to pick out the rock border around the flower bed. He tapped once, twice, three times before being rewarded with a hollow sound. Picking up the fake rock he turned it over, looking for the opening. How predictable of Mrs. Gordon, he thought, hiding a key in case someone needed a spare. He was surprised the woman didn't wear pearls while she vacuumed. After a moment's fiddling he was rewarded with a slight popping sound as the cover came off, and he shook the key out into his hand.

Quietly he opened the screen door. He was sure she was asleep, but he didn't want to risk spoiling the moment. He'd waited too long for this. He slipped the key into the lock and turned, and the next moment he was standing in the kitchen. It was almost anti-climactic. He had come prepared to use more forceful ways to enter, but this would do.

He waited a moment to let his eyes adjust to the dim light from the LEDs on the appliances. He knew the house, so he didn't bother with the light. He crept out of the kitchen, heading towards the front of the house and the stairs. The glow from the street lights gave him just enough illumination to maneuver around the banister and up the steps.

In the hallway outside her bedroom, he paused to listen for her breathing, savoring the moment. He pushed the door open and took one, two steps into the room.

A rustle and a click were his only warning before the bedside table lamp switched on, blinding him.

She had been staring at the ceiling counting sheep. When she had heard the creak on the steps she'd though it was Jeff getting home. At the sight of the ski mask, shock and terror raced through her like lightning.

"Chris, no!" She tried to leap to her feet and got tangled in the blankets. The next moment she was pinned to the mattress, one hand crushing her throat. The other hand flashed something silver in front of her eyes: a large hunting knife. The peripheries of her vision faded to black as her world narrowed to the gleaming blade. Slowly it lowered to her throat, replacing the hand that had pinned her. The edge pressed into her flesh and she tried to pull away, deeper into the mattress. She forced herself to look up into the eyes staring out at her from behind the balaclava. The expression in them left no doubt about his intent.

Her attacker leaned back, one knee on the mattress, the other

172

foot on the floor. His free hand stroked back her hair, and he smiled as she flinched at his touch. He was laughing at her, she realized, and the thought turned her fear into rage. "No!" she yelled, grabbing at the arm holding the knife. Simultaneously she got her legs up under his torso and kicked with all her might. Her attacker stumbled backwards, bumping the door closed, and Andrea scrambled to her feet, kicking her blankets away.

He lunged at her, and the two of them fell onto the bed. Andrea ignored the knee jabbing into her gut as she focused on clinging to his gloved hand, trying to keep the knife away from her. The next second he was gone, his weight lifted from her body and the knife arm pulled loose from her grasp. Andrea lifted herself on one elbow and stared in shock: another man was in her bedroom now, his back to her. He had slammed her attacker against the wall and was twisting the knife arm. The attack of an assailant his own size must have surprised the man in the ski mask, because he dropped the knife. The other man kicked it away, allowing the would-be rapist to get in a vicious body-blow. Andrea's rescuer doubled over, and the attacker ran through the open door into the hallway. The second man coughed before staggering upright and launching himself into the hallway. Andrea heard them collide, slamming into the wall. She grabbed the phone from her bedside table and dialed 911.

"Please help me! A man broke into my bedroom, and someone else is here, and, and, they're fighting! Please, you have to help me!"

"It's okay, miss. Can you give me your name and address?"

"It's 555 Smithville Road. Hurry, please."

"Okay miss. Are you some place safe? Can you lock yourself in? Miss?"

Andrea had stopped listening. It had to be Jeff. He must have come home after all. She could hear them fighting in the hall. With trembling legs she walked to the door and peered out. In the darkness she could just see the two figures wrestling at the top of the stairs. She reached for the hall light switch and hesitated. From the phone on the bed she could still hear the dispatcher's voice calling her back to safety, but she couldn't stand the thought of hiding, waiting to see who won. With a flick light flooded the hallway, but the two figures did not pause in their struggle. In their whirling dance they turned, and Andrea got a good look at her rescuer.

"Chris!" At her voice he turned his head to look at her.

"Andrea! Lock yourself in! Agh!" The shift in Chris' attention allowed his assailant to get in a lucky punch, and Chris fell over backwards. The intruder stumbled, catching his foot on Chris's outstretched legs, as he turned towards the head of the stairs. Rage flooded through Andrea. With a savage snarl she leapt forward, catching up with the man in black and shoving him in the back. He grabbed the railing, but his forward momentum carried him down the stairs. There was a sickening crack as he lurched to a halt. His grip on the railing had caused him to twist as he fell, thudding against the wall, and he let out a howl of pain before collapsing into a sobbing heap.

Andrea jumped at a light touch on her shoulder. She whirled around, fists clenched and one hand drawn back to throw a punch. Chris stepped back, raising his own hands palms up in a signal of surrender.

"Easy, Rug Rat, easy," he said. "I'm not going to hurt you. Did you call the cops?"

She nodded, eying him warily, adrenalin still racing through her.

"When they get here, tell them everything that happened, but when you get to the end tell them he tripped over me and fell. Got that? You rushed out of your room just in time to see him trip as he tried to run down the stairs. It's important."

"But..." She lowered her fists, but continued to glare at him.

"No buts, Andrea. If you tell the police you shoved him, and they put it in the report, he might turn around and sue you. Trust me."

"Okay." Andrea nodded. She glanced down the stairs, but her assailant hadn't moved. She looked back at Chris for a moment, and then struck him in the arm with her fist. "You jerk. Where have you been?"

Chris flinched from the blow. Despite her anger Andrea felt tears threatening to fall. The look on Chris' face softened. "Around," he said, his eyes flicking between her and the huddled figure on the stairs. Andrea took a deep breath to steady herself.

"We need to check him." Chris pointed to the man in black, and Andrea nodded. The tears were still threatening, but she was in control. She tried to smile, but it felt weak.

The groans and curses from the base of the stairs had been growing quieter, but Andrea was in no hurry to get closer. "Stay here," Chris warned. She nodded.

The masked man had pulled himself to a semi-sitting position with his one good arm, and his left foot was twisted at an impossible angle. The ski mask was still in place, but blood was soaking into it from his nose. Chris reached forward and pulled off the mask. The man on the floor reached up to stop him, but swore in pain as he shifted his position. As the knit mask cleared his face, Andrea cried out in surprise. "Greg?"

Chris dashed back up the stairs and caught her as she started to sink to the steps. He pulled her close and she collapsed against his chest, tears of rage and horror choking her. In the distance she heard the police sirens, their wail piercing the night.

Four hours later Chris was sitting in a small room with a large mirror, waiting for the police to come and take his statement one more time. Despite being alone, he could feel eyes on the other side of the glass watching him. Andrea had been separated from him by the emergency response team, who insisted on checking her over. Chris had encouraged her to go, worried that she might be hiding an injury or at risk for shock. He had been giving his statement to the first officers on the scene, enjoying the status of loyal friend and hero. Then Tony Keubler showed up. He was an old high-school classmate, now a cop, who had been nearby when the call came in. He'd spoken to the first responders, and suddenly all of the looks directed at Chris turned from admiring to suspicious.

Since then Chris had lost track of the number of times he had been asked to re-tell his story. He was sitting with his head in his hands when he heard the door to the interrogation room open. He didn't bother looking up. He had been up all night, and he wasn't ready for another round of questions.

He braced himself for the scrape of the chair on the other side of the table. Instead he felt a light touch on this shoulder, and his head snapped up. Rachel Gordon was standing over him.

"Chris, are you all right?" When he nodded the most beautiful smile warmed her entire face. The joy and relief that flooded through him threatened to lift him off the ground. She opened her arms and he stood up into the embrace, startled to find he towered over her. He held her tight, closing his eyes, and drinking in the familiar scent of her perfume. He opened his eyes, and saw that Andrea had come in with her mother.

"Are you all right? How did you know? How have you been? Listen to me, I sound hysterical." Rachel reached into her purse for a tissue.

"That's all right. Please, sit down." Chris motioned to the chairs, but no one moved. He turned to Andrea. "Hi Rug Rat. How are you?"

"I've been better." She smiled, but it didn't reach her eyes. He tried to direct her to a chair, but she refused.

Rachel looked at Chris with concern. "You told the officer that you just happened to be passing the house when you saw someone moving around. Why?"

Chris fiddled with the sleeve of his sweatshirt. "I figured it sounded better than saying I was following them."

"But why were you following me? How did you know? What did you know?" Andrea had walked around her mother and stood glaring up at him.

Chris took a deep breath and considered how to answer. This wasn't going to sound very good.

"I had heard Andrea was on the Varsity softball team this year, so I went to a game to see her play. It was the one against Central High. I saw you with Greg." He closed his eyes, remembering again the surge of concern when he saw his "little sister" hugging someone, remembering the concern turning to alarm as he saw the way Greg watched her walk away. "I didn't like the way he looked at you, so I asked around about him. I found out he has a habit of not taking rejection well."

"So why didn't you tell me?"

Chris snorted. "Yeah right. 'Hi Andrea, haven't seen you since I was sent to jail. By the way, your new boyfriend is a rapist.' Like you'd have believed me."

"So you decided to stalk me?" Andrea's voice rose, slightly hysterical.

Chris shrugged. "I didn't have any proof."

"You do now," Rachel said. "It turns out there was a complaint filed by one of the girls at school. She withdrew her complaint when she realized how hard it would be, her word against his. But the police are going to call her back today to see if she's feeling a little braver."

"Good." He looked at Andrea again, still worried. "Are you sure you're okay, Rug Rat?" The use of her hated nickname again earned him a punch in the arm. He winced and looked away, suddenly feeling the urge to cry a little himself.

Andrea tucked her hair behind her ear as she looked around the sterile room. "Come on, we can drive you home."

Chris looked at her, startled. "I'm free to go?"

"Of course," Andrea said. "Tony and I had a little chat." The exhaustion in her eyes was replaced by a look Chris remembered well. Tony's ears were probably still ringing. "The police won't be bothering you anymore."

Chris sagged a little with relief. He looked awkwardly at

Rachel, not sure what to say next.

"You should come home with us," Rachel said, slipping her arm around his shoulder. "You can stay in the guest room and tomorrow you can tell us what you've been up to."

The lump in his throat kept Chris from replying. "You're part of the family," Rachel said.

"Of course you are." Andrea's smile was weary but genuine. "Just don't expect me to call you Big Brother."

The Fair Copy

by Vicki Delany

Charlotte stepped over the corpse of the dog rotting in the gutter. It was not long dead, thus barely offensive to the nose; she hoped someone would come and clear it up before the day got much hotter and the stench became too unbearable. She negotiated a painstaking path through the refuse and horse droppings, clutching the precious package to her chest.

It had rained heavily the previous night, turning barely passable streets into swift-moving rivers of human debris. The main street of their town was one of the steepest in all of England. After even the most moderate of rainfalls the road became a treacherous thoroughfare in which a careless walker might instantly find herself seated in the muck, being dragged downstream by the current.

A group of wide-eyed children ran shrieking past in pursuit of a mangy dog. They were dressed in an ill assortment of rags; most of them had no shoes. They kicked up clumps of wet mud as they passed and a spray of dark water landed on her skirts. She brushed at it idly and turned to watch as the children and their prey continued up the street. She hoped they didn't catch the dog; it would not hesitate to bite any child who dared venture too close.

An old man carefully attired in black frock coat and stiffly starched white shirt stepped out of the public house on the corner at the precise moment the pack of children careened by. He was not as tolerant of splashed mud as was Charlotte. With an outraged bellow the man swung his cane wildly. Charlotte could hear the blow from where she stood and see a flash of bright blood spring through the dirt on a boy's cheek. The child howled and released a torrent of foul language at the old man, who stood on the public house steps waving his cane in front of him like a sword. The boy decided against further contact with the enraged man and the cane and took off after his friends. They disappeared around the corner.

Charlotte continued to make her way. She leapt nimbly aside as the door to one of the tiny houses flew open and a bucket of slops was tossed into the street.

Charlotte and her sisters rarely ventured into the village. They much preferred the quiet of their home and the peace of the open moors. But Charlotte was determined to take her parcel directly to the postal carriage herself and see it safely on its way.

A sizeable inn was located on the other side of the village, and it was from this inn that the post was loaded onto the carriage to begin the journey into London. When Charlotte arrived at the stable yard, she found a group of people milling about waiting for the next carriage to London.

"Morning Charlotte." Dr. Blackwell lifted his hat at her approach."It is a pleasant surprise to see you here, my dear." He looked with undisguised interest at her parcel.

Charlotte did not intend to indulge the good Doctor's curiosity. "Good morning, sir."

"What's that you have there then?" Mrs. Bridges moved closer to have a look. Where the doctor was too well-bred to ask such a question outright Mrs. Bridges was not. She was a tall, beefy woman with a red bulbous nose and a wild mop of grey hair. Her dress was years old but it was mended with care and was as clean as any dress could be in this town on this day. Her sleeves were pulled up to reveal heavily muscled arms, clear evidence of a life spent in the mines or the wool mills.

"A parcel bound for London." Charlotte knew Mrs. Bridges well. Most of the Bridges' children attended, with varying degrees of regularity, Charlotte's father's Sunday School. Mr. Bridges had died years ago in a mine accident leaving his wife to raise their five living children. With some help from Charlotte's father and his Church committees, but mostly her own hard work, she had provided a fair life for the children.

"How's your family, Mrs. Bridges? I do hope they are all well."

"Oh yes, Miss Charlotte, they is. My Tommy has a job at the mill, did you know?"

"No, I had not heard."

"With him and Hugh and John working, and George being married, there's only Mary for me to worry about."

"I'm sure you have nothing to concern you about Mary. She's a fine girl."

"Aye, she is. But I would like to keep her out of the mill. Give her a better life than that."

A shout came from across the yard. "Not another one of those stupid books!" Charlotte groaned inwardly as Richard Fellows made his way through the mud toward them.

"Let's see, what rubbish is it this time?" Richard lunged for the parcel, but Charlotte pulled it out of the way. Charlotte's father and Mr. Fellows, the largest mill owner in the district, were the bitterest of enemies. War raged constantly between the mill owners on one hand and the clergy and local doctors on the other over any initiatives the latter might propose to improve sanitation in town or living conditions of the workers. Many dark nights Charlotte listened at her father's study door as he ranted against the intransigence of the mill and mine owners. Charlotte had grown up detesting Richard, and her feelings had never changed.

"Can't I have a little peek, Charlotte? Maybe it's a good book you've written. I won't know until I read it. If it's a good book, then I'll have to stop teasing you."

Charlotte tossed her head. "Well, it is not a book," she lied, "but if it were and if you liked it, then I would know that there must be something wrong with it."

Richard laughed heartily.

"A book! I would certainly hope not." The Reverend Eustace McNally gave his habitual frown over the top of his glasses. "I have heard rumours that you and your sisters have been writing books, Charlotte. You girls will never get yourselves husbands as long as you spend all your time with that silly writing."

"Now, Reverend," Richard leapt to Charlotte's defence, "All ladies have to have a little hobby, something to occupy the mind."

Charlotte moved away from the group, heart pounding. She glanced at her parcel, wrapped so carefully in the very best heavy brown paper, tied tightly with good strong string. She'd put a bit of sealing wax on the folds, to ensure the parcel wouldn't start to come apart on the journey. All her hopes and dreams lay within the brown paper wrapping. She'd worked so hard, struggled so long, to craft this novel, it was beyond bearing that Richard could dismiss all her labours as "a lady's little hobby".

"You listen to me, Charlotte," the Reverend was shouting now, "writing is no business of a woman's. A woman must engage in no activity which will distract her from those duties of home and family which God put the fair sex on this earth to perform."

"Yes, Reverend," she said dutifully. How strange, she thought, that her father could so encourage the art of writing in his own daughters, but Reverend McNally was determined to extinguish it.

"A book, is it?" Mrs. Bridges came over to sit on a pile of hay beside Charlotte. "It must be wonderful to write a book, Miss Charlotte."

"It is very wonderful indeed." Now came the not-very-wonderful part. The terrifying task of submitting her book to the publisher. She had produced one novel already, and it had been rejected several times. Her book travelled the rounds of publishers in a package along with novels written by her two sisters. Their books were accepted. Charlotte's was not.

But the publishing house of Smith, Elder had sent, along with their rejection, a kind letter praising her work and suggesting she submit a more appropriate novel. Fortunately at that time she was finishing up another work. It was this second manuscript that was now so lovingly cloaked in brown paper, about to begin the long journey to the London offices of Smith, Elder.

"My Mary can read." Mrs. Bridges said proudly, "Do you think she could write a book one day?"

"Why yes. I'm sure she could." Charlotte knew how very unusual it was that the daughter of a mill worker be able to read.

"Does it pay well?"

"I don't know," Charlotte said. "As of yet I have not been fortunate enough to have anything published."

"It must pay more than the mills, though."

"Much more than the mills."

They could hear the carriage long before it pulled into the stable yard. Horses' hooves clattered on cobblestones and wheels groaned and joints squeaked. The driver pulled his horses to a stop, shouted greetings and leapt down. Two stable boys rushed out of the barn and quickly unhitched the horses. One boy led them to water and feed while the other brought fresh horses.

"Girl, the roads are bad today so I'm in a hurry. Get me a mug of ale and a plate of your mistress' good stew, and I'll be on my way," the driver shouted to a little kitchen maid. She rushed to do his bidding.

Richard and Reverend McNally tossed their bags to the driver. They would be making the trip into London. Mrs. Bridges had a letter from her employer for the post. Dr. Blackwell and Charlotte handed him their parcels.

"This is very important," she said softly, "please look after it."

"All my parcels are important, Miss," he said, with a kind smile. "I look after them all.

"Let me have my lunch, gents, and then we'll go." The driver went into the inn.

Charlotte stood in the mud for a few moments. She considered waiting until the carriage left before going home.

"Why don't you come to London with me one day, Charlotte," Richard said. "We could have a grand time."

Charlotte tossed her head once more. "I have far too much to do around here." She mustered all her dignity as she walked away, knowing Richard was watching her. She stepped firmly into a fresh horse pat.

She left the stable yard, face burning, to the sound of Richard's laugher.

"Emily, the most terrible thing has happened." Charlotte burst into the drawing room where her sister sat reading by the open window. Outside the sun was shining and a light breeze stirred the curtains. "I got a letter today, from Mr. George Smith of Smith, Elder, the publishers."

"Oh, no! My dear, did they refuse your wonderful book?"

"Worse, Emily, worse. They did not receive it. Mr. Smith writes to enquire when he can expect the manuscript which I have promised him."

Emily lowered her book and stared at Charlotte in horror. "You mean it is lost?"

"What could have happened to it?"

"Are you sure you addressed it properly?"

"Of course I addressed it properly!" With a moan Charlotte dropped into a chair, "What am I to do? I suppose I must begin working on another fair copy. But I fear that by the time I've finished, the opportunity will have passed. So much work, lost."

Emily placed her book on the piecrust table beside her chair and rose to her feet. She smoothed her gown. "You do not want to begin again. We must find it."

"I put it on the carriage. How can we ever hope to locate it now?"

"First, we shall speak to the carriage driver. To ensure that your manuscript did, in fact, arrive in London. It is just past nine o'clock now. The carriage to London will not have arrived yet. If we hurry, we can catch it."

So great was their concern to speak to the carriage driver the sisters did not even bother to change into more proper attire for venturing out of the house.

They arrived at the inn long before the carriage. Charlotte paced fitfully up and down the stable yard. Emily had brought a book and made herself comfortable on a bale of hay.

Precisely on time the carriage pulled to a halt outside the inn. To Charlotte's relief the driver was the same man to whom she had given her parcel. His feet had barely touched the cobblestones before a breathless Charlotte rushed over.

"Please. Do you remember me? I gave you a parcel bound for London, about three weeks ago?"

"You asked me special-like to look after your parcel."

"It never arrived. Do you know what might have happened to it?"

"Never got there," the driver repeated, rubbing his beard thoughtfully. "I remember you handing me your parcel right enough. Don't remember it after that. You know, Miss, I don't think it got off at London. That was a very light trip, that was. Only them two gentlemen what got on here the whole trip. No, your parcel didn't get off at London. I didn't take it off. I don't know who else would. Hope you find it, Miss." The man tipped his cap to Charlotte and went into the inn for his mug of ale.

Charlotte stood beside the carriage in despair. Her manuscript was lost. She had her first copy, but she had made many changes as she painstakingly wrote out the fair copy. Re-writing would be so much work. By the time it was again ready the offer from Smith, Elder might be withdrawn.

"That's good news." Charlotte started at the sound of her sister's voice.

"Good news, whatever do you mean?"

"I mean, dear Charlotte, that the manuscript is not lost somewhere in the depths of London. If it did not fall off the carriage, and I pray it did not, then it must still be in Yorkshire."

"Easy for you to say. Your manuscript is already on its way to being published, as is Anne's. It's mine which is lost."

"I know, dear. Therefore we must find it."

The sisters walked slowly home. Charlotte's steps felt heavy, leaden. Emily took her arm.

Charlotte asked to be excused from luncheon. "I shall walk and try to gather my thoughts."

The parsonage lay directly at the foot of the moors and it was to the moors where Charlotte and her sisters and brother ventured in times of despair. She walked for a very long time, thinking of little else but her package and where it might be. The fierce wind tore her hair from its pins and whipped at her cloak. The pleasant sunlight of earlier in the day was long gone, the sky heavy, the only colour provided by clumps of purple heather clinging to the tough soil. She could see from one horizon to the other, as the dark, rolling clouds moved swiftly across the sky. No other person invaded her solitude.

By the time she was ready to return to the Parsonage Charlotte had come to the conclusion that it was not a matter of "what" might have happened to her parcel, but "who" might have happened to it.

The next morning Charlotte left home immediately after breakfast and marched resolutely to the Fellows' mill office.

The thin, pasty-faced clerk showed Charlotte to the waiting room.

She paced up and down, scarcely noticing the quality of the furnishings. Fortunately she did not have long to wait. Richard soon appeared, straightening the shoulders of his handsome jacket and extending his hand in greeting. "Charlotte, to what do I owe this most pleasant surprise?" He seemed genuinely happy to see her.

Ignoring his broad smile, warm greeting and outstretched hand, Charlotte rounded on him. "I want it back, Richard."

"Whatever are you talking about?" Remembering good manners, he added, "would you care for tea?"

"Certainly not. You know why I am here. I want my parcel."

"Parcel?"

Richard looked so baffled that Charlotte's certainly deserted her.

"My parcel was taken off the carriage before it reached London and I want it back."

"But Charlotte, dear, I do not have it."

"You don't?"

"Why ever would you think I would take your parcel?"

"As a joke. You said you wanted to read my book. Richard, you are always playing jokes on me. I do not find this amusing in the least."

"Dearest Charlotte, do you not know by now that I tease you only because I am so very fond of you." He moved to stand in front of her and took both her hands in his. "Never would I play a joke on you that would hurt you."

So sincere was his expression Charlotte believed him. She pulled her hands away. "Did you see anyone going through the mail?"

"I went into the inn to have a quick mug of ale. The parcel was on the carriage then. Perhaps something happened to it whilst I was in the inn."

"I am sorry to have accused you." She hurried out the door.

"Please think about what I have said," Richard called after her. "I care for you very much, dearest Charlotte."

But so troubled were her thoughts, Charlotte did not hear him.

She called next at the surgery of Dr. Blackwell. His waiting room was full, but Charlotte pushed her way in and demanded to see the doctor on a matter of great urgency.

"Sir, I must ask if you removed my parcel from the London carriage which we met three weeks ago?"

The doctor pulled his glasses down his nose and stared at her over the tops of the rims. "Certainly not. Good heavens, girl. You can't come into my surgery and make an accusation like that."

"Did your package arrive at its destination safely?"

"It did."

"Mine did not. Did you stay with the carriage until it departed?"

"I placed my package in the hands of the driver then took my leave. I have better things to do than stand around stable yards all day. If you will excuse me."

Charlotte ignored the hint. "Did you see anyone take my package down off the carriage?"

"I did not. You had best be careful, young lady, before you go around town accusing people of theft."

Charlotte turned and marched out of the surgery. The puzzled doctor shook his head at her retreating back and straightened his glasses as he settled his ample form back into his consulting chair. Young people today had no respect for their elders.

At home, Charlotte knocked lightly on the door to her father's study. The Parson looked up from his desk and adjusted his glasses as she entered.

"Father, I'm convinced it was Reverend McNally who stole my manuscript."

"A serious accusation, Charlotte. Are you certain?"

"Fairly certain, Father. You know he does not approve of women writing."

"That doesn't make the man a thief."

"No, but he did have strong words to say while we waited for the carriage."

The Parson rubbed his eyes. "You must do what you think you have to do, my dear. Reverend McNally will be returning to our village tomorrow. He's interested in my plan of setting up a new school. We have to get as many of the mill children into school as we can, before they are lost to us. You have my permission to speak of this matter to him. But, please, attempt to be discreet."

"Thank you, Father." She kissed him lightly on the cheek.

Charlotte dressed with great care for her confrontation with Reverend McNally. She was anxious to give him no further reason to disapprove of her, but hoped to get him to hand over the manuscript by clever use of good reason.

"Reverend McNally," she began. "It would appear that my package never arrived in London. You were on the same carriage, I believe."

The Reverend was a remarkably handsome man, with thick dark curls and eyes the colour of the sky over the moors on a hot summer's day. He was not much older than Charlotte; he had risen quickly in the Church. Charlotte's father was of the opinion that he would rise farther still.

Charlotte gulped. "I was wondering if you noticed anyone take my parcel."

"No."

"It is very important to me. Months of arduous labour were in that parcel. Are you sure?"

"You verge on being offensive, Charlotte. I have said I saw no one, therefore I did not."

Charlotte rolled her good white gloves into a tight ball and passed them from hand to moist hand. "Did you, uh, perhaps happen to move my parcel yourself?"

"I did not touch your parcel. But let me tell you, it is no great sorrow if you have lost the wretched thing." He rose to his feet and stood over Charlotte. "I have told you before, Miss, that women are not suited to writing. Perhaps this will convince you. If you have misplaced your manuscript, it is because your womanly constitution is not strong enough to enable you to organise affairs of the larger world."

"I did not lose my package, sir. It was stolen from me. Allow me to ask you directly: did you steal it?"

"Allow me to answer you directly: I did not."

"Were you with the carriage the entire time it stood in the stable yard at the inn?"

"No, I went with young Mr. Fellows for a spot of ale before the journey. If you check with Mr. Fellows I expect he will tell you we sat together at a table until we were called to leave."

Charlotte's heart sank. The Reverend would never say he was with Richard if it was not so.

"Thank you for your time." Charlotte gathered up her gloves.

"If your package was taken, I am sorry. It is terrible times we live in, thieves and drunkards are everywhere. But I will remind you once again it is not wise for you to continue with this writing foolishness."

"And let me remind you, sir, that not all the wisdom in the world is lodged in male skulls." Charlotte slammed the door on her way out.

It was a thoroughly discouraged Charlotte who returned to the Parsonage that afternoon. She took her first copy out of the cupboard and arranged the pages neatly in front of her. Settling herself down at her desk in the drawing room, she smoothed a fresh piece of paper and dipped her pen in ink. She sat with the pen in the air: maybe she should just give up. Charlotte put her head in her hands and wept.

The door opened softly and Emily slipped in. "Did you make any progress today?"

Charlotte sobbed. "I don't think Richard has it. I do believe he would have taken it for a joke. You know how he is. But once he realised how important it is to me, he would return it. Dr. Blackwell would have no reason to take it, and Reverend McNally is a perfectly horrible man but he is not a liar. If he stole it you can be sure he would tell me that he burned it for my own good."

"Who else was in the stable yard that day? Think Charlotte."

"The kitchen maid came out, but only for a brief moment. The two stable boys were busy with the horses. Mrs. Bridges gave the driver a letter."

"Ask them all if they saw anything. Perhaps they did. Servants notice everything, you know that. Ask Mrs. Bridges also."

Once again Emily accompanied Charlotte to the inn. They spoke to the kitchen maid and the stable hands. All swore they knew nothing about any parcel. They did not have the coach in sight the entire time and no one noticed anyone hanging about apart from those waiting for the carriage.

"Perhaps Mrs. Bridges saw something of interest," Emily said as they made their way home. She swung her skirts deftly out of the way as a horse trotted down the hill, tossing mud in every direction. "Tomorrow is Sunday. She is sure to come to church, you can speak to her then."

Sunday morning, Charlotte planted herself at the entrance to the church and scanned the crowd for Mrs. Bridges. Finally, as the service was about to begin, she saw the large woman making her way down the path. Charlotte was about to step forward to speak to her when her arm was seized in a firm grip.

"My dearest Charlotte, how are you this fine day?" Mrs.

Edward Smith, the oldest member of the parish, smiled up at Charlotte.

"I am well, Mrs. Smith. And yourself?"

"Not well at all, dear. Not well at all. My joints are beginning to act up again. The onset of autumn. Every September I am positively cursed by my joints." Charlotte attempted to edge away but Mrs. Smith's grip was firm. She was not about to release an audience when she had hold of one. Mrs. Bridges slipped past them into the church, eyes downcast. Mrs. Smith chattered on.

The service was agony. So great was Charlotte's impatience she almost leapt to her feet to cry, "Get on with it, Father." When it was finally over, Charlotte rushed down the aisle while the others were still getting to their feet.

"Mrs. Bridges, I must talk to you."

"I have to get home, Miss Charlotte." Mrs. Bridges fairly raced down the path through the graveyard.

"It won't take but a minute, please."

Mrs. Bridges stopped beside a particularly large and impressive gravestone.

Charlotte asked the same questions she had been asking for days. To her acute disappointment Mrs. Bridges gave the same answers as everyone else. She had seen nothing.

"Are you sure?"

"I am sure, Miss Charlotte. This is the stainless truth."

Charlotte did not return to the house but rather continued through the graveyard onto the moor. She walked through the desolate landscape for hours, finding some small comfort in the familiar surroundings. She bent down and picked a small flower growing amongst a small bunch of heather spreading like a stain across the tough moor grasses. She raised the bloom to her noise and smiled.

Charlotte returned to the parsonage only long enough to beg Emily accompany her. Emily complained that Charlotte would ruin her Sunday dress but Charlotte insisted they hurry. In the gathering dusk they rushed through the streets of Haworth. Charlotte had been to the Bridges' home twice, both times bringing a meal when Mrs. Bridges had taken ill. She was not sure if she could find the way, but was determined to search all night if need be. Candlelight was flickering behind closed windows when the sisters finally knocked on the door.

Mrs. Bridges stood in the entrance, wiping floury hands on a well-worn apron stretched to its seams over her amble bosom. Her mouth hung open in shock at the sight of the well-dressed young ladies standing at her door.

"Good evening," Charlotte said, "I apologise for the lateness of the hour, but may we come in?"

"Yes, Miss Charlotte. I expect that you should."

The house was small, exceeding small. The sisters stepped directly into the kitchen. The Bridges' daughter, Mary, sat at the well-scrubbed kitchen table, a pile of close-written pages spread across the surface in front of her. She looked up at the visitors, then bowed her head and placed her hands over the papers on the table.

"You know why I'm here, Mrs. Bridges," Charlotte began.

Emily looked at her sister in some confusion, startled at the severity of Charlotte's tone. Charlotte had not revealed the purpose of this visit.

Mrs. Bridges stood behind Mary, and placed her hands on her daughter's shoulders, "I'm sorry to cause you such trouble, Miss Charlotte, surely I am." Mary began to slowly gather up the papers.

"Why did you take it, Mrs. Bridges, why?"

"I thought maybe my Mary could read your book. See how writing is done. Then Mary could be a writer. Keep her out of the mills, if she were a writer of books."

"But Mrs. Bridges, this is my book. It can never be Mary's. Do you understand that, Mary?"

The girl nodded, her face a picture of misery. Mutely she placed the papers in their wrappings and handed the rough bundle to Charlotte.

Charlotte grasped the pages tightly.

"This was not Mary's idea," Mrs. Bridges insisted, "but mine alone."

"I know that. I won't tell anyone about this, Mrs. Bridges. I have my manuscript back now. That's all that matters to me."

"I have an idea," Emily said suddenly. "Young Mary will be old enough to seek her living soon. If you continue to read, Mary, and maybe write a few simple stories or some poetry, I will speak to Papa. I am sure Papa would be able to find you a good position as a governess before you are much older."

Mrs. Bridges beamed. Mary smiled shyly. "I would like that very much, Miss Bronte."

"How ever did you guess it was Mrs. Bridges who took the parcel, Charlotte?" Emily asked as the sisters made their way back through the twisting streets toward Haworth Parsonage.

"When we spoke in the churchyard earlier in the day, Mrs.

Bridges swore she was telling the "stainless truth". Of course Mrs. Bridges' speech is very Yorkshire plain. She has no education. At the time I thought it a fancy turn of phrase for her to use. Then it came to me: there is a line in my manuscript, which reads, "I would not say he had betrayed me; but the attributes of stainless truth was gone from his idea." Clearly Mary read the phrase to Mrs. Bridges and she liked it and remembered it."

Emily laughed, "Well, I am glad that's over."

Charlotte loosened the wrapping slightly and peeked at the first page. She smiled at the sight of the title boldly written in her own careful hand. Jane Eyre.

Murder Most Royal

by P.M. Jones

Sunday

A five-ton delivery van was stopped in the road, the driver leaning over the steering wheel mesmerized by the sight of the laughing woman who had crossed the road in front of him moments before. The film crew took advantage of the bottle-neck caused by driver's stupor and followed her onto the sidewalk leading to the open doors of Toronto's St. Lawrence Market.

The outdoor vendors paid little attention to the presence of a film crew. It was a common thing in Hollywood North, to see cameras, cables and crews clogging up the roads. They did, however, notice the captivating woman. She was impossible to miss.

The woman did her bit—a hair-tossing, bantering piece of fun—mugging for the cameras, which loved her. She was to be a celebrity judge in a televised cook-off for one of the food channels.

The film crew wrapped for the day. The woman was picked up by a hired car, whisked away to the Ritz Carlton. She was scheduled to meet for drinks in the lounge at six o'clock with her publicist and a rep from a publishing house who was vying for the rights to distribute her next book. The woman thought the entire thing was a lark. She never took anything seriously which didn't have a direct impact on her real job. A job which was nothing but serious.

As the street vendors packed up, eager to be done after a long day which had started at four a.m., Freddie Rawlins called out to his neighbour. "Hey, Armstrong! I could use a hand with these goddamn chairs, if you've got a sec."

Freddie bitched to himself under his breath while waiting. He always did a better trade in small items, twenty bucks or less—jewellery, old paintings, handbags—but the bigger items

193

attracted the eye of shoppers and had a huge profit margin, so he lugged this type of thing back and forth every Sunday.

Frank Armstrong complied, helping to heft the plastic and chrome moulded seats into the back of Freddie's van.

"You see what Maggie was up to this morning?" Freddie asked Armstrong, without waiting for his reply. "Came waddling by my tables around eleven. Scared her off when I caught her trying to pocket some silver earrings. Maybe we should rename her Magpie," Freddie told him. Both men laughed, agreeing the name suited the old bag-lady with a wobbly shopping cart and an eye for anything shiny.

Monday

A miniscule article, on page nine of the newspaper reported a sixty-seven year old woman of no-fixed address had been found dead in St. James Park. The last few words escaped the notice of most everyone. Police were asking anyone to step forward who had information on the stabbing death of the homeless woman.

Tuesday

Detective Mack Petersen was not happy.

Why had he been saddled with investigating a murder with zero leads? Payback? Still? It wasn't Mack's fault that Captain Frost's girlfriend had preferred him to Frost thirty-odd years ago. He and Frost had both been fresh from the academy, wet behind the ears at the time. Never mind that Mack had married Olivia and Frost had soon rebounded, getting hitched to a nice girl himself. Captain and Mrs. Frost now had a very nice cottage on East Lake and three very nice kids.

Olivia had passed away fifteen years ago, without cottage or kids.

A hardened cop, biding his time until retirement, Petersen reminded himself he only had a year and a half to go. It had become his mantra, mentally chanting the phrase whenever he felt like telling some asshole to go screw himself.

This came to Petersen's mind every time he resented a case he had been assigned to. It rarely occurred to him that he was given the hardest cases because he was very good at what he did.

Whatever the reason, Petersen knew he had a job to do, and he set out to do it, never suspecting that a case was unfolding which would dredge up details from before the first World War, thieves, royal lineage, and introduce him to the most renowned detective in the western world.

At six-fifteen p.m., Mack picked up the shrilling phone on his desk, sighing into the receiver, "Detective Petersen."

"Hello? I'm calling about, uh, something I might'a seen last weekend? The dead bag-lady. This the right person to talk to?"

"You got the right guy. Who am I speaking with?"

"Stan Loogey. I drive a truck for D.O.C. Delivery. I saw in the paper you was looking for information."

"Uh-huh," Petersen said, settling himself back into his chair. "Go ahead."

"Well, I don't know if it's important or not, but I saw this woman, a gorgeous woman, crossing the road, right in front of my truck. She was one hot piece of..." Mack cleared his throat.

"Tied traffic up both ways and made me late for the whole rest of the day," Stan chuckled with amusement.

"And?"

"And I did my delivery, took forever, and when I came out, I saw a bag-lady holding on to her shoppin' cart, trying to keep this other guy away from it."

Petersen rolled his eyes. Great. Spectacular lead in a homicide.

"You felt compelled to report this, why?"

"Cause the man trying to take the old babe's cart was dressed in a suit. It was odd. Just thought someone should know, is all."

Petersen took down the details Stan provided. Average height, average weight, short brown hair, suit. Pointy toed shoes were the only thing Stan could point out as 'distinguishing'. Stan noticed the shoes because the man had put one foot up on the cart as he tried to heft it away from Maggie, who was holding on for all she was worth. Not much to go on, but sometimes that was all it took.

Wednesday

The tedious task, of interviewing those who knew Maggie, unfolded. Petersen waded his way through the streets, climbing endless flights of stairs to walk-up apartments, finding out little to nothing about the woman, other than her nickname, Magpie, and the fact she made a habit out of pilfering from the vendors at the antiques market on Sunday.

Her shopping cart had been found beside her body, the contents tipped out. The only thing that stood out as slightly unusual was one navy blue velvet box, with a regal-looking insignia embossed upon it. Empty.

Petersen pulled up in front of the last residence on his list. It belonged to Freddie Rawlins, another street vendor. Petersen looked over at the house—a bungalow. Thank God.

The door was pulled open before he hit the porch. "Frank Armstrong called," Freddie said, bracing the screen door open. "Can't tell you much about Maggie, other than what Frank told you. She was a nut, but she was okay. Aside from her sticky fingers, she was harmless. Don't know who'd want to kill old Magpie..."

Petersen took notes, wondering why the hell he was bothering. He turned to leave.

"One more thing, Mr. Rawlins. By any chance, are you missing a navy blue velvet jewellery box?"

Freddie's eyes slid to Detective Petersen's, narrowing slightly. "Just the box huh? Nothing inside?"

Petersen had the answer to that question

"You know what was inside the box before Maggie palmed it?"

"Hell, ya. It was a necklace. Had a big yellow glass stone. I had it priced at one-fifty. Probably too much, but hell, the box had a fancy stamp on it and the chain was solid silver for sure. I knew the stone wasn't worth a tinker's damn, but it looked like it could pass for a genuine antique. If she weren't already dead, I'd kill Maggie for snatching that one."

Thursday

Petersen ambled in at five to nine. He had been popping antacids all morning. In the rush to fill his grumbling gut without having to put any more wear and tear on his barking dogs last night, he'd taken a spin around the drive-through for a bacon cheeseburger and fries. The effects of the hasty culinary decision emanated from within his paunch like Mount Vesuvius on the brink of eruption.

Studying a print-out waiting on his desk, Petersen's interest was slightly peaked. Who would have thought the old broad had a jewel case in her cart embossed with the House of Habsburg? Austrian Royalty, the information sheet said. Huh. He wished he'd questioned Freddie on where the box had come from, then realized it would've been an exercise in futility. He'd met plenty of Freddies in his day. He tucked the blue box into his middle drawer, wondering if he should have listened to his hunch and submitted it as a formal piece of evidence. It had been hard to tell what was relevant and what wasn't in that cart full of stuff Maggie had hauled around.

At two-forty five, feeling much better thanks to a re-hydrated bowl of ramen noodles loaded with enough sodium to spike his blood pressure, Petersen looked up from his computer and tried not stare.

A woman wearing a red silk wrap-around dress and killer heels stood looking down at him, smiling. She had jet black hair, smoothed into cascading waves, full luscious lips and fair skin that looked like it had been airbrushed into perfect china-doll smoothness.

Petersen mentally processed her physical details in less than five seconds. He squared his shoulders and straightened his spine, sucking in his gut without conscious thought.

"Can I help you?" he asked, gruff-voiced.

"Perhaps," she said, sitting down on the wooden chair beside his desk. She perched herself on the edge of the seat and leaned toward him. "I think it shall be I helping you, but let's not get off on the wrong foot." Her eyes were almost as dark as her hair, but not unfriendly. Intense though.

"I assume you've come here to give me some information on a case?" Petersen said formally, bristling at the attitude. He re-focused his gaze away from hers while he moved coffee mug and papers aside in search of his notepad.

"No, not really," she said. She tapped a piece of paper on his desk with a long blood-red fingernail. "This is why I'm here."

It was the print-out of the crest on the blue box. What the hell was going on here? Mack wondered. Bag ladies, royal crests, sexy woman from the pages of a Bond novel.

"I didn't catch your name," Mack said, pencil poised.

She threw her head back and laughed, with a low-throaty chuckle. "Guess you don't get out much Detective Petersen. Or may I call you Mack?"

Petersen's brow furrowed. She looked familiar, but he knew he'd have remembered meeting her before...

"Monique Elena Alvarez Black," she said, in her purring voice. Her lips moved around the words like she was savouring a rich piece of dark chocolate. Slightly accented, but of indeterminate origin. They shook hands. Her grip was firm and cool.

"Can we cut the bullsh... can we cut to the chase here, Miss Black?" Petersen said.

Monique smiled, like she was indulging a small child begging for a sweet. "Of course, Mack. And please, call me Monique. I need a little something from you, and I, in turn, will give you something.

I am here about Maggie. The homeless woman stabbed last Sunday."

Monique's manner had abruptly changed. She was all business now. Petersen eyed her with curiosity, trying to place her.

"I'm going to solve your case for you, Mack. I just need one tiny thing from you in exchange."

The realization hit him like a sledge-hammer. Monique Black was the Private Investigator. Famous, beautiful, smart and sought after by those with power, money and infamy. He'd seen her in some magazine. She was a self-promoter and supposedly good at what she did. Why she would be interested in this case was a crap shoot.

"Why, on God's green earth would I want help?"

"Oh, Mack. You're no fun at all. Why wouldn't you?"

Petersen had to think hard about that one for a minute. Maybe it was because this woman was so passive-aggressive, it rankled his male pride.

"Well, Miss Black," Mack emphasized, "I've been doing my job for... a lot of years, and I don't reckon that I need anyone to solve my cases for me."

Monique pursed her lips, drawing them up into the most charming little moue Mack had ever seen.

"Well, Mack, how about a little wager then? You seem like the type of man who wouldn't be afraid of a little bet. I am very, very good at what I do, and I will prove it to you in exchange for one small thing."

Petersen knew he was being hustled, but there was little he could do about it. Ego dictated that he couldn't refuse. Plus he'd love to take her down a notch or two.

"Sure," he said, smiling. His brown eyes were focused now, taking her probing gaze in straight on. Mack loved a challenge. "What do you have in mind?"

She smiled again, showing even white teeth behind the rosy lips.

"I will tell you five personal things I have learned about you, since walking in here. If I'm correct, you give me the jewel case. If not, I will slink away and never bother you again."

"How do I know you didn't research my life before you got here?"

Monique threw her head back and laughed again.

"I can assure you, I knew nothing about you but your name before I sat down."

Strangely enough Mack believed her. Plus he had nothing to

lose.

"Okay. Deal."

Monique nodded her head, almost regally.

"First, you are a single man without children. Widowed. You wear a wedding ring which is too tight, clothes which could be... improved on, and the single photograph on your desk is of a woman – quite pretty by the way – the photo is at least twenty-years old. I would say you loved your wife very much and she died, oh, let's say fifteen years ago."

Mack's eyebrows shot up, his gut clenching slightly.

"Second, you are counting down the days until you retire, which will be, most likely, about a year and half from now, at which time you are planning to hit the open road on the motorbike you are rebuilding at home. A Harley."

Mack's eyes were now slightly wider, though he was trying to keep his poker face. "How do you figure?"

Monique explained, in her soft husky voice. "You have a calendar tacked to the wall behind your desk with little tick-marks on each day, and a new one, a sixteen month calendar, tacked up beside it. This leads me to conclude you are counting down to something – looking forward to it. Judging by your demeanor, you are not a man who gets overly excited, so it will be something big. You don't seem the Mediterranean Cruise type, so it must be retirement."

Monique paused to take a breath. "The motorcycle was easy. Your coffee mug has a Harley Davidson logo on it, your fingernails tell me you a backyard mechanic, and under that stack of reference books on your credenza is a worn looking book entitled 'Bike Mechanics for Dummies'. Simple, no?"

Petersen's eyes hadn't left hers. How she had catalogued all this within the two minutes she had sat at his desk before the game began, he didn't know.

"My third observation is that you prefer dogs over cats, though you own no pets. You probably plan to get a dog when you retire as well. A Golden Retriever or a Lab."

"And why do you assume that?" Mack asked, feeling a little spooked. It was like she was plucking insignificant bits of information out of his brain... things he'd never told anyone.

"You are very... macho. Men with machismo always prefer dogs over cats – usually big hairy dogs. You have no animal hair on your clothes and your long working hours do not allow you to keep a pet, regardless. A man who has lived alone for so long, must long for some sort of companionship, but you still wear your wedding ring, so I deduce you have no desire for your companion to be a woman. So it must be a dog. Most police departments work with Retrievers and Labs, and they are faithful, intelligent companions... this would appeal to you. Plus they have a good long lifespan with no serious health issues inherent to the breed. This would also be of importance to you."

"Anyone ever tell you you're a little scary?" Mack said.

Monique laughed again, tossing her hair over her shoulder. She loved to be complimented, and she took what he said as just that.

"Shall I tell you what you had for dinner last night?"

"Please," Mack said, eyes narrowed slightly but with an unmistakable hint of amusement in them.

"I am going to hypothesize... something greasy. Fast food, I would say. Bacon cheeseburger and fries, from a drive-through?"

Petersen almost fell off his chair. "What... how?"

"I must confess, I was taking a shot in the dark with the specifics. But your body language told me I was on the right track, regardless. I apologize for the bit of 'parlour trick' thrown in there, but you are rather amusing," Monique said. She sighed resignedly, as if it were a bore to detail how she drew her obscure conclusions.

"As for how I knew about your meal, the only item in your trash can is a small bag from the drug store and there is an open bottle of Tums on your desk with a quarter of it gone. Greasy food is the most common cause for this type of stomach ailment, and knowing you are working on a case leads me to believe you skipped lunch yesterday, probably had sore feet from traipsing all-over, and drove through for fast food on your way home, rewarding yourself after a hard day's work with the worst thing for you on the menu. See? Simple."

Mack nodded his head in concession. She was good. Better than good.

"My last observation is that you, too, are very good at your job." Monique sat back in her chair. "I don't need to explain why I come to that conclusion, I hope?"

"It'd be interesting to hear it—but no, I don't need to know why you think so. I know I am, and that's good enough to get me a decent night's sleep."

Monique flashed him a dazzling smile. "The jewel case, Detective Petersen?"

He reached into his desk drawer and pulled out the blue box and handed it to her without preamble. "You can call me Mack now."

Friday

The day was hotter than Hades, though Monique Elena Alvarez Black sat outdoors in the chic little patio at the back of the Ritz Carleton, looking completely unaffected by the staggering humidity. Flowers were wilting, servers were sweating and Monique was waiting patiently, sipping iced-tea.

Detective Mack Petersen came pushing through the door, cursing inwardly at Monique's choice of meeting spot. The bar just inside the door was cool and practically empty and he was perspiring profusely in his button down, jacket, tie and slacks. He chanted his mantra inside his head as he made his way over. A year-and-a-half. A year-and-a-half. A year-and-a-half.

"Monique," Mack said, by way of greeting. "I'll have the same," Mack called over his shoulder, waving his hand in the direction of Monique's drink as the waiter approached. The server looked glad to have only traversed half-way across the wooden decking in the ninety degree heat.

The space they sat in was ultra-modern, with low, white-leather out-door club chairs, square dark-stained tables, bamboo in glass and chartreuse cat-grass trimmed flat, sitting in long boxes on high tables around the patio. Sounds from the busy streets were audible, but minimized by a stretch of parkland behind and the buildings on either side.

Monique sat perched upon a stool at a high table for two. Mack sat down across from her as she took out a long brown cigarette and lit it. Now he understood the need to be outdoors.

"Shouldn't smoke," he said to her gruffly.

"Tsk-tsk, Mack. We can't begin judging our friends now, can we?" Monique said.

"That stuff will kill you. You're one of the smartest people I know, so I'm sure you've realized that," Petersen qualified.

"You ex-smokers are the worst," Monique said, taking care to blow her smoke sideways. "And really, Mack, if we're going to sit here and lecture each other, I have a few things to say about your diet, your daily caffeine and beer intake and lack of exercise. You do want to make it to retirement, don't you?" Monique's smile was saccharine and just a little smug.

"Okay, so moving on. You said you've got news? Found another clue in our case?" Petersen asked, wanting to get to the nitty-gritty, out of the heat, and into the air conditioning.

"I like that. You said 'our case'," Monique said, smiling with her eyes. He bristled slightly, but his lips twitched at the corners, ever so slightly.

"I do have news... but it isn't another clue. I've solved the case." Monique stubbed her cigarette out as she said it, matter-of-factly.

"Oh really? When? This morning? Was the left shoe of the bell-hop worn down on one side, leading you to the killer? Or perhaps the clerk at the front desk scratched his nose as you walked by, leading you to conclude he was lying about something?" Mack laughed at his own joke. Monique's face held a smile of indulgent humour at his mockery.

"Really, Mack. No need to be silly over it. It was a simple matter, to tell you the truth. Not one of my more difficult cases. We'll deal with it shortly," Monique's eyes grazed over him. "Good. Handcuffs. I'm glad to see you've come prepared. And, is that a gun in your pocket, or are you just happy to see me?" Monique tittered at her own joke, Mack snorting a laugh in response. Vexing woman.

Detective Mack Petersen and Monique Elena Alvarez Black strode into the lobby of the Ritz and rode the elevator up in silence, Mack following her lead. The doors pinged open to display multiple sets of soaring double doors, leading to banquet and conference rooms.

A thin little man with a sparse head of mousy brown hair, a tan coloured suit, funny looking shoes and tortoiseshell glasses snapped to attention, like a meerkat poking its head from its hole, as they strode toward him.

"Monique! Wonderful! We're in here. Tons of press. We'll get international coverage—all the big names are here," the flighty little man said, his words jumbling together as he herded them into a conference room. A long table had been set up on the far wall, skirted and laid with pitchers of water. Books sat atop the table, covers displaying Monique Elena Alvarez Black's bewitching smile and 'Best Seller' emblems were positioned front and centre. A large poster of her latest book cover adorned the wall behind.

"My publicist, Jerome Whittington. Press conference," Monique stage whispered to Mack.

"Thanks," he replied sarcastically. Monique shot him one of her trademark smiles and made her way up to the podium.

A brief introduction was made to the press by the publicist, who positioned the microphone in front of Monique before stepping off the platform.

"Ladies, gentlemen," Monique addressed the crowd with a slight nod of her head. "Thank you all for coming. I know you've probably got a list of questions you'd like to ask." Hands shot up in the air. "First I'd like to take care of something rather more important than a book tour. That something... is murder." Silence descended upon the room, as if all the air had been sucked out of it through the large vents which sat high up on the walls.

The double doors at the back of the room clicked shut. The sound of a lock turning filled the hushed atmosphere, as two uniformed police constables stood guard.

Monique placed the blue velvet box on top of the table. Petersen wondered where she had produced it from. Her handbag was too small to have carried it here. Petersen moved slowly moved across the side of the room, as it suddenly dawned on him who she was about to finger for the crime.

"I was hired to retrieve a certain object of immense value. I have found it. It's here in this room. The person holding it is a murderer. Shall I go on, Jerome?"

Jerome Whittington's thin, pointed face blanched as every head turned toward him.

"I don't know what you're talking about," Jerome stammered. His eyes darted about, then widened, catching sight of Detective Mack Petersen's imposing form standing a foot away.

"Mack?" Monique's eyes turned toward him. "If you'd care to check Jerome's inside jacket pocket, you'll find the Diamond of Habsburg neatly wrapped in a white handkerchief."

Petersen turned and pinned Jerome with his gaze. Jerome froze. Mack inserted a hand into Jerome's suit pocket and pulled out the hanky. He unwrapped it carefully, exposing the stone to the room. Prisms of light danced off the facets of the gem like sunshine, dazzling everyone in sight with the sheer size and beauty of it.

"Check his other pockets, Detective, please. I'm quite certain you'll find a one-way ticket to Panama," she said to Mack. "In his suite upstairs, you will find the knife he used to kill Maggie. Check his toiletry bag. It has been washed, but traces of DNA should prove to be a conclusive match to Maggie's blood."

Monique directed her attention to the gap-mouthed reporters. "You see, the homeless woman who was murdered last weekend was actually Baroness Margaret Von Strauss. A poor relation, as I'm sure you've all gathered, but a relation nonetheless, to the royal family of Austria from long ago."

The members of the press where all talking at once, shouting questions, snapping photos and acting very uncivilized, to Monique's sensibilities. She sat serenely, like a queen upon her throne, until everyone quieted down. It took no more than one minute.

"I shall explain," she said to everyone.

"Baron Jordan Grumenhauer has been looking for this flawless, twenty-two carat yellow diamond for many years. Having recently hired me, I began tracing the origins of the stone and found that an aunt, belonging to an obscure branch of the Habsburg's family tree, had immigrated to North America many, many years ago. The main branch, the male line of the Austrian Royal Family, died out just at the beginning of World War One. Baron Grumenhauer is one the few known descendants left from the female line of the Royal Family.

"Margaret Von Strauss, also known as Maggie, or Magpie to her closest acquaintances, was rather tricky to track down. Though find her, I did. I shan't bore you with the details right now... it'll be in my next book," Monique told the room in all seriousness. Mack snorted a laugh.

"In her possession, was this blue velvet box containing the coat of arms of the Habsburg family and the exquisite Royal Diamond. Sadly, Margaret was, how do you say it... not quite right in the head." Some nervous chuckles burst out of the crowd before silence descended once again.

"As I was saying, poor Margaret held onto the necklace and the box which her aunt had given her upon her death. Margaret never understood the value of it—that she had roots... family." Monique paused to take a sip of water. The only sound in the room was that of pencils scratching furiously on note pads and fingers on keyboards tapping away like a band of castanet players.

"A short while ago, Margaret traded the box and the necklace to a local street vendor. In return, she received some silver bric-a-brac, hoping to get some money by selling the silver pieces. This we learned from Margaret herself, as told to my associate last week. She knew where the jewel case and necklace were, but said she had to wait until Sunday to retrieve it, not disclosing the location. Where she had left it I deduced by simple geographical and logical conclusions. I positioned myself in the appropriate place, ready to assist Margaret and ensure protection to her and the valuable treasure she didn't know she possessed.

"Unfortunately, my publicist was much more vile than I gave him credit for... he located my notes, which he then read and began scheming over. Obviously, a diamond worth a few million dollars is motivation enough to kill for, and unfortunately, he got to Margaret Von Strauss first."

The silence burst, voices puncturing the air like a balloon

pricked with a pin. Monique held up a hand, quieting the room with one pointed look.

"I'm afraid, ladies and gentlemen, that this is all I have to say on the matter at present. I do not wish to jeopardize the case which the police will be making against this heinous individual." Monique gave Jerome a look like he was a piece of filthy gum stuck to the bottom of her shoe.

Everyone filed out, a mixture of excitement and complaints that the details were left incomplete... especially those details of the more enthralling aspects of the crime.

Two uniformed officers had taken custody of the accused, leaving Detective Mack Petersen and Monique Elena Alvarez Black standing alone in the room.

"How did you know it was Jerome I was going to identify?" Monique asked.

"Ah, so you noticed me sidling up to him, did you?" Monique gave him a look which said, of course—don't be stupid. Mack smiled.

"Well, rather ironically, I noticed his shoes. It clicked in when I realized he matched the description of the man trying to wrestle Maggie's cart away from her just before she was killed. Sorry for that crack about the bell-hop earlier, by the way."

Monique threw her beautiful head back and laughed, her low throaty chuckle reverberating off the walls of the empty room.

"I'd appreciate a ride to the station, Mack. And after I've given my statement and evidence, mind if I stick around for a while? I'll need all the details for this chapter in my new book."

Mack offered her his arm as they strode together out of the Ritz. "You can bet on it, kid."

Full Circle

by Sylvia Maultash Warsh

Sylvia Maultash Warsh was born in Germany to Holocaust survivors. She earned a B.A. and an M.A. from the University of Toronto. Her short stories and poetry have appeared in Canada and the United States. She has taught writing to seniors since 1990. She writes the award-winning Dr. Rebecca Temple mystery series set in 1979 Toronto. The first, To Die in Spring, *was nominated for an Arthur Ellis. The second,* Find Me Again, *won an Edgar and was nominated for two Anthonys. The third,* Season of Iron, *was short-listed for a ReLit Award. In a departure from mystery, her fourth book,* The Queen of Unforgetting, *is an historical novel set north of Toronto in 1973. In this book, the theme of the 17th century tragedy of the Hurons is juxtaposed with the Holocaust of the Jews. Warsh's fifth book is* Best Girl, *a 'Rapid Reads' novel aimed at reluctant adult readers.*

Did I deceive her? Of course I did. She didn't deserve the truth. And I knew what she'd do with my little secret. Marla never could keep her mouth shut. Just like she couldn't keep her clothes on. Now she had an excuse. Hot flashes. I wanted to tell her—Look Marla, I went through the change before you; did you see me throwing off my knickers first chance I got? When she was sixteen, it was one thing, but now the mountains of her boobs have collapsed and headed toward the corral of flesh surrounding the top of her bikini underwear. You wouldn't want to accidentally come across her before a meal.

I was lucky about one thing though: I could only see half of her. This was my deception, or rather my sin by omission—I neglected to tell her about that morning when I woke up at the beginning of the summer holidays and half of me was gone. The left half. At first I thought it was only my face that had disappeared in the mirror—half a head of chin-length hair, one brown eye. Didn't take me long to find I was missing my left arm too, and my left breast, and then the whole left side of the room. I remember poking my right hand in and out of the void like a kid who's discovered a new law of nature. And I had, really. It went like this: Just when you think everything's okay and you least expect it, watch out from behind because something's going to come barreling down at you, flatten you, and not look back. Well, it needs some work for the textbooks.

In my desperation I had called up Marla. Biggest mistake I ever made.

"So Julie, you remembered I was alive."

"Look Marla, let bygones be bygones. I have a proposition for you. You like Toronto, don't you?"

The town she lived in, a hundred miles away, had one main street and was best known for its high security prison. Complaining all the way, she'd moved there with her husband; and now the alimony he was paying her went further there. Toronto was an expensive place.

"How'd you like to move here? Live with me in my house?"

I heard heavy breathing on the other end. The equivalent of Marla thinking.

"I thought, we're both alone. It's been two years since Morris died, and I'm... I'm not happy living alone. You're my closest cousin." (She was my only cousin) "What'd you say?"

"I'm speechless. Except to say I can't afford it. You know what that slime ball pays me each month? I can barely keep up the rent in this one horse town."

"Marla, I'm talking about you moving in. Free. No money changes hands. You can save what the slime ball gives you. Spend it on lipstick."

Again heavy breathing. I would never have offered her this if I had been in one piece. But I needed help if I was going to keep up a semblance of normality. I could no longer drive or shop for myself. Walking in a straight line was an effort. The doctor said a blood clot had cut off the flow in the right occipital lobe of my brain, a mild stroke that had left me with hemianopia, a fancy word that meant there was nothing wrong with my eyes, but my brain could only interpret half of what they saw. Apparently I was lucky I hadn't lost the use of my arms and legs. Okay, lucky, so in September I planned to go back to teaching my class as if nothing had happened. If the principal found out what I couldn't see, she'd cheerfully pack me off with an early pension. Twenty teachers were waiting in line for my job, twenty teachers she could pay less because they were wet behind the ears, unlike me who had thirty years seniority and, according to the union, commanded top dollar. I couldn't tell my only friend, Trudy, because she was a teacher at the school and would be obliged to pass it on. So I needed help. Why should I pay someone to look after me when Marla would do it for free?

"What'd you say, Marla?"

"What's the catch?"

"You've got to drive me back and forth from school. And my doctor's appointments. You'll have to do the grocery shopping. And share the cooking."

"I don't do floors."

"I have a cleaning lady."

An intake of breath. Regrouping of thoughts. "What about your shots. You still diabetic?"

As if that kind of thing went away. "I do that myself." I looked down at my right leg which was getting the brunt of the shots. I must get used to injecting blind. "You might have to go to the drugstore for me. In my car, of course."

"How old is it?"

"My car?" Was this what it was coming come down to? "Just three years old. Morris only drove it a year before..."

"Okay. So tell me what's really going on?"

A little truth couldn't hurt. "It's my eyes. You know at our age things start to go wrong. Well I've gotten so short-sighted I can't drive."

"Can't you get glasses?"

"Marla, I can't drive, with glasses or without."

She showed up one day in her 1986 Chevy, rusted bits of the front fender held together with rope and duct tape. I could hear her long before I could see her, the caterwauling of her muffler shrank the suburban quiet of the street. It was a mystery to me how she got that car to eat up one hundred miles of the 401 highway and gave me a new respect for her determination.

"You look terrible," she said, depositing two large suitcases in my front hall. She glanced around dismissively at my modest furnishings.

"It's nice to see you too," I said. I could only see all of her when I turned my head completely to the left, as if I were looking over my shoulder.

Half of her would've been plenty: long platinum hair, a thick layer of pancake makeup, chunky black mascara. She'd aimed for that tasteless kind of glamour since she was sixteen. But now the woman was fifty-eight and her waist had disappeared into her hips. Who was she trying to impress with those short shorts?

"You could use some makeup," she said, squinting beneath the branches of her eyelashes. Then she noticed my cane. "Good God, Julie!" she cried. "You've turned into an old woman!"

I remembered now why I had always cried when Marla came over to play when we were children. "I told you, I have trouble seeing."

I had dug up the cane from the remnants of costumes used by my students in school plays over the years. It was lightweight and unobtrusive and allowed me to walk without bumping into things that lay in the baffling void to my left.

I watched Marla drag three large green garbage bags through the front door.

"Lookit all these pictures!" she said. "These your classes? I guess if you couldn't have your own kids, you can put other people's up on your walls."

My small hallway was plastered with class photos from the past twenty-five years, rows and rows of eight-year-olds grinning, me sitting joyfully on one end in the front. That was how those kids made me feel. Joyful.

"I got something better to put up on your walls," she said, giving me a start.

She began to pull framed paintings out of the bags and lean them against the wall on the carpet. Some autumn landscapes with too much orange; but worse, some were copies of famous paintings, one of those naked women by Goya, and of all things, the Mona Lisa.

"I'll bet you never guessed your cousin was an artist," she said.

She waited for me to comment, but I was too stunned by their mediocrity to make a go of lying.

"Aren't these something? I did them myself."

I blinked at the canvases, grateful that half had fallen out of my field of vision.

"Yourself?"

"Bet you can't tell, even if you look close."

I sidled up to the Mona Lisa and touched the surface. Real paint. Marla didn't have a creative bone in her body. I silently apologized to da Vinci. "Paint by numbers?" I said.

"You guessed."

Marla moved into the spare bedroom with frightening finality. She had sold all her furniture but a TV to the widow who was subletting her apartment and stuffed her car with the trinkets she couldn't part with. Only two books had survived this culling, one a biography of Jayne Mansfield, and the other a thumbed five-year horoscope.

She insisted on installing her turquoise rendition of Gainsborough's Blue Boy in the kitchen. The little rouged child-face, frighteningly false, oversaw our first dinner, a couple of microwaved "Thin Cuisine" dinners I kept in the freezer for emergencies.

"You remember when we were teenagers, Julie? We used to talk about what we'd do when we grew up, how many kids we'd have and what our husbands would be like?"

"You wanted a rich husband," I remembered, "and servants so you wouldn't have to take care of your kids."

"Did I say that?" Marla opened one of the bottles of wine that had languished in the buffet since Morris had died. She'd asked for scotch but we had never drunk hard liquor. Besides, with my diabetic diet and medication, any spirits were out of the question. She was enjoying the wine.

"Yeah, well. Look at me now. No husband. My kid can't stand looking at me—his father pays his bills and that's all he cares about. You didn't miss out not having any. What do I get out of having a kid? Doesn't even call to see if I'm alive. You're lucky you don't have all that aggravation."

For a change Marla was delicate enough to omit my medical failure, the cysts on my ovaries that kept me from ovulating regularly and consequently from being able to conceive. I had desperately wanted children. I was sure it was why Morris had died so young—the bitter disappointment in life of not passing on his genes, or having the pleasure of seeing a child of his own flesh and blood grow up before his eyes. He always felt he'd missed out. The irony was I should have been the disappointed one. And I was, for a while. But I got over it because I had my children in school. I had no time for disappointment. I was busy watching them learn and play and become human beings. I had been mother to thousands and would be to still more as long as the principal was kept ignorant of my condition. I had nothing left but the children. Marla had no idea how important she was.

Marla also had no idea how to shop. She would come back with an assortment of junk food as varied as the corner store. I would send her to the grocery with a list of items to buy, including more than enough money to cover, and she'd come back with the kind of stuff store managers pile near the check-out counters to catch the eyes of children who then browbeat their mothers. All I got for my specific instructions about the four-in-a-pack vegetable burgers near the green beans was a four-pound box of frozen hamburgers. She didn't know a Red Delicious apple from a Macintosh, or a low-fat Mozzarella from a heart-clogging Havarti. On the other hand, she had a working knowledge of Oreo cookies, nacho chips and an expensive brand of rum and raisin ice cream. I wondered if I would have to accompany her to the store and supervise her shopping. It turned out that shopping was going to be the least of my problems.

Less than two weeks after she arrived, a station wagon pulled up in front of the house. I was sitting on the porch in the July sun, trying to read a children's book. Since I could only see half, I had to practice turning my head full to the left, or moving the book to my far right in order to read. Somehow I would have to make up for my disability by September if I was going to carry on as usual.

A bulky man in a golf shirt got out of the car carrying a box of tools and headed toward me.

"Afternoon ma'am, someone called about a leaky faucet." He was standing in front of the sun so that I could barely make him out.

"You must have the wrong house," I said in my naiveté.

He peered at the house number and said, "Is this Reynolds Drive?"

"Just a minute," I said, struggling to my feet. My tee-shirt stuck to my back with sweat.

Marla blinked innocently as I stumbled in the door. "Did you call a plumber?" I asked.

"Oh, come to think of it... The toilet doesn't flush right upstairs."

"I never have any problems with it. Where'd you get this guy's number? He isn't dressed like a plumber."

"Oh, I ran into him at the grocery, and when I heard he was a plumber..."

"You gave a stranger our address? Did you look him up in the phone book at least?"

"Geez you're paranoid. He's okay."

"How do you know? He could have a gun in that tool box."

Marla sighed. "He doesn't have a gun. I know him," she said finally, "from before." She turned toward the door. "He's okay. Don't have a conniption."

That's when I began to see the light. "There's nothing wrong with our toilet."

She shrugged. "A girl gets lonely. He's a nice guy." She straightened out her platinum waves. "Come on, I'll introduce you."

After Frank and I shook hands, Marla could see her little explanation hadn't gone far in appeasing me. Frank, a flabby, primitive type around sixty, watched her face as if the sun rose and set on it. Half of him was a lot more than I cared to see. To her credit—maybe it was self-preservation—Marla strolled him out the door and down the street to the park.

I stood at the screen door. They had disappeared around a corner. She'd known him from before, she said. But she'd only been in Toronto two weeks. She could've met him here. But not likely. I was betting on an earlier friendship in her former town. Which meant he had a two hour ride home and would probably stay for dinner. This was something I hadn't counted on. The woman was fifty-eight. I thought she would've grown up by now.

I microwaved some frozen cannelloni while Marla and Frank partied at the local Pizza Hut. Relieved at the temporary restoration of my privacy, I ate under the watchful eye of the Blue Boy. It was a pleasure to go to bed without the constant buzz of the TV Marla had installed in her bedroom so she could watch till two a.m.

It was after one when I heard the front door open. The picture of Frank hurtling down the highway in the middle of the night to get home fizzled into thin air when the whispering started. I sat bolt upright. She couldn't have. I tiptoed to my door and listened. Footsteps up the stairs. Giggles. Whispers. I stood listening till her door closed, then sat down on my bed to think. I had brought this on myself. I knew what Marla was like—only I thought she would've mellowed with age. This was inexcusable behaviour. She wasn't a teenager anymore. I was too angry to sleep and opened a book on my night stand. The page on my right blurred in the fuzzy light of the lamp, the one on my left was sucked into the void. I wasn't going to follow it there. I was going to lay down the law to Marla in the morning. She was living in my house and would have to follow my rules.

I woke in a sweat long after I had intended to get up. Jumping out of bed, I cursed Marla for turning my life upside down. I didn't look forward to confronting the loving couple. I needn't have worried.

I could see Marla out the window, sunbathing in the backyard in her striped bikini underwear. Alone.

Try to wake up, I thought. First, insulin out of the fridge. Fumble with the disposable syringe, inject the dose into your thigh. Okay, you're all right now. Don't put it off.

I opened the back door. "Marla, about what went on last night. I can't have it."

"Oh, that was nothing, Julie," she said without looking up. "Frank had too much to drink—I couldn't let him drive home like that. I let him sleep on the floor."

How stupid did she think I was? "Look, I don't want it to happen again."

"Don't worry. He's not my type."

Well it turned out he wasn't her type. But Bill was. And Al. And George.

By August I was dead tired of her alleycatting and lies. She made up a different story each time she had company overnight. Al had locked himself out of his apartment and couldn't get back in without waking the super. George's car wouldn't start and he couldn't get a garage till the morning. Bill was so depressed he'd threatened suicide. I'd had enough of Marla and her over-the-hill Romeos. I was tired of being taken for a patsy. Just because I couldn't see, didn't mean I was blind. I had made up my mind to hire someone to take Marla's place. You get what you pay for.

One afternoon when I was walking in from the garden with my watering can, Marla was on the phone in the kitchen. Her back was to me.

"Didn't she tell you I was moving in?" Pause. Listening to the voice on the other end. "Yes, I'm looking after her. We're cousins, you know. Anyway, I took a St. John's course twenty years back."

My life flashed before me but I couldn't move. It was like one of those dreams where your limbs have turned to stone.

"Oh, she's a strong one. She'll outlive us all." Listening.

It was Trudy, I was sure.

"Well, I don't know what you call it, but it makes her crabby."

I tried to open my mouth. Something must've come out because Marla turned around and saw me.

"Anyway, I'll tell her you called," she said quickly,

Marla tossed her head like a schoolgirl to dislodge an errant wave of platinum. She picked up a magazine from the table. "That was your friend, Trudy," she said. "She's worried about you."

I grit my teeth to see straight. It had been a close call. "Marla, this isn't working. I'll give you two weeks to find another place."

Marla turned the pages of the magazine. "Don't be stupid, Julie. You need me."

"I want you out of here. I'm being nice about the two weeks."

Now she looked up. "Julie, what exactly is wrong with your eyes? You're not short-sighted. It's more than that, isn't it?"

"What difference does that make?"

"How're you going to teach? I've seen you turn your head when you need to look at something. I'm surprised the school will let you keep teaching."

"I'll be fine," I said through clenched teeth.

"They don't know, do they? You haven't told them. Is that smart? Course, you've been teaching a long time. You wouldn't know what to do with yourself if they canned you."

"They're not going to can me."

"Not if they don't find out. And who's going to tell them, right?" She looked at me pointedly.

"You wouldn't," I said.

She raised a black-penciled eyebrow. "Trudy said she teaches with you. I guess you haven't told her."

I glared at Marla, wondering what it would take to make the visible half of her disappear.

I stared at the absurd copy of the Mona Lisa in my living room. The tiny blocks of colour were too bright, cartoonish. Her smile was even more enigmatic since the left half of it had dropped into oblivion. I could smile like that if I had to and nobody would know what I was planning. Because there would have to be a plan; the status quo was unthinkable. It had been a big mistake to bring Marla here.

I'd seen it almost from the start. I always fixed my mistakes. That was what I taught my children in school—mistakes must be fixed. There was nothing I wanted more than to see my children again. Only three weeks and I would be reunited with all my little chicks. If I could fix my mistake.

I caught her in the middle of a rainy day. "Marla, guess what's on TV tonight? 'Diamonds are a Girl's Best Friend.' Remember, with Marilyn Monroe? It's one of my favourites. Why don't we order some Chinese food and make it a girl's night in?" I guessed she was sick of pizza.

That night while she was mesmerized by the flickering shadows, I pulled out a brand new bottle of scotch and placed it on the tea table beside her sweet and sour chicken balls.

"Where'd you get that?" Marla's eyes narrowed with anticipation.

"The liquor store delivers," I said sweetly.

She didn't notice that I wasn't drinking. I kept my highball glass filled with ginger ale; hers I topped up with scotch whenever the level dropped. By the time the movie was over, she didn't know what planet she was on. I was hoping she wouldn't conk out before I got her upstairs. She'd be a dead weight. I propped her up with my right arm around her middle and we staggered up to her room.

"Marla... do you want to get undressed?"

I realized my fears were groundless when she started to snore. I counted myself lucky that she slept naked—once I undressed her, at least I wouldn't have to struggle on her pajamas. It was time for the next step. A fresh disposable syringe and a dose of insulin. I measured it out carefully—it wouldn't be my regular dose. How much more would I need?

Marla was snoring softly under the covers. She looked almost harmless. But I knew better. I knew she was all that stood between me and my little chicks, my sweet children who would look up from their desks the first day of school and watch me with expectant and innocent eyes, knowing I would give them all I had because I loved them more than anything. She would not separate me from my babies.

Marla turned and groaned as I approached but her eyes stayed closed as coffins. I lifted the sheet from the bottom to expose one of her feet. It was awkward separating two of her toes with my left hand—I had to turn my head fully to that side to see. I didn't have another hand to hold her steady if she moved, so I held my breath as I poked the needle of the syringe in between her toes, then pushed in the plunger. She moaned and I thought: so this is how life ends, we don't get much of a chance at it, do we? Some people would say Marla got a good kick at the can, considering. With her busy social life, she never got up before noon, so I wouldn't check on her till then. The police wouldn't arrive till a full twelve hours after the time of death. Lots of time to settle my nerves. Not that they'd find anything. They'd know she went into shock but there would be no obvious cause of death. Insulin was a natural substance and left no trace. Only oblivion.

An oblivion that stretched three hundred and sixty degrees.